SCARED TO DEATH

OTHER BOOKS BY JEFF LENBURG

The Three Stooges Scrapbook, Updated Edition
Career Opportunities in Animation
Genndy Tartakovsky: From Russia to Coming-of-Age Animator
Hayao Miyazaki: Japan's Premier Anime Storyteller
John Lasseter: The Whiz Who Made Pixar King
Walter Lantz: Made Famous By a Woodpecker
Matt Groening: From Spitballs to Springfield
William Hanna and Joseph Barbera: The Sultans of Saturday Morning
Walt Disney: The Mouse That Roared
Tex Avery: Hollywood's Master of Screwball Cartoons
The Facts On File Guide to Research, Second Edition
The Encyclopedia of Animated Cartoons, Third Edition
Who's Who in Animated Cartoons
The Facts On File Guide to Research
How to Make a Million Dollars With Your Voice with Gary Owens
The Encyclopedia of Animated Cartoons, Second Edition
All the Gold in California and Other People, Places & Things with Larry Gatlin
The Encyclopedia of Animated Cartoons
Once a Stooge, Always a Stooge with Joe Besser and Greg Lenburg
Baseball's All-Star Game: A Game-By-Game Guide
Peekaboo: The Story of Veronica Lake
The Great Cartoon Directors
Dudley Moore: An Informal Biography
Dustin Hoffman: Hollywood's Antihero
The Three Stooges Scrapbook with Joan Howard Maurer and Greg Lenburg
The Encyclopedia of Animated Cartoon Series
Steve Martin: An Unauthorized Biography with Randy Skretvedt and Greg Lenburg

SCARED TO DEATH

A Lori Matrix Hollywood Mystery

JEFF LENBURG

MOONWATER PRESS

SCARED TO DEATH: A Lori Matrix Hollywood Mystery

Published in the United States by Moonwater Press, P.O. Box 2061, Litchfield Park, Arizona 85340.
www.moonwaterpress.com

Originally published by iUniverse. Copyright ¤ 2005 by Jeff Lenburg. All rights reserved.

Library of Congress Control Number: 2014946638

Publisher's Cataloging-in-Publication Data

Lenburg, Jeff.
  Scared to death : a Lori Matrix Hollywood mystery / Jeff Lenburg.
pages cm
ISBN: 978-0-9903287-0-4 (pbk.)
ISBN: 978-0-9903287-1-1 (e-book)
  1. Murder Investigation Fiction. 2. Hollywood (Los Angeles, Calif.) Fiction. 3. Actors and actresses Fiction. 4. Television news anchors Fiction. I. Title.
PS3612.E522 S33 2014
813'.6 dc23

                                                        2014946638

For previews of upcoming books by Jeff and more information about the author, visit: www.jefflenburg.com.

Printed in the United States of America.

To Don Bresnahan, for telling me never stop believing, no matter how bad the hand you are dealt.

CONTENTS

Chapter 1

This was the time of day that made Lori Matrix wish she were anyone else but the most popular news anchorperson in the Los Angeles television market. At nine o'clock on a Monday morning, she was driving up the Moorpark Drive on-ramp to the Ventura Freeway and heading for Hollywood and the studios of KTRB-TV.

Her morning started with a story conference where the producers and assignment editors developed stories for the six o'clock news. This ritual always made her feel a little like James Cagney must have felt in that old black-and-white flick in which he was being dragged to the electric chair. However, he only had to do it *once*.

God knows she was not hired because she had a degree

in journalism from the University of Michigan, or because her late father was Mike Fishbein, the greatest city editor the *Detroit Free Press* had ever had.

She had that Cosmetic Look every station wanted. She was not just the product of it. She epitomized it. It was what had landed her the job at KTRB in the first place.

Networks were hiring models and actresses and Lori had been a successful model in New York for two years after trying unsuccessfully for the better part of one summer to land a job, any kind of job, on a newspaper, any kind of newspaper. Some hotshot TV news consultant had decided this twenty-eight-year-old blue-eyed, blonde-haired womans brand of journalism as perfect for TV news after watching her Jensen Swimsuit commercial. It had been the skimpiest suit she had ever worn, and the thought of it still embarrassed her.

The fact that she wanted to cover hard news--and perhaps one day do those in-depth interviews with world leaders that Barbara Walters does--had always eluded her. Lori got all the soft features, and so-called "women's stories." While some incompetent was covering the aftermath of the massacre in Haiti, she was doing a "cute" film piece on Santa Monica's muscle beach.

She remembered the words of the program director, Solly Kornfeld, the only person on the lot who knew she was the former Ann Fishbein.

"Sure, we know you got a brain, but it ain't a brain we're sellin'. Look, kid, we can go out and buy a hundred reporters and writers who can write and report rings around you. They're easy to get. But there's only one Lori Matrix, babe. Who's got your build, your style, your sex appeal?"

The story conference was already underway when Lori headed past her tiny cubicle in the newsroom--described in her contract as "extremely comfortable, spacious, and if possible, luxurious facilities, providing Ms. Matrix with a pleasant environment in which to do her work"--and entered the conference room.

Tommy Ewart, the five P.M. news producer, looked up and said to no one in particular, "God, what wouldn't anyone give to take a bite out of one of those gorgeous buns?"

"Can I pass?" asked Sally Greer, the six P.M. news producer. "I've got this silly thing about spoiling my lunch. And besides, I think I'm straight."

Billy Gamm, the executive producer, looked up from his schedule sheet and joined the chorus of hellos and hi's to Lori as she took her seat. Then it was back to business.

"Let's get this turkey underway," Gamm said firmly. "I've got to get a haircut. The Champ is throwing another one of his orgies after the six o'clock news."

The Champ ("The Boss"), otherwise known as Clinton Cramer Leaf, the vice president and general manager of KTRB-TV, Los Angeles, was in his counting house counting the overnight ratings while visions of interviewing pretty and over-sexed young things who wanted to be reporters danced in his well-coifed head.

Peter Coyle, the assignment editor, stabbed the schedule in front of him with a forefinger and said, "The City Manager is going to dedicate that new wing of the Los Angeles General Hospital. It's supposed to have good visuals, lots of modern equipment and stuff for treating drug addicts."

"Is Hizzoner's daughter going to throw out the first needle?" Ewart laughed.

"She has so many punctures on her arms she leaks in the shower," Gamm added with a bemused smile.

"Jesus, what a sensitive, understanding bunch of bastards," Coyle exploded. "They ought to have a wing for cynics."

"St. Luke's Hospital has a capping ceremony for nurses," Greer added.

"And there's a graffiti mural contest in East L.A.," Lopez offered hopefully.

Circling an item on his rundown, Gamm said, "No. Let's cover this one. It's a bunch of old movie stars who've formed a social club and they're going to meet the first Thursday of each month and look at each other's classic films, starting tonight."

"Yeah," Ewart said favorably. "It might be interesting to see something like that. Any big names?"

"The biggest," Gamm enthused. "Martha Von Tours. Rita Reno. Charles Evans Fine. Peter Olson. Rex Hampton. Bette Oliver."

"I thought they were all dead," Greer wondered aloud.

"I never heard of any of them," Ewart admitted.

"We'll send Lori," Gamm said, smiling at the thought. "She'll make a great contrast to those old broads. We can film the talkie part of the meeting, and then show the old birds looking at the old nitrate films, and maybe we can borrow a clip, put it on video tape, and run it with the interview of the star that appears in it. Sound good?"

It sounded good to everyone, except Lori. The news that she would be covering the old actors' feature story drew a familiar reaction.

"Shit! When in the hell do I ever get to cover a hard news story?" she demanded.

Gamm smiled, patiently. What a shame, he thought, that she tried to take her role as a TV news reporter seriously.

"Listen, beautiful," Gamm said gently. "I know you've got what it takes to cover the harder stuff, but everyone works his way through the softer features on the way."

"Oh, come on," Lori replied honestly. "I've been at it two years now. And I'm still covering fashion shows and baby contests."

"And doing it beautifully," Gamm said, playing to his star anchor's ego. "Do this one for me, baby, and we'll see if we can line up something harder for you tomorrow."

Lori reluctantly took the piece of paper from Gamm's hand, scanned the scribbling on it, and sighed.

"Okay," she agreed. "I'll be there. But remember what you said about giving me a hard news story tomorrow."

"I'll remember."

Lori nodded, and turned to head back to her office.

Gamm locked his eyes on her retreating ass beautifully encased in the super-tight black jeans, and he found the slight jiggle intriguing.

Ewart slipped up beside him and helped him look at the departing buns. "Now there goes a reporter with a really interesting background."

Lori had guessed the address in Bel Air would belong to some giant old mansion not unlike the one used in the filming of *Sunset Boulevard*. She had seen the classic flick five or six times, and found Gloria Swanson's performance in it fascinating every time.

But this was not Sunset Boulevard. It was more California

Modern, not at all the kind of place she would expect to find an old movie star like Rita Reno living in.

Moments after the musical doorbell stopped reverberating among the lilac bushes, another surprise was in order. Rita Reno answered the door herself. She had to be at least sixty-five or seventy years old. Her soft gray hair, helped a little by a good color rinse, and bright, clear blue eyes gave way to a figure that made her look like a woman of thirty. The well-disciplined voice also was that of a much younger woman.

"Miss Matrix. How nice of you to come. You're the only one."

With just a trace of disappointment in the carefully modulated voice, Lori smiled warmly and thanked Reno for allowing her to stop by. She quickly introduced the crew, Bob Reese, on camera, Alfredo Cadenza, on sound. The tiny woman shook their hands warmly and directed them into an anteroom off the main dining room, where they began organizing their equipment. Rita guided Lori into the main dining room. There, looking just a trifle uncomfortable, were the other members of the cast, looking, Lori thought, not unlike figures in a wax museum.

Reno paused at the threshold and made a little gesture and Lori leaned down so the former Hollywood screen siren could whisper in her ear.

"I know you must think we're all a bunch of old wrecks. But one day you'll discover that the difference between young and old is just a handful of years you can't even account for."

Lori protested as best she could, sotto voce. "You look lovely, and it's an honor for me to be here. It really is."

Lori found herself meaning it. It was the greatest assembly of sheer film talent she had ever seen in one place. Not the least of it was contained in the one hundred and ten-pound body of this lively little woman, who seemed to defy aging,

Lori had seen several of Rita Reno's pictures. Her thirty-year career in motion pictures and five husbands had left her with close to seven million dollars. However, it was not enough to satisfy a punctured ego or to remove the frustration that had built up over the years. Reno bore a marked resemblance to Bette Davis all her life, and that proved to be a major obstacle in her career. When the really choice roles came along, whether it was *Of Human Bondage* or *Petrified Forest* or *The Corn is Green*, Bette got the starring roles and Rita, typecast as a Bette Davis-type, got the leftovers.

One by one, Reno introduced her guests.

Colleen Kantor, reputed to be the richest woman in the film colony. No one under thirty probably had ever seen a Colleen Kantor film, unless they were one of those buffs that had haunted the Fine Arts and other revival theaters that regularly screened the old black-and-white classics from an earlier era. Not one of Kantor's pictures had ever appeared on television.

At seventy, Kantor still believed television was a gimmick, a passing fancy. She was one of the rare ones who owned her own pictures without ties to the apron strings of a studio. She never sold even one of her films to the networks. All her pictures had made money, and Colleen was an even better businesswoman than she was an actor. Ask any of the dozens of corporate heads that lease her buildings along Wilshire Boulevard constantly faced with rent increases.

Sylvia Carl-Stapleton. Everyone knew her as Mrs. Murphy, that sharp-tongued, heart-of-gold lady who pushes her brand of coffee on young newlyweds in television commercials. Sylvia was in the ninth year of that commercial contract with the Ajax-Hanley agency that represented Murphy's Coffee. Only her friends knew that if it were not for that commercial contract, the gracious old lady in the beaded, other-era dress would be occupying one of those grim little stucco senior citizen hovels in the Wilshire District and eating at the corner cafeteria.

Martha Van Tours. The Flaming Girl of the thirties, rumored to have broken Douglas Fairbanks' heart and a dozen box-office records during her day. Martha wore a wig, not out of vanity, but because she had lost most of her hair as the result of restorative surgery following an automobile accident in the fifties. She seemed shy, withdrawn.

Charles Evans Fine. He was even taller than he appeared to be in the original version of *Lawrence of Arabia*. Fine's career nearly ended in the McCarthy era when his leftist politics caused every major studio lot in town to blacklist him. Nevertheless, he made a comeback as a director in the late Fifties, and won an Academy Award for that picture which launched Frank Sinatra's comeback. Fine was one of Hollywood's most respected actors, and rumor had it that Marlon Brando personally launched his career because of he was a friend of Brandos mother.

Peter Olson. Lori knew all about make-believe and the movies, but the man who made Dracula a household word still caused a slight shudder in her as he rose, graciously kissed her hand, and fixed those pitch black eyes on her.

"You must come to my study on this dark night," he said, in the phony Hungarian accent that had made him famous in a dozen classic horror films. Then he laughed at his well-worn private joke, and Lori laughed along with him.

Rex Hampton. God, Lori thought, no wonder a dozen Hollywood beauties from another era had lost their heads over this one. His features looked like they had been chiseled out of granite, and he was every bit as handsome as Cary Grant. In fact, he had starred in several Grant pictures. Hampton gave Lori one of his warmest smiles, and she felt a kind of erotic glow that she did not even need to analyze.

Bette Oliver. She was the only one who did not rise, and Lori took her outstretched hand and wondered at the tiny size of it. They exchanged meaningless pleasantries, and as Oliver offered her some hors d'oeuvres, Lori realized that her movements were extremely restricted, and then she remembered from her research Oliver had painful, crippling arthritis.

The introductions over, Lori removed a notebook from her oversized handbag and took a microphone from soundman Cadenza to conduct a brief interview with Rita Reno. This after cameraman Reese had carefully positioned Reno in the foreground of a shot that would reveal most of the others sitting in a semi-circle in the background, facing the still empty screen that dominated the room.

Lori listened for the familiar whir of the hi-resolution video camera and catching the approving nod of the cameraman out of the corner of her eye, she fixed her best on-the-air smile on Reno and said, "Tell me how this all came about. Was it your idea to have these once-a-month showings of classic films?"

Reno's smile out-dazzled that of Lori.

"Yes. I thought, here we are, a group of veteran actors who have made perhaps fifty classic films and we share, oh, perhaps nine Academy Awards among us, and wouldn't it be interesting to come together and mutually enjoy each other's finest moments on the screen."

Lori said, "You're not just a wee bit competitive about this, are you? I mean, after all, actors do have healthy egos."

"Oh, we have egos all right," Reno admitted, managing a smile for the camera. "But none of us here has to prove anything anymore, do we? No, we enjoy each other's successes, and the films are all so different, you can't really compare them, can you. Could you, for instance, say that the original 'Mutiny on the Bounty' was a better film than The African Queen,' or that 'Elizabeth and Essex' were a better motion picture than one of those many marvelous things that Fred Astaire and Ginger Rogers did?"

And that is the way the interview went. Rita Reno was charming, informative, and exuded warmth that matched anything she had ever projected on the screen.

Lori was delighted. She had about ten minutes of footage to edit down to two minutes or less in the on-the-air version, but she knew she had some fillets that would delight the film editor and her producer.

The cameraman did several reverse questions, and that amused the old actors. Lori stood in isolation and asked the cameraman the same questions she had asked Reno. Later, the video editor would cut those questions into the interview. It was how viewers would see the interviewer as well as the interviewee's full face when the story aired on television.

Reese had to do a couple of dry runs on the lighting as the projectionist began the showing of Rex Hampton's 1942 blockbuster, *Captain Morgan and the Devil*. A World War II flick in which Hampton not only had to out-fly the greatest Nazi ace of the war, but also had to wrestle with the devil that was coming to collect on a bargain Captain Morgan had made with him. The unearthly compact had stipulated that if Morgan should become the greatest Allied air ace of World War II, and shoot down Germany's greatest ace, he would agree to crash his plane and turn his soul over to the devil. The film made a superstar out of Rex Hampton, who went on to big-budget pictures.

Fifteen minutes into the picture, Reese had all the shots he needed to complete Lori's feature story. He had taken long shots of the room, showing the backs of the assembled actors as they watched the screen, then he had taken individual close ups of each actor, watching the film.

Reese always came up with something creative on his own. In this instance, he held his camera on a long close up of the younger Hampton on the screen. Then he rolled fifteen or twenty seconds of a matching shot of Hampton watching himself intently. Reese knew the editor would see what he was after and would dissolve from the younger Hampton to the older Hampton for an interesting filmic effect.

Television news crews rarely have enough time to devote to anything, so at seventeen minutes into the picture Lori caught Reese's anxious look and read it correctly. They had invested all the time they could afford on this story. They would have to move on to their next assignment. Lori nodded and Reese began quietly removing his equipment. She then slowly began picking her way in a semi-crouching position in the chair in which Rita Reno was sitting.

Suddenly, Lori froze. A long, anguished cry came from the back of the room. The voice was that of Rex Hampton. Lori swiveled her head just in time to see Hampton leaping to his feet, his right arm jerking forward, as if he were trying to point to the screen. Then something else he tried to cry out stuck in his throat, and his body pitched forward and he crashed face forward on the floor.

Cadenza, closest to the major light switch in the room, dived for it and flicked it on, flooding the room with light. Peter Olson, sitting on Hampton's right, was already on his feet and bending over Hampton's still form. Martha Von Tours quickly joined him and the others crowded in.

"What is it," she asked frantically, "a heart attack?" Von Tours would know. She had suffered two heart attacks in the last three years.

It looks that way, Olson said, gently turning Hampton on his back. The mans face seemed drained, and he lay deathly still.

Olson put two fingers over Hampton's right temple and Von Tours stopped him, saying, "No, no, you do it this way."

Then she felt for the pulse in Hampton's right wrist. She found none, and checked for a pulse in his left wrist.

Charles Evans Fine, a veteran of two wars, pronounced Hampton dead, and Rita Reno had handyman, George, call the paramedics. They arrived nine minutes later and verified everyone's worst fears. Hampton was, indeed, dead, apparently the victim of a massive heart attack. The news heightened the pall over the gathering. As paramedics carried out Hampton's body, now covered with a red blanket, Rita Reno sank into an overstuffed chair and began crying gently. Bette Oliver tried to comfort her.

"Darling, he was in his seventies," she said, consolingly. "His heart never was very good. It could have happened any time, any where."

"But it happened here," Reno said resentfully, wiping the tears from each eye.

Von Tours, who entered the scene, noticed the tragedy. "Yes, it's a terrible thing," she told Rita, "but we've got to make the best of it."

Reno looked angrily at Reese, who was putting the lens cap on his camera, having taken shots of Olson and Von Tours huddled over the body, and the paramedic carrying the body out to their red and white van. What had started out as a soft feature had turned into a hard news story, and Lori had an exclusive on her hands. No other L.A. station had covered the event.

Quietly, Lori slipped out of the room and the direct line to the assignment desk at the station, and got Peter Coyle.

"Pete? Lori. We're wrapped at the old movie star get-together in Bel Air, and you might tell Gamm to consider putting it a whole lot higher in the show than he originally planned."

"Sure," Coyle said incredulously. Lori was an amateur; she got overly enthusiastic about every goddamned story they sent her out on. "Why don't I tell The Wizard it may even be the lead of the show? All we got is the President's news conference, another blackmail statement from OPEC, and a triple-shooting in East L.A."

"Try this," Lori said, trying not to gloat. "Rex Hampton, superstar of the forties, drops dead watching the movie that won him his first Oscar. And under, maybe, mysterious circumstances."

"You're shittin' me!"

"No. He did. He dropped dead, right in front of us. And we got it all. Well, not him falling to the floor, but everything after that."

"Jeez," Coyle said, in one of his rare impressed moods. "Let me tell Gamm. Nice goin', kid."

A nice goin' kid from Pete Coyle was equivalent to an Emmy from any news director in town. Lori beamed and hung up. Pete Coyle said, "Nice goin', kid!" The same Pete Coyle who still had Dan Rather and Tom Brokaw on his wait-and-see list.

Chapter 2

Sergeant Mark Bennett removed the Los Angeles Police Department phone memo from his uniform shirt pocket, unfolded it, and read it again, slowly. "Lori Matrix, KTRB reporter, called. Wants to talk to you re: fatality, Rita Reno house, Bel Air. Ryerson."

Bennett sighed, refolded the note, put it back into his shirt pocket, and leaned back in the squeaky chair, placing his hands behind his head. He stared at the ancient spittoon without seeing it, the same spittoon his policeman father had used for its original purpose when he occupied this same 11th precinct detective squad room fifteen years ago. Now the spittoon was a planter, hanging from a corner of the cluttered room.

Bennett knew who Lori Matrix was. He had seen her on the street several times. Once with her station's mini-cam unit during the attempted hijack of a Japan Air Lines plane by that sixteen-year-old disturbed computer genius who wanted to take the plane directly to Las Vegas so he could try out his new roulette theory. Another time when the Knights of Freedom and Justice called KTRB-TV, bragging that they had planted four bombs on the first floor of *The Los Angeles Times* building. The last time he had seen Lori Captain Terry Smothers was retiring and she had charmed the old man out of his shoes, unexpectedly handing him a dozen roses she had paid for herself and planting a kiss on his weathered cheek

Bennett could not help wonder what Lori was like off camera, someone so beautiful and famous, someone who was a knockout like her.

At that moment, a redheaded, Irish lieutenant stuck his frizzy dome around the door interrupting Bennett's thoughts.

"Young man, I'm looking for Dick Tracy. Might you be him?"

Bennett smiled and closed his eyes briefly. When he opened them again, he was staring into Pat Malone's eyes.

"Come in, Pat. And close the door on your thumb."

Malone came in with that curious half-smile on his lips. The man never was completely serious about anything.

"The boys downstairs say you're going to visit a very lovely lady today now...a Miss Matrix. Is that right is it?"

Pat could ask three separate questions, or the same questions three times, in a single sentence.

Bennett said, "Yeah. Strictly business."

"Strictly business, of course," Malone noted. "Was it me

16

now, ah, I'd be wearin' some maddenin' scent and trying my best to steal the lady's heart."

"Or her drawers," Bennett remarked, without missing a beat.

"Whatever," Malone said. "What would she want with the likes of a poor homicide sergeant like you?"

"Malone, for Christ sake, stop playing Irish. You graduated from Southern Cal, not Notre Dame, and I happen to know your ancestors came over on the Mayflower."

"Or swam behind it," Malone said, suddenly devoid of his brogue. "No kidding, Mark, what does this Lori Matrix want to see you about?"

"I don't know for sure," Bennett replied, walking over to the dusty mirror next to a cracked washstand. He peered into the mirror, showed his teeth to it, and said, "The word I get is that she has this thing for me."

"Perfectly understandable," Malone offered. "Probably saw you on the Medal of Valor awards show. Her station ran the whole boring thing just so their camera crews can park in the red zones without gettin' tickets."

"Possible," Bennett said. "I was awfully good on that one. I remember after they got through reading whatever it was I was supposed to have done, I looked the chief right in the eye and said, Thank you, sir.'"

"And said it beautifully, I might add," Malone laughed.

"Thank you," Bennett retorted appreciatively. "And then, wouldn't know all those inarticulate bastards who followed me up on the stage had to play copycat and say the same goddamned thing one after the other. Thank you, sir.' Thank you, sir.' Thank you, sir.' It's enough to make you sick."

Bennett took a stab at his curly black hair with a long

comb broken in half to pocket comb size and prepared to leave. Malone walked over and gave him a playful punch on the arm.

"Watch your step, son. She may be one of those women who are looking for no more than a nest egg in her old age. It would be quite a feather in her cap if she could snag a cop and get him to share that magnificent pension with her."

Bennett waved a forefinger in the air. "By God, you're right. I'm almost sorry I'm wearing my best suit."

"Shit, yes," Malone boomed. "But do the second best thing. Don't let her see the J.C. Penney label and maybe you can convince her it's only a cheapie."

"Right," Bennett smirked, "and thanks for all your good advice."

"It's nothing, old friend," Malone said. "And one more thing. Keep your fly zippered. Nothing fails to impress a television star like Miss Matrix more than a cop who walks in with his weenie dangling out his pants."

Bennett opened the door and paused in the doorway. He turned and smiled sweetly at his old friend.

"Mr. Malone, I wonder, are you familiar with the expression...Kiss my ass!"

Bennett slammed the door behind him and he could hear the old man laughing almost until he reached the revolving door at the front of the police building.

Bennett had never been in the Silver Cloud Inn. Honest cops could not afford it. Police sergeants especially did not appear in places like the Silver Cloud Inn unless it happened to be on business. Police business. Unless, of course, they had captured the Hillside Strangler single-handed and

18

collected all these rewards, or maybe they were on the take and had just looked the other way as one hundred and fifty pounds of marijuana went waltzing past your nose and your eyesight suddenly de-escalated to zero. That is why Bennett's hand was in his left pocket, reassuringly fingering the twenty-eight dollars there.

He had hardly set foot inside the door when he sensed that something was different about the place tonight. It had the posh look and feel he expected, the velvet atmosphere, sure. But there was a feeling of electricity in the air. And he could see the reason for it.

In full view was Lori, seated in the center booth, unofficially designated the celebrity booth by the management, because the occupants of all those other booths could see it. She looked radiant in a rich blue dress of some kind of shiny material that complimented her figure. She was wearing a tiny tiara in her long blonde hair and every head in the place seemingly turned in her direction. If she was aware of the attention, she gave no hint of it.

Lori was writing in a small booklet wired at the top, a reporter's tool Bennett had seen many times before. The maitre d' did not even ask Bennett his name. He simply brought him over to the table and as Lori became aware of his presence, she looked up and her smile seemed to light up the room.

"Sergeant Bennett!"

It never sounded like that to Mark Bennett before. He nodded, and smiled a little. She asked him to sit down and he nodded again.

A waiter in a red velvet jacket had materialized as very good waiters do, and handed Bennett an oversized menu.

He was glad he had it. He felt the need of a prop.

One look at the prices and Bennett knew the twenty-eight dollars in his pocket would be completely adequate. For a tip. How he would bail his twenty-year-old car out of the valet parking lot he could only wonder. Perhaps the valet would consider his Timex watch as a down payment. After all, it was a self-winding model, even if the crystal was broken.

Lori seemed to sense his discomfort, as well as his attempt to disguise it.

"This is business for me, Sergeant, so I hope you'll understand when I say I've got to pick up the check. Can't set a precedent and let my cheap network think I'm going to pay for dinners at places like this out of my own pocket."

Bennett smiled, and hoped she had not seen the lump in his throat a few moments before.

"Well, of course, if you really mean that. Otherwise..."

"Oh, I really do."

Bennett thought, "Otherwise, what? Otherwise, I'll wash the dishes or pull out my service pistol and back out of the joint."

Lori was studying her menu and Bennett was studying her. The bright blue eyes looked as big as half-dollars on his thirteen-inch color flat screen TV. Here, just eighteen inches away from him, they looked like saucers. The skin was smooth as cream and flawless, the hair shiny and he imagined he could even smell it; it looked so clean and fresh. His examination was quick but penetrating. However, when Lori looked up from the menu, her eyes connected with his flattering glances. They talked menu talk for a little while and Lori ordered a wine very unfamiliar to Bennett.

When he checked it on the menu, he knew why. It cost eleven dollars a bottle. Four-ninety-five was about a police sergeant's limit, and it had better be somebody's birthday.

Between the wine and some kind of flaming dessert Bennett could not identify and was too proud to ask for an I.D. came a marvelous end cut of prime rib that Lori did not even have to request. She automatically got the best wherever she went. Restaurant and club owners were always delighted to have a local celebrity on their premises and frequently the management tried to pick up the tab, something Lori never allowed.

"Sergeant..."

She was hoping he would say something like, "Call me Mark," but he did not.

"Sergeant...I wanted to talk to you, to tap your expertise and get your opinion and advice, on what happened at the Rita Reno house."

Bennett knew very well what had happened there. Bill Ross had done the paperwork on that one and had mentioned to him how much he had admired the deceased as a boy.

Lori said, "It's true that Rex Hampton was nearly seventy years old and had a record of heart trouble. It's not surprising that he would have a heart attack. It could happen to any of us at any time. I think."

She wanted Bennett to say, That is right, go on. He simply looked at her with what was becoming a frustrating way. Not insolent, not anything. Just looked at her as if he was looking at a wall.

"Anyway," she continued, "what I wanted to talk to you about is the way it...well, looked."

"And how was that?" Bennett asked, puzzled.

"All right, well, when someone has a heart attack, they might leap up, as he did, but I've had two specialists tell me that it's more likely, much more likely, that someone having a seizure like that would clutch their hands to their chest and keel over. And there was that other thing."

"What other thing?"

"The way his right arm seemed to strike out. Actually, what it looked like...God...you're going to think I'm crazy."

Bennett smiled more out of confusion than amusement.

"Keep going."

"Look, let me just tell you exactly what it looked like, from beginning to end. We're watching Hampton's picture. There's this sudden shriek...from him. We turn around and he's jumped up from his seat and for the life of me he is pointing right at the picture, at something in the picture, something he sees, and whatever it is that he sees brings on this...this heart attack."

Bennett studied her face for several long seconds.

"You're saying the man saw something in the picture, in the film, that, what? Scared him to death?"

Lori shook her head in frustration. "I don't even know if there is such a thing as being scared to death. I just think there is. But that's exactly what it looked like. Something in that picture startled him. He jumped up, pointed at it, and...kaplooey."

"Kaplooey?"

"Keeled over. Dead. What do you think?"

Bennett smiled, patronizingly.

"Please don't be offended, although I'm sure you will be." Bennett paused for a second. "But I think you've fallen out of your tree. Too farfetched. And I don't believe in the occult."

"I'm not offended, but I didn't say it had to be anything occult. I just meant...oh, shit, what's the use. I'm probably dead wrong, anyway."

Bennett continued to play it straight with Lori.

"Hey, I don't know whether you're right or wrong or what. I understand what you're saying. I'm just saying the likelihood of it is, well, unlikely. Bad use of language, eh?"

Lori flashed her best smile and then turned serious. "How the hell would I know, I'm in television news. We rarely use the language in my business."

They both laughed again. Lori devoured her fifth piece of sirloin and pushed the plate from her.

"Don't tell me you don't like that," Bennett wondered aloud. "I never tasted a better piece of meat in my life."

"No," Lori said. "I'm getting fat as a pig and I've got to start using a little self-discipline."

Bennett looked quickly at the svelte figure. Yeah, she was right. Five-foot eight and what? Maybe one hundred and ten beautifully distributed pounds. A real pig all right.

"Well," Bennett confessed, "since I'm rarely seen on television, and I make most of my personal appearances in whore houses, family fights, and robberies in progress, I'm going to clean my plate like my mother always told me I should."

Lori smiled approvingly. She liked this man. She liked the fact he had not come on to her, not once. And not once, as with most men she knew, had she caught him trying to look down the front of her blouse and examining her breasts.

Bennett did indeed clean his plate. They finished their wine and walked to the parking lot after Lori paid the bill and left a generous tip--so large Bennett misinterpreted it as an offer to buy the place.

As they waited for the valet to bring up Lori's Porsche, she looked over Bennett's five-foot-eleven-inch frame. He looked rock hard, in top condition. And Lori noticed that women noticed him, too. If he was not handsome, he was just this side of handsome. And there was something sexy about him. More than the athletic build, more than the curly dark hair.

Bennett would not let Lori take his parking ticket. She wanted to pay for that too, but that seemed just a little too much. He had his pride.

"Listen, can I call you...on business...some time again?"

"Sure," Bennett said. "I'll think over what you said, but..."

"I know, I know," Lori admitted hesitantly. "Farfetched."

Bennett shrugged and smiled. Then Lori propositioned him.

"I'm covering the next meeting of that little group on the fourteenth. Want to come along? I can bring you in as a member of my crew?"

Bennett shrugged it off. "Thanks, no. But if you come up with another corpse, give me a jingle."

Lori nodded. She knew he was putting her on, not taking her seriously, and she was not even sure she was taking her own theory seriously. It was she admitted, if only to herself, an improbable theory.

The Porsche rumbled up and the valet popped out and held the door open for Lori. As she got in, her skirt moved up her thighs, revealing amplitude of perfectly formed leg.

24

The valet sighed. Bennett pretended not to notice.

Lori pointed a forefinger at Bennett and he pointed one back at her. Bang! Then she roared off.

The valet, an over-acned young man with a runny nose, sidled up to Bennett and said, "Jeez, what wouldn't you give to fuck that, huh?"

Bennett looked at him. "What, again?"

At the precise moment, another valet brought up Bennett's car, and he popped into it wondering how long the valet would have that same look on his face. He liked to think, hours.

Chapter 3

Rita Reno did not answer the door this time. An overweight Mexican-American woman with a kind face and gentle humor showed Lori and the crew into the home. Charles Evans Fine greeted them. Lori and Fine sat down at his suggestion. The news crew busied itself setting up the equipment. Fine looked concerned, the gray brows slightly knitted, the long, sensitive fingers fidgeting with the front of his jacket.

"Rita's not been feeling well since...you know."

"I'm sorry to hear that," Lori said understandingly. "She looks so well, I would never guess her health was anything less than perfect."

"It's not her physical health," Fine explained, lowering his voice just above a whisper. "She's been very upset that something like that should happen right in front of her. She told me she had never seen anyone die before, not even a relative or loved one."

"I know what a shock it must have been. But the showings...the club, it will go on."

"Yes, of course," Fine brightened. "It was just an unfortunate coincidence that poor Hampton should cash in during our first meeting. I thought I'd mention these things because, well, it's liable to be just a little somber in there tonight and, well, you know."

It was an obvious plea for tact and sensitivity and Lori recognized it as such. She nodded, and Fine knew she understood.

Lori got up and whispered to the crew out of Fine's hearing. "Okay, guys, we have to kind of pussyfoot around this one. The last time out, as I told you, one of them keeled over so let's kind of walk on eggs in there, you can see why."

They could. They were a newly hired crew, anxious to please. And working with Lori for the first time made them a whole lot more reticent than they normally would be.

The crew set up the lights. After indicating they were ready, Lori ended a conversation she had begun with Reno and with a signal from Reno, the projectionist performed his magic and the old black-and-white flick, *The Girl from La Jolla*, began. Lori noted that Martha Von Tours had top billing over the movie title, unusual in those days, and a testament to her enormous popularity in the early thirties.

The story line of *The Girl from La Jolla* was painfully familiar, but Lori remembered what another film director once had told her in another interview, "'Play it, Sam' and other clichés of today were fresh when first heard. They lasted and became clich s because they were good enough to last. Even 'They went that away was fresh once, new once."

In *The Girl from La Jolla*, Martha Von Tours was the shy little girl from Kansas City, trying to make it on Broadway. Why a shy little girl named Ginger from Kansas City would wear a skimpy costume like that, with her boobs and buns jiggling in and out when she danced, Hollywood never felt compelled to explain. She met a handsome prince from some obscure and completely imaginary European kingdom, and the prince was smitten and there were all sorts of cute little business-including several songs because this was a forerunner of the big movie musical.

From the moment the film began, Lori had experienced an inexplicably eerie feeling. A feeling others in the room apparently did not share. As the film moved along, the original somewhat somber atmosphere had changed, and the assembled guests had been in a rather light-hearted mood, exchanging pleasantries and code talk about the business that Lori did not quite understand, and passing around hors d'oeuvres and both hard and soft drinks.

When the picture ended and the lights came up, everyone applauded, not just polite but enthusiastically.

Lori was sitting in the back of the room, the better to observe everyone, and when the lights came back on almost every head turned to Martha Von Tours. Lori, seated behind Martha, leaned forward as she saw the sea of smiling faces turn toward Martha, and said, "Oh, that was fine, really fine."

Then she saw the smiles suddenly fade.

Peter Olson, closest to Martha, rose and said, "Oh my God, no!" The others were soon on their feet, and Lori leapt to her feet and came around to face Martha. Her eyes were wide open, and she seemed to be staring at the now empty screen. Peter leaned over and brought his face close to her.

"Martha? Martha, my dear, are you all right?"

Peter touched her cheek lightly, and she fell over, her head hitting the empty seat next to her. He caught her body before it could strike the floor.

She was dead.

The second tragedy in two weeks was the lead on the 11 o'clock news and on all three owned and operated network stations. The independents played it up with equal fervor.

Two major superstars of the past, each dying of a heart attack at a showing of his/her picture in the Bel Air mansion of Rita Reno. Only Channel 7 had footage of paramedics wheeling out the body. Channel 4 arrived just after the coroner's man and got no more than the paramedic van pulling out of the driveway.

Channel 2 had a brief interview with a harassed and hurried Charles Evans Fine, who downplayed the silly reporter's suggestion that something occult might be involved.

"A most unfortunate coincidence," is what Fine had called it, and just about everyone saw it that way.

Except for Lori. She had a strange feeling about the first death and this latest death confirmed her original feelings, even though this time the victim, if she called Martha Von Tours that, had not cried out. She had simply died where she sat, silently, noiselessly.

Jeff Lenburg

The office loved the story. Patricia Mahoney, the 11 P.M. producer for Channel 7, thought so much of it she allowed it a full two minutes--the very same amount of time she had given the attempted suicide of Pope John Paul and the prison escape of Charles Manson.

There were follow-ups the next day on the five and six o'clock reports. Rita Reno would talk to no news people except Lori. She had come to know and trust her, but refused to do an on-camera interview. Lori did an audio report with her, tape recording her remarks, and the two news shows played them over hastily assembled stills from Rita's major pictures.

Rita delivered a tribute of sorts to the late Martha Von Tours. She said how unfortunate the coincidence of a double death was, and told Lori--and through her the public--that while the second death would not stop the group from continuing to show their pictures to each other, she could no longer host the club in her home. Rita revealed that Charles Evans Fine had volunteered his beautiful Malibu Beach house for their next and subsequent meetings.

Lori had difficulty keeping her mind on her routine after Martha Von Tours' death. She had placed a call to Sergeant Bennett and received no reply. At the end of the day placed another call to Sergeant Bennett. This time, it paid off.

"Can I possibly see you?"

"Sure. When?"

"I was thinking, like tonight."

"Tonight? It's a quarter-to-twelve."

Humorously, Lori said, "Won't your mommy let you out after dark?"

"Cute," Bennett grinned. "Very cute. You take Twinkies

31

intravenously? All right, if it's urgent. Meet me at Kelly's Bar in fifteen minutes."

"Right," Lori said, and hung up.

Then, muttering quietly under her breath, she said, "Oh, shit!" She suddenly remembered she did not know where Kelly's Bar was.

Well, the desk knew everything, she remembered. She would ask them. Coyle knew Kelly's Bar very well.

"It's a crazy place. No place to take a woman, of course. It's filled with nutsy harpies and their friends. One of those joints where they sing authentic Irish tunes and pass the hat for the IRA," Gamm offered. "Worth your life to start an argument in there. The Irish fight for the fun of it, you know, and only God knows why. Sixth and Hillhurst. Lovely neighborhood. The muggers give it a wide berth, and know they'll be mugged if they go down there."

With that recommendation racing in her golden head, Lori took off for Kelly's. It was just as Coyle said it would be, plus two. It looked like the siege of Stalingrad, in all-civilian dress, and sounded like the inside of a railroad roadhouse.

It was an uncommonly quiet night. Only three men were rolling in the sawdust on the floor, and one of them appeared to be making a valiant effort at stuffing an empty half-gallon beer bottle into another's left ear, while the third was seeing how far up the first man's nose he could push two fingers of his left hand.

The bar was jammed with imbibers. Some singing, most arguing, a few simply engaged in nearly reasonable conversation, and another reciting of Dylan Thomas to three teary-eyed old hags. All of them close to collapsing from the strong drink, the bond that drew them together in the first place.

The bartender was a fragile, three hundred-pound Celtic elf who left Dublin under a cloud, charged by an over-sensitive judiciary with abusing a public vehicle. What he had done was to punch out all the windows of a downtown bus in a fine fit of Irish temper after his girlfriend told him she was leaving him for another man--her husband. For an incurable romantic like Patrick O'Donough it was just too much to bear.

Bennett was there ahead of Lori, fulfilling her first wish. So he was able to reach out and draw her in just in time. A huge oaf with two teeth missing from his upper ivories had made an instinctive lunge for Lori, but mumbled "beggin[1] your pardon I am" when he saw Bennett.

Almost everyone in the place seemed to know Bennett, and that restored a little of Lori's sense of security. Bennett guided her skillfully to a corner table that he had reserved. Kelly himself was there to shoo off any intruders and Bennett placed Lori in a chair facing the wall and sat down close to her.

"What will you have?" he asked Lori.

"A Tequila Sunrise," she said firmly.

"Two Bushmills," said Bennett to Kelly, and Kelly smiled broadly and shouldered his way to the bar.

Bennett leaned closer to Lori. "When you first visit an Irish bar, it's good policy to order something very Irish. Order a Tequila Sunrise in here and they're liable to paper the wall with you."

Lori looked at Bennett with a warm, sweet smile. "In other words," she mused," when in Rome..."

"Something like that. And what do we have to talk about tonight?"

Lori frowned a little and hoped Bennett had not noticed. But there was nothing about her that went unnoticed by him.

"You thought I was a little foolish when I feltwell, funny about the first death at Rita Reno's. Now there's been another, and I'm doubly distressed. Sound crazy to you?"

Bennett smiled. He did not smile often, and Lori liked his smile.

"You've got every right in the world to play amateur sleuth. Everybody does."

Lori did not like that, not one bit.

"That's patronizing. What you're saying is 'I'm a little dope whose opinion isn't worth anything.'"

"Not at all. Calling you an amateur in the police business is no insult. I'd be an amateur in the news business."

Lori still seemed offended by his comment. Her voice conveyed her disdain. "Some people think I still am. I'm trying to prove they're wrong."

"So you'd like to solve a murder, just like in the movies. Is that it?"

"Now you are laughing at me."

Bennett reached over and lightly squeezed her shoulder, "Honest, I'm not. Okay, let's talk seriously."

But before they could begin, Kelly returned with two two-ounce shot glasses of Bushmill's and two glasses of water for chasers.

Bennett thanked Kelly, who pushed away the five spot Bennett aimed at him.

"No mick cop has ever paid for the first drink of the night in Kelly's. Up the Irish."

Bennett nodded appreciatively and he and Lori held up their glasses to Kelly, who accepted the toast with a sweep of his hand and a histrionic bow. Then he melded back into the melee.

Bennett watched him go. "A hambone. Used to be with the Abbey Players, no less. Or so he claims."

"Which gets us back to the actors," Lori said.

Bennett looked at Lori thoughtfully. She might look a bit fragile, but she hung on like a bulldog when an idea possessed her.

"You're suspicious." Bennett made his remark in a way that his voice betrayed him.

"You're being sarcastic."

Bennett said reassuringly, "Not at all. Look, two meetings, two people drop dead. You have the right to be suspicious. I'm..."

"Suspicious too?"

"No," he paused, "curious. And there's a difference. I only get suspicious officially. I see no evidence of foul play, no reason to be suspicious. But, yes, I am curious. It's an interesting coincidence."

"If it is a coincidence."

Bennett studied Lori's silky features. There definitely was a brain behind all that smooth skin and those terribly bright blue eyes.

"All right," he said convincingly, "let's examine your suspicions. This film society group meets, and an elderly man dies of a heart attack. He had a record of heart trouble. Nothing to raise eyebrows, right?"

Now Lori was studying Bennett. Was he mocking her, making fun of her amateur sleuthing? Or worse, was he here now only because he was like every other man she had ever met, fantasizing how she would be in bed? Or was he trying to see her as she saw herself. As a serious person, someone accepted at face value, despite all that image garbage, that glamour bullshit?

"Now there's another meeting, and another film is being shown. And this time an elderly woman dies, of natural causes. On that, we have the coroner's word. But in both cases, autopsies were performed at the request of the heirs to the respective victims' estates. Now you tell me, why should I think anything other than what apparently happened... happened?"

Lori sighed, a sigh of resignation. "Meshugaas!"

"Huh?"

"It's crazy, I know. This whole meshugaas is driving me crazy. Maybe I should drop the whole thing."

Bennett thought, she must have been sleeping with a Jewish guy. She has picked up the entire lingo.

"Hey, think what you want," Bennett countered. "Unless I see some hard evidence to the contrary, I've got to accept what I think is the truth. Two elderly actors have died of heart attacks. Period."

Lori took a long draught of her drink, and then set it down slowly. She smiled, sweetly, like a cobra about to strike.

"All right, Mr. Detective, you win. There is nothing wrong. Nothing at all. But my gut instinct tells me something. Want to hear it?"

Bennett figured he had little choice in the matter.

"Why not?"

Lori tapped his chest with her forefinger.

"There will be another showing on the first Thursday of next month. If someone else dies, will you call it a coincidence?"

Bennett shook his head. This crazy lady was possessed with the notion that something very strange was going on. Not just something...odd, but something, what?

Lori could read his thoughts. His face betrayed them.

"Come on, now," she said, looking for a straight answer, "I'm asking nicely. Would a third death, under almost similar circumstances, convince you that something very, very unusual was going on?"

"Are you talking about the supernatural?"

Lori looked very long and hard at Bennett before she answered. "Yes."

He did not laugh. He did not even smile. And when he spoke, she knew he was deadly serious.

"I don't believe in ghosts, goblins or the occult."

"I don't know whether I do not or not," Lori agreed. "And I don't know if that's what I'm talking about, or not. Look, I'm a reasonably intelligent, college-educated woman who's been around, at least a little bit. And something deep inside me tells me we're not dealing with normal events."

Bennett smiled a little now. "Hey, I'm the one who's supposed to believe in leprechauns and things that go bump in the night."

"Let me tell you something," Lori admitted. "I don't believe in the supernatural. And I'm not clairvoyant. And as far as I know, I don't have ESP or anything like that. But as surely as we're sitting here, I'm telling you, someone else is going to die if another meeting of that club convenes. And I don't know why."

"All right," Bennett said, "I will be there, with their permission, the next time they meet. And if something happens, well, let's just wait and see if something does."

Chapter 4

If Lori had discussed her innermost thoughts with Charles Evans Fine instead of Sergeant Bennett, she would have been pleasantly surprised to discover that Fine was experiencing the same strange feelings she was.

But he didn't feel he could say anything to his live-in mistress, Barbara Dawes. Barbara was twenty years his junior, and she wasn't decorating Fine's beautiful seaside home because of her knowledge of brain surgery and classical music. She was a sensuous, still-beautiful woman, unsuccessful as an actress but marvelously successful as a mistress. She had lived with four other men before Fine, and served each of them well. They had done very well by her, too, and she was satisfied with her life.

By the financial arrangement she had had with each of her men friends, Barbara was cared for better than a wife was. When she decided to leave, she left, and each time walked away with a generous sum of money as a going away present. There was nothing written between them. Nothing had to be.

Barbara always earned her keep, and she chose only honorable men with reputations to protect. She liked Fine the most of her previous alliances, and had no plan to leave him. Now in her mid-forties, she knew her beauty was fading and she was growing slightly less secure than she had before.

Fine watched Barbara fussing over the seating arrangements for tonight's meeting and wondered, as he had many times before, if she really had been faithful to him. Not that he would do anything about it if she were not. He was sixty-two years old now, and much of the anger and jealously and insecurity of his earlier years had left him. Her fidelity, real or fictional, was a matter of only passing interest to him now. She had served his needs. She owed him nothing more.

"Charley?"

"Yes."

"Where do you want to sit?"

Fine got up from his favorite easy chair and strolled into the sun-drenched living room. He paused, as he had done a million times before, to take a sweeping romantic view from his window. That, and the gentle breeze, was why he bought this place twenty years ago. Now, with California beachfront property escalating out of sight, he couldn't afford to buy it again, not at today's inflated prices.

"I think next to Pete." He meant Peter Olson, of course, the man made famous as Dracula in the movies. This was Pete's night. They were showing *The Land of the Living Un-Dead*, a title that always amused him because of its redundancy. And if it was Olson's turn to drop dead, by God, Fine was determined to find out what would cause it. Like Bennett, he didn't believe in ghosts. But he had lived long enough to know that many strange things occur for which there seems to be no rational, scientific explanation. For some reason he remembered his father once saying to him, "You can't see the wind, but you know it's there." That gross simplicity seemed to have relevance tonight, but his mind was too full to turn it over and examine it.

Barbara was saying, "Would you mind very much if I ducked out on the meeting? I mean, if you would, I'll stay."

Fine laughed. Sometimes she was like a little girl, more like a daughter than mistress.

"Of course not. You'd probably be bored out of your pretty little skull picking among us ruins."

"Ruins!" She came over and put her arms around his neck, leaned up, and kissed him, not casually but passionately.

"I'd shove Paul Newman out of bed for you."

Fine laughed again. She was so good for his morale, always.

"That's one of the kindest exaggerations I've ever heard," he said. "But I like it. No, you run along. I don't really care to live in the past and there's no reason for you to take up residence there, not even for a few hours."

"You're sure?"

"I'm sure."

Barbara was going to visit one of her girl friends, or take in a movie. Whatever it was, she would decide to do to escape the meeting. But she stayed until just half an hour before the first guest arrived, and had everything in perfect order, as she always did. There was a huge pot of coffee perking on the kitchen range, the bar was serviced and ready for entertaining, and there was a mountain of little goodies, most of which she had baked herself.

Barbara was a product of the lower classes and was never the equal of his more intellectual friends. She was never self-educated, and there was gaping holes in the store of her knowledge. But she did not mind her flaws if he did not. And what she lacked in the intellectual area she more than made up with her kindness and caring. He watched her pretty figure as she walked to the driveway, and waved goodbye from the window.

His director's eye approved the way nature backlit her flowing red hair just before she crossed the nose of the car out of the driveway and toward the main road. Then he walked back to his picture window, concentrating again on the strange happenings that were beginning to occupy most of his waking thoughts.

He had lost two members of his peer group. Truth was, neither had been really close friends. But he liked and admired them. He knew Peter Olson better than he had known Rex Hampton and Martha Von Tours. They had worked together in two pictures, and Olson was one of the few Hollywood actors who had had the guts to speak up on behalf of the Hollywood Ten and other leftists and liberals blacklisted in that ugly era that saw Fine's career go into an eclipse because of his politics.

Fine had a terrible feeling in the pit of his stomach that something bad was going to happen tonight. It went against all logic, against his own judgment, and yet, there it was, this gnawing, aching something that made him wish that the fast-sinking sun could just freeze-frame and hang there until someone, somewhere, figured this thing out. But time will not stand still, and wishing does not make it so. Eight o'clock arrived, and so did the first of the evening's guests.

Bette Oliver arrived on the arm of Peter Olson and brought the news that one club member would not be on hand tonight. Colleen Kantor had asked her to present her regrets. The events at the last two meetings were more than she could handle. She wanted it known that she was not superstitious, although most show people are. She had just decided not to go on with the film showings. Fine understood. He had serious reservations of his own, but did not convey them to Bette or Peter.

Rita Reno arrived ten minutes later and, moments after that, Sylvia Carl-Stapleton, fresh from a cocktail party in Beverly Hills, and higher than a kite. Fine distributed cocktails all around and ten minutes before the film was to begin, the doorbell rang again. Fine was delighted to see Lori but looking over her shoulder, he saw no film crew.

"They're at a gigantic furniture warehouse fire in West Covina!" she offered.

Fine smiled. He was pleased that no television news crew would be on hand tonight. He had kept the location of their meeting a secret this time so the media would not be a distraction. He only invited one member of the press: that young charming newswoman Lori Matrix.

Lori arrived, all alone and a without a crew, moments

before the movie was about to begin. She said hello all around and got Fine aside again at the first opportunity to tell him she had discussed the happenings--that's what she had taken to calling the two deaths--with a police sergeant. Fine did not know whether that was a good or a bad idea. He did not think, at this point, it helped or hurt.

Just as Carl-Stapleton began sinking slowly in the west, thanks to too many cocktails beforehand, the projectionist flicked the lights off and on from Fine's custom-made control booth, the signal for the guests to take their seats. Fine sat next to Peter Olson with Rita Reno perched on the other side. Lori took an easy chair next to Bette Oliver After the lights went down and out, the opening title to *The Land of the Living Un-Dead* splashed onto the screen.

The twenty-five-year-old soundtrack had not weathered the years as well as its star, Peter Olson, and it was fuzzy, as if the orchestra that had played the background music was deliberately trying to miss every third note. Olson, in a festive mood from three martinis, leaned over to Fine and whispered, "Now that's my kind of music!"

"Still beats that rock and roll stuff," Fine said, revealing one of his generation gap prejudices.

The others sat in silence. They were pros, and did more than simply view and enjoy films. They analyzed them silently as the frames slipped by. They took note of editing techniques, and lens changes, and set decoration. Those kinds of things and many more had been the whole of their lives. They looked at films like a master chef looks at a seven-course dinner. Everything had special meaning for them. Nothing escaped their expert scrutiny.

Lori had the strangest feeling watching this old film. She

had seen it first on television, and it had scared the daylights out of her. But she was one of those children who enjoyed being scared, if she was making the choice. She had got on a vampire kick early in her teens, and had made a point of seeing all of Peter Olson's horror films at theaters that specialized in old movies. She knew this particular story very well, but even knowing what was going to happen next did not soften the blow when it came. She was frightened all over again and enjoyed it.

Lori thought, "How little we really change. When this film frightened me last, I could not have been more than ten or eleven years old. Now I'm twenty-nine and I'm still scared to death. We never grow up."

The scene had everyone on the edge of his seat, even Peter Olson himself.

Olson looked marvelously eerie dressed in a long black cloak. His hair was jet black, and he looked not unlike a young Bela Lugosi, after whom Olson had modeled his character.

In the most important scene in the film, Olson stood on the edge of a cliff, trying to decide whether to throw himself off into the abyss, and end the psychological torture of the battle between good and evil that raged within him.

Suddenly, Olson's young assistant appeared out of the murky fog that surrounded the mountain. He pleaded with Doctor Morda (his name in the film) not to take his life.

"No, no!" The anguished scream came not from the young actor in the film, but from Olson, sitting fifteen feet from the screen. Before anyone else could move, Olson was on his feet, running at the screen. Lori had only half raised to her feet when Olson went crashing into the screen, his outstretched hands clawing at the silky smooth material. The weight of Olson's body barreling into it tore the screen from its moorings in the ceiling and it came crashing down, enveloping Olson's tumbling form. In seconds, Lori and Fine reached the front of the room to extricate Olson from the torn screen. His face seemed drained of all its color. Fine called his name, repeatedly, without a response. He felt for Olson's heartbeat, and then checked his pulse.

Kneeling over Olson's body, he told a wide-eyed Lori, "I think he's dead."

Rita Reno screamed and fell back in her chair in a faint. Bette Oliver stared straight ahead, unbelieving, And Sylvia Carl-Stapleton, roused from her drunken stupor, kept saying, "What's happening?" over and over again.

By the time Bennett arrived, Sylvia was either sober or a far better actress than any critic had ever given her credit for. But she was useless as a witness. She had been unconscious throughout the entire incident.

The coroner's men removed the body, and Bennett gave them instructions to talk to no one. He also irritated Lori by telling her she was also a witness and while she could call her newsroom, once, she could not leave the premises and he prohibited access by all television news crews.

After she called the desk and told them what had happened, she hung up and turned to Bennett.

"Sergeant, I'm an officially credited member of the news media in this city and you are not going to keep me a prisoner in this house."

Bennett looked at her. "I suggest you sit down and calm down."

It was so abrupt and cold it took her by surprise. And to her surprise, she found herself sitting down.

She wondered what had happened to the quiet, almost shy policeman she had known, and she suddenly realized she had not known this Mark Bennett at all. He could be charming, all right, but now he was all cop, almost too self-assured, too organized. He was tough, cold, efficient, and it bothered her.

Bennett began talking quietly to a uniformed officer and when he finished, he turned to Lori again.

This time his voice was lower, more personal, but still very firm.

"This is what you wanted, a full-scale, formal investigation, wasn't it?"

He did not wait for her to answer.

"I've joined you in your suspicions, even though there isn't enough hard evidence for a homicide investigation. But three deaths in a row, under similar circumstances, are enough to direct the department's attention to the matter."

Bennett had inspected the built-in projectionist's room. Nothing was unusual. The film, since rewound, was back in its original tin canister. The projectionist said he was on a cigarette break and returned just after Olson had suddenly keeled over. Therefore, he would not be a credible witness.

Bennett spent the next hour and half interrogating each guest, and dismissing each one afterward with almost the same words.

"Thanks for your cooperation. I'll probably want to talk to you again. Since you're all material witnesses, I'm going to ask you not to leave town without notifying me first."

Rita Reno was the last to leave and declined Loris request for an interview. She did make it very plain that she would attend no more screenings, which came as no surprise to Lori. The latest incident seemed to write finis to the entire project.

Fine saw Rita to her car, and then returned to his home. Bennett examined the elderly director's face. It was drawn, the tension of the evening having taken its toll.

"Mr. Fine, I think you've all been through enough of an ordeal without my adding to it. I would like to talk to you, too, but perhaps that can wait until tomorrow."

Fine nodded. He looked exhausted.

"Sergeant, there are some things I want to talk about, but you're right. Now is not the time. Miss Matrix, I'm afraid you got a whole lot more story than any of us bargained for. Perhaps, later, we can talk about it."

Lori agreed, and Fine disappeared into an anteroom to get her coat. Lori avoided Bennett's gaze. They stood in silence for the few moments it took for Fine to reappear and when he did, Bennett took Lori's coat from him and held it for her. She managed to put it on without once looking in his face.

"We have things we've got to talk about," Bennett said. Lori turned, and then caught herself. Bennett was not addressing her; he was talking to Fine. She felt a touch of heat come into her cheeks and hoped Bennett had not noticed it.

"But not tonight," Fine said, his voice sounding tired.

"Of course," Bennett responded. Even a casual glance at Fine would reveal the man was obviously under great strain.

Lori put out her hand and Fine took it.

"I'm so sorry, Mr. Fine," she said sincerely. "In a few days, I'd like to talk to you again, if I may."

Fine nodded and frailly turned to Bennett.

"Give me a call tomorrow."

Bennett said, "Fine, Mr. Fine," and Fine smiled and nodded.

To Lori's annoyance, Bennett then took her by the arm and they walked to the front door. She gently freed herself and opened the door before Bennett's hand could reach the knob.

He looked at her, a suppressed smile on his face.

"Thank God for women's lib," he said. "It's bringing back all those nice little courtesies that men so frequently seem to forget."

Lori smiled sweetly.

"You can be a horse's neck when you want to, can't you."

It was not a question, it was a statement of fact, and Bennett grinned.

Following a brief lull in the conversation, stopping and facing Bennett, Lori interrupted the silence and blurted out what was on her mind.

"Do you think there is any question of foul play in these three deaths?"

Bennett paused briefly and answered as she had hoped. "I'm almost certain of it."

Chapter 5

The next morning, Bennett was back at the police station to see if he could come up with any news clues or leads before meeting up with Lori at Charles Evans Fine's home to question to him about last night's death.

Bennett gathered his case file to meet with Captain Henry Hansen to brief him on what he knew so far. It was known throughout the station that Hansen did not like Bennett. He didn't like any officer in his command who exhibited too much independence and Bennett was notorious us for playing the cop game according to his own rules

Now Bennett was at it again in his investigation of murder where murder did not exist in the deaths of three old actors. Hansen had seen the autopsy reports. Death from natural causes. Heart attacks. No trace of poison or any foreign matter. No wounds, no injuries. Nothing to suspect that anything unusual had occurred, unless the person is Mark Bennett, of course

That is why Hansen had pushed the homicide division button in front of him and the knock on the door would be Bennett.

"Come in."

"Captain."

Hansen always thought there was a sneer in Bennett's voice when he said captain. He knew Bennett resented him. Hansen was a political officer who had come up through public affairs and public relations. Bennett was a street cop. The kind of disdain a combat soldier had for an administrative officer.

"Sit down, Bennett, and tell me what in the world you're doing looking at this Rita Reno thing."

Bennett sat down, crossed his legs, and reached down and untied his shoelace and then tied it again. Hansen lightly drummed his fingers on his desk pad. Finally Bennett spoke.

"Captain, I know you've checked the autopsies and they show nothing. There are no clues, no suspects, and possibly no reason to think that Homicide should have any interest in these three deaths."

"Exactly my thinking, sergeant. And that's why I'm asking you what in the world you're doing spending your time on this matter, these matters."

Hansen always chose his words carefully. His public relations background had served him well. Bennett wondered if he had, in all his eighteen years on the force, ever collared a drunk or heard a gun go off not fired on the police range.

"Well, captain, first I think you'll readily admit that three deaths in a row, under almost identical circumstances, might be a little suspicious."

"Might...or might not," Hansen responded, picking up a lead pencil and tapping the nails of his left hand with it.

"Granted," Bennett agreed. "But I thought it was worth a run-by if nothing else."

"And is the run-by over now?"

Bennett detected the sarcasm but chose to ignore it.

"I had this thought, captain. Perhaps there's nothing here at all. Nothing. On the other hand, these three deaths are the special interest of Lori Matrix..."

Suddenly, Hansen was interested. Very interested.

"In what way?" he asked.

"Well, originally, she was assigned to the first film showing at Rita Reno's house as a feature story. She saw Rex Hampton check out. She was there when Martha Von Tours took the gas. Then, finally, when Peter Olson keeled over after running full tilt at the screen."

"Yes, yes," Hansen offered. He was now anxiously holding on to every word. "And what does she think, what has she said about all this?"

Bennett kept his answer simple and straightforward. "She suspects foul play, but can't put a name to it."

"She has a theory these people were murdered, in other words?"

"Not quite a theory," Bennett explained. "Just a hunch, a feeling. Whatever."

That set Hansen to thinking for a moment, and Bennett let it sink in. Then he said, "I figure it this way, captain. Say we *don't* look into the deaths, okay? Suppose this Matrix woman goes on the air and says something about lack of police interest. Or energy. I mean, we could look bad, couldn't we?"

"Good point," Hansen acknowledged, retreating in his chair. "These TV people can be a real pain in the ass. They don't play by the rules like the newspaper people do."

"Right," Bennett added. "So I figure, since Matrix contacted me personally and tried to get me interested, I'd better go along with it, for a while at least."

"Well, of course, and that's what I want you to do," Hansen blurted.

"Exactly what I figured." Bennett smiled and then began to get up.

"You spend a little more time on it," Hansen ordered. "I'm sure what always happens will happen again."

"What's that?"

Hansen rose from his chair before answering. "Some asshole students will riot in Westwood or someone will shoot Solly Behmer again or it will snow in Pacoima and this lady reporter will forget all about these three stiffs."

"Right," Bennett said, inching his way to the door.

"Be sure to check with me from time to time. Don't keep me in the dark. This is a team effort," Hansen added, getting in one last word.

"Sure, captain. Whatever you say." Bennett walked out and closed the door behind him, and did everything he

could to contain his laughter. "Whatever you say, captain?"
Right. Who was kidding whom?

Molly Rector, Hansen's pretty secretary, gave Bennett her
best smile as he walked by.

"You know, he secretly loves you."

Bennett's smile was equally dazzling and equally
insincere.

"He's my leader. Why, it's almost a spiritual experience
just talking to him."

"In a pig's eye," Molly blurted.

"Exactly."

"Listen," Molly said, showing a sudden display of interest.
"If you buy me a drink after work today, I won't tell him
that you call him Captain Dumbo behind his back."

Bennett knew a dozen good blackmailers had put four of
them in jail. Molly was the best in the business.

"You got a deal. You don't tell the captain about my
little joke, and I won't tell him you wear a Wonder bra."

"I do not," Molly insisted, indignantly.

"Of course you don't," Bennett remarked, pausing for an
effect. "That's obvious to everyone."

"Forget the drink," Molly pouted. Flat-chested Molly. "And
don't expect any more favors from me."

"I can't remember the first one," Bennett quipped, and
quickly reached and closed the door behind him just before
the ashtray crashed into it.

Forty-three minutes between her next story assignment in
El Segundo covering a women's aerobics competition, Lori
and Bennett were sitting in Charles Evans Fine's living room,
accepting a cup of coffee from Barbara and waiting for the
old director to appear.

Barbara had been trying to tell them quickly and quietly that she was very concerned about her husband. He seemed worried, preoccupied, even distracted.

"Of course, it's all this, this thing."

No one quite knew how to refer to the three deaths.

Lori wanted to help, but did not know how to pick her words.

"I'm sure he'll be okay. It's been a series of shocks. But everything ends." Lori wondered how this would end.

But before they could continue the conversation, Fine had appeared at the bottom of the hallway stairs. Bennett rose and took his outstretched hand.

"Good to see you, Sergeant."

"And you, sir."

Lori placed his hand in Fine's and he welcomed her warmly. "Nice of you to come."

They all sat down and Barbara discreetly melted into the labyrinth of rich old woods.

Fine sighed. Bennett noted he looked tired, possibly after a restless night.

"Sergeant."

The voice was tired, too.

"Yes."

"Do you believe in history repeating itself? Because that is what may have caused these deaths."

Fine had Bennett's attention.

"Just what do you mean by that?" he asked.

A heavily veined hand waved at the air. "You'll think I've grown senile, perhaps I have."

Lori politely interrupted wanting to know more. "That's alright. Tell us what you're thinking."

Fine got up with an effort, looked long and hard at the young newswoman and police sergeant, and then began pacing between his chair and the picture window.

"One of us is a murderer."

"A murderer?"

"Yes."

Bennett studied the older man's face. He seemed rational, but that could be deceiving. There was no doubt he believed what he was saying, but what was that worth to a detective who dealt in hard facts?

"All right, which one?"

Fine shook his head. "You don't believe me. You think I'm just an old fool who's been under too much pressure and now I'm just spouting off, raving."

"Not at all. But you've raised a very serious charge," Bennett explained, "and I want to know if it's simply a wild idea, or if you have something that I should know about."

"I have something."

It was obvious this was all very difficult for Fine but he was not going to say what was on his mind until he was ready. Bennett shot a quick glance at Lori who looked as though she was not about to say anything. Bennett decided it might be a good idea to remain silent. He was right. After a full minute, Fine opened up and when it finally came, it came in a gusher of words.

"It was a great many years ago, and it's almost been forgotten by just about everyone who knew about it. And few knew about it. She was a beautiful young woman, everyone agreed to that. And she had many lovers. I was one of them."

By the quizzical looks on Lori and Bennett's faces, they

were thinking whom the hell and what the hell was Fine talking about? Since Fine was talking, again they remained silent.

Fine continued, "It happened on his boat. Rex had his yacht, a beautiful thing. Oh, you could find pictures of it in the fan magazines of the thirties if you looked it up."

"Rex? Rex Hampton?" Bennett wanted to shake him by the shoulders and make him be more explicit.

Fine went on. "It was one of those crazy Hollywood parties of the late thirties that used to make grist for the gossip mills and famous columnists, Louella Parsons, Hedda Hopper, Jimmy Fidler, and others, you know. Anyway, she met him on Rex's yacht, and fell insanely in love with him in a single evening. The very woman we all loved, would have given anything for, and this oaf from Kansas has her in the palm of his hand in a single evening."

Lori thought, what is it that makes this man string out this story so? Is he afraid to come to grips with the reality of it, if it is real, or is there too much of the ham in him not to hold center stage as long as he can, teasing the audience, and finally releasing the key speech?

"They became lovers, and then one night she walked in on him unexpectedly while he was making love to a cheap little tramp from the valley. She always carried this little pearl handled .32 caliber revolver. She shot them both."

That was enough for Bennett. His patience was exhausted.

"For Christ sakes, Mr. Fine, who in the hell are you talking about?"

"Rita Reno. She's murdered before. I think she may have murdered again."

Lori was shocked and speechless. Bennett sighed deeply. He waved Fine to a chair and he took it. There was a long silence, and then Bennett leaned forward, fixing his official detective's gaze on the old director.

"You're telling me that Rita Reno killed a man."

"No, the woman...Sally Kenne. Shot her dead."

Bennett shook his head as if to clear out the cobwebs.

"Rita Reno kills this, this woman, Sally..."

"Kenne."

"Yeah."

"When was this?

"1939."

"1939. All right, what about the man?"

Fine blurted it out. "The man was named Carson or Carslon, I can't remember now. He ran out of the room and was never seen, or heard from again. He was a drifter, a tramp."

"And did Rita Reno go on trial?"

Fine nodded. Bennett then pressed for more.

"She went on trial. Convicted?"

Fine nodded again.

"Did she do time?"

"No. There were no eyewitnesses. She pleaded self-defense and was clean. The woman, the dead woman, had a terrible reputation. Rita told the court that she drew the gun to frighten them, but that the woman tried to take it from her and was killed in the struggle."

Playing cop, Bennett was on his feet now. Lori watched and listened.

"Then how do you know that Rita Reno wasn't fighting for her life, didn't kill this woman in self-defense?"

"Because she told me, in the strictest confidence," Fine confessed.

"And you're telling me this now because..."

Because I think she may have lost control and is now trying to kill everyone who knows the story."

Bennett began to pace searching for what to say next. Lori made her case known. "Do you mean to tell us that Martha Von Tours and Peter Olson and Rex Hampton and you all knew this same story?"

"I do."

Bennett sat down again and gripped the arms of the chair. "That's the worst kept secret since the days of Sonny Tufts. It's absolutely crazy, improbable, and maybe impossible."

Trying to soften the blow of Bennett's caustic remarks, Lori reached out and placed her hand on top of Fine's to comfort him. Fine looked sadder at this moment than any time she had ever seen him before.

"I'm sure this is awfully difficult for you, and I admire you for speaking up," Lori said. 'You are one very courageous man."

With a look of horror on his face, his hand trembling in hers, Fine said with a straight face. "So you think I'm crazy?"

Lori looked Fine straight in the eye. "No, I think you could be right. And that makes us both crazy."

Chapter 6

Leaving Charles Evans Fine's palatial mansion an hour later, Lori agreed to meet up with Bennett later to compare notes after his meeting with Rita Reno, who was next on Bennett's list of witnesses to question.

Early that afternoon Bennett pulled his old Dodge Neon into Rita Reno's driveway. He knew he was going to hate this. She had sounded a little apprehensive on the phone. No one ever wants to talk to a police officer, and Bennett guessed his call would have her thinking about that 1939 shooting aboard Rex Hampton's yacht. She would be on her guard, perhaps even hostile. Bennett guessed little or nothing would be served by questioning her about an old murder, or manslaughter, but he did not know where else to begin with the investigation that hardly deserved the name.

The massive door to the old three-car garage was open and Bennett noticed it as he got out of his car. There was something very shiny and black in there and he looked around, wondering if he might indulge his curiosity.

He walked over casually and began to examine it. It was a Mercedes, that was obvious, and in beautiful mint condition. But what year?

Bennett almost jumped out of his shoes when a man's head popped out from under the car. It was an old head, and it was followed by a torso and legs clad in the dirtiest jeans he had ever seen.

The man huffed and puffed to his feet and grinned.

"Can't shake hands, get you full of grease."

"She's a beauty all right. Yours?"

"Don't I wish," the man said as he wiped grease from his hands with an oily rag. "I'd give my house and kids for this baby. No, I work down at Cecil's Mercedes on Wilshire. Come up here now and then to check her out, turn over the engine. She belongs to Miss Reno."

Bennett walked around the car, slowly admiring its dark brown finish.

"What year?"

"1937. Only a half dozen left in the world, I think. It's a Grosser Mercedes. With a 7.7 liter straight eight engine. Created in 1930. Emperor of Japan has two of 'em, but don't know where any of the others are. Nazis made 'em for the top brass. Worth a bloody fortune."

Bennett walked around the car and admired its condition

and beauty, all the time keeping up the conversation.

"Rita Reno. Does she still drive it?"

"Drive it," the man said. "Hell, she's never driven it. Doesn't know how to drive. Never did. Nah, it just sits here. She keeps it like you or I would keep a book that we especially like."

"Some beauty."

"Yeah," the mechanic said with a crazed look in his eyes, "I'd kill for it."

Bennett thanked the man and realized he had not even asked him his name. Well, no matter, he would never see him again. And this way he did not have to tell him he was a cop. The more people he did not have to tell, the better Bennett liked it.

A woman who introduced herself only as Mary answered Bennett's knock on Rita Reno's door, and she guided him into the living room. She was a very heavy lady. Only about five feet tall but she must have weighed nearly 180 pounds. She waddled when she walked, and she caused the floors to squeak.

"Rita, it's your Sergeant Bennett."

Rita nodded, smiled pleasantly, and motioned Bennett to a chair. She was pouring over old scrapbooks, and Bennett could see her name on the pasted down headlines and programs. There must have been five thousand individual pictures, judging from the size of eight or nine books lying in front of her.

"We're all hams, you know," she admitted, powered by ego. When we slip from public grace, we retreat into our clippings and reviews, and that's where we live again."

"Yes ma'am," Bennett said, not knowing how else to respond.

Bennett wondered if she had not dressed for the part that she seemed to be playing. She was wearing an old beaded dress that looked something like one he had seen in a museum somewhere. It was definitely from an earlier era, that was clear, but he knew nothing about women's clothing. Was she ready to talk about the past? Is that why she had gotten out the old scrapbooks and put on a dress she probably had not worn in the last thirty years?

"How about a cup of coffee, sergeant?"

"No thanks, ma'am."

Rita was ladylike and proper but she was not one for formalities.

"Please don't keep calling me ma'am. I hate it when an attractive young man calls me ma'am. It only reminds me how ancient I've become."

Oh, she is a charmer all right, thought Bennett.

"Call me Rita."

"Yes, ma'am..."

They both laughed. And Bennett was beginning to see why so many men of fame and wealth had fallen in love with the tiny lady who looked like a model for a Dresden figure.

Rita astonished Bennett by forming her hand into a gun the way children do. And she made the same sound that children make.

"Bang, bang," she said, smiling. "That's what you're here to talk about, isn't it?"

"Why, uh, yes, it is," Bennett countered, shocked and surprised by her honesty. "Can we do that?"

"Of course, we can. I'm too old to be deceitful any more. About the only way I can impress a man as young as you these days is to show him how honest I can be."

Yes, Bennett told himself, she was something special. Still is.

"How did you know I wanted to talk about something so far back in your past?" he asked.

Rita smiled. "I knew you were talking to Charles. And I guessed that he might tell you about the, uh, incident. Why? Because the only others who were close to it are now dead."

"You don't seem worried...Let me put that another way. You don't seem concerned that I want to talk to you about it."

Rita edged up in her chair. "Why should I be? I was let off, cleared. And God knows it wasn't the only scandal to come out of Old Hollywood. There was that Fatty Arbuckle thing, and those Franchot Tone stories and Louella on Hearst's boat and, well, it's all on the public record and so is my arrest and trial."

"I know," said Bennett. "I went into the files and read it all."

"So, what can I tell you that you don't already know?"

Bennett got straight to the point. "Tell me if it was murder or self-defense."

Rita laughed, involuntarily. "I don't believe you," she said. "You really think I might have deliberately shot that girl to death?"

"I'm sorry," he replied seriously, "but it's possible."

"And what if I did?"

"I don't know." Bennett interrupted his answer to rub his jaw with his left hand. A nervous habit of his even he found irritating. "If I knew that you had done it deliberately, and not in self-defense, it might indicate that you're capable of..."

"Of murder." Rita underscored each word for dramatic effect. "Of course. And don't you know by now that we're all capable of murder, given the right circumstances?"

Rita made a good case for herself. "I guess you're right," he said.

Rita seemed to be enjoying all this, which was hardly what Bennett had expected when he walked in.

She continued to be on the defensive, and Bennett found all he could do was listen.

"Indulge an old lady for a few minutes. Suppose I admitted to you, I did murder that girl. What would that tell you, really? That I killed three of my best friends. And even if I had, how in the world did I do it?"

Now it was Bennett's turn to smile. "You know something, lady? You're right. There is absolutely not a trace of proof in the world that they died in any way, except the way they did. So this conversation is really academic."

"But interesting."

"Yes."

Rita eased back in her chair. "I'm glad. All right, just for laughs, I'll tell you. I did it. Deliberately. But I didn't even know when I pulled the trigger. My lawyer probably would have gotten me off on temporary insanity. Or diminished capacity as they call it these days. But he chose to defend on the basis of self-defense since the only witness disappeared."

"Doesn't that ever worry you?" Bennett asked. "Somewhere out there may be a man who is an eyewitness to that shooting who might resurface any time."

"I don't think so," Rita said, seeming sure of herself and her statement.

"And why not?"

"Because he was killed in World War II. I had that verified a long time ago."

Rita built a strong case for herself, and there was little Bennett could do. She was always one-step ahead of his questioning. It was as if she could read his mind.

Finished, Bennett rose to go.

"So soon?" Rita said, surprised.

"I've got a lot of things to do." Bennett puts out his hand and a tiny hand grasped it.

"That Matrix girl," Rita said tenderly. "I'd get a hold of her if I were you and never let her go."

Bennett was surprised. He never expected such a comment.

"And what do you suppose someone who makes one hundred and fifty thousand dollars a year and looks like a movie star would want with a cop stuck in grade who drives an old Dodge Neon?"

Rita came close and tapped Bennett on the chest.

"I know what I'd want you for," she said, flirtingly. "And she's no different than I am, or any other woman."

Bennett actually thought he felt himself blush for the first time since he was a child.

"I, uh..."

"Just remember what I said," Rita said, inching back on her heels.

Rita showed Bennett to the door. He stood on the threshold, looking down at the diminutive figure. Then he leaned over quickly and kissed her lightly on the cheek.

Her eyes twinkled. "Oh, if I were twenty-five years younger."

"You know what?" Bennett said. "I think you are!"

Rita watched the detective get into his old car and rumble off. She walked back into the house and sat down again in front her scrapbooks. For the first time in years, she felt old. Very old.

Back at police headquarters, Bennett picked a telephone note out of his "in" basket and dialed Lori Matrix at KTRB-TV. A secretary said she was looking at video footage and could not be disturbed. He left his name and number. Fifteen minutes later, she was on the phone.

"I know you're probably busy," she said, sounding hurried. "Is there any chance we could meet and talk after the six o'clock news?"

There was. Bennett agreed to come down to the television station and pick her up. The Porsche was in for service. Again.

Although Lori had left word with the guard to pass Bennett through, he was suspicious. Lori received dozens of obscene letters and phone calls each week, and frequently there has been some weirdo waiting around the main gate, hoping to see in person the woman he loved from afar. In the last six months, the police had picked up two lovesick cuckoos, one seventeen, and the other fifty-four, who had run after her car as she drove off the lot. Bennett put the keystone cop's mind at ease by showing his sergeant's badge and he ushered him into the newsroom.

Bennett had been in newsrooms before, and they always amused him. He had worked on his high school newspaper and for a time had aspired to a career in journalism. However, he was unable to attend college, and laboring under the illusion that a degree in journalism did not guarantee a job in the news business, he had entered police work instead.

It was much later that he discovered many of the news people Bennett admired the most had never even taken journalism in college. One of them told him it was more trade than a profession, something learned at the side of someone who already knew, much like the old apprentice method of teaching medicine and other disciplines. He chose to believe that on the basis of reporters with whom he had done business. The ones with the most experience seemed to ask the right questions and get the story right the first time. It was, like the cop business, something you learned by doing, not reading about.

A skinny young thing in faded jeans stared at Bennett from behind horn-rimmed glasses and said yes, Lori said he was coming and he was to wait in her office.

The six P.M. show was already on the air, and Bennett was surprised that so few people in the newsroom were watching it. They were reading newspaper and magazines, or rummaging through desks or talking about whatever news people talk about. Only one in ten was watching the show they had just helped to get on the air.

Bennett was surprised again to see how tiny Lori's office was. Hardly deluxe quarters for a big news star. When her co-anchor Huey McLane came in, he learned that it was not her office exclusively. She shared it with the man who brought L.A. *The Morning Report*, a news and variety show that aired at 9 A.M. each day to try to hook the valley housewives into watching daytime television.

Me Lane was in and out with a nod, not knowing or caring who Bennett was, and, finally, Lori appeared. She looked angry, and she was.

"Oh, hi. I'll be right with you."

She stalked over to her desk, sat down, and dialed an inside number.

"Ronnie? Who edited that piece of shit on the six? You know, the women's aerobics competition. Cassidy always takes those damned tit and crotch shots on those kinds of stories, the chauvinist bastard. And no one ever uses them for obvious reasons. Did you see what I saw? Did you? There were at least three of them left in it. I was goddamned mortified."

Lori slammed down the receiver and sunk in the chair, almost forgetting that Bennett was sitting there. Then, she suddenly became aware of his presence and got up.

"Oh, I'm sorry," she said, deflated. "That kind of crap just gets to me. I'm sorry. I didn't mean to sound off like that. You must think I'm some kind of ogre."

Bennett did not think that called for a comment, so he did not offer one.

"Well, I'm not. And I sure as hell don't like playing star and bitching about the show but come on, I have to sit there and narrate those stories and the public doesn't know the difference. If our cameraman is trying to demean those women marching around in the rain to make a point, the viewer thinks I'm the one who's doing it. You know what I mean?"

Bennett knew what she meant. She grabbed a short coat, swung her long blonde around on her head, and they headed for the parking lot.

Bennett wondered how this glamour girl would enjoy riding in the old Dodge Neon with the torn upholstery and erratic springs. He opened the door and then asked her to wait a moment while he threw two empty Coke cans onto the floor in the back. He decided he was not going to apologize for the car.

They lived in two very different worlds. If she did not like his old clunker, she could take a cab. Why was he being so defensive? She had not said a word about the car.

"Where would you like to go?"

"Anywhere we can talk. Say, would you mind my apartment?"

Bennett thought, now how many men in this town would like to hear those words from this sex symbol?

"Whatever."

"Good. That way, I can whomp a couple of sandwiches while we talk. You hungry?"

"A little."

"I'm ravenous. Missed lunch because of that aerobics competition thing I was bitching about."

They drove the last four or five blocks to Lori's apartment in silence, mostly because she wanted to hear KFWB, the all-news radio station. She was interested in a story about Idi Amin, but she failed to hear it on the roundup that was airing at the time.

Lori lived in The Palms, a deluxe security apartment building in West Los Angeles. It had a doorman and more doors and keys than Bennett had seen since the last time that he had delivered a prisoner to Terminal Island. Everyone in the building was rich or a celebrity or both. They were willing to pay handsomely for their safety and privacy.

When Bennett turned the old car over to the doorman, he thought he saw the man sniff, as if he had smelled a bad odor. Maybe he just imagined it. They eventually reached the final door and went through it. Lori took his jacket and disappeared with it. She called out from the bedroom.

"I've got beer and cold chicken or chili and scotch or bourbon or what?"

Bennett was looking over her place with a keen eye when he shouted back his answer. "How about chili and beer," he said.

"You got it," Lori said, reappearing behind him.

"How did you do that?" he asked.

"Oh, it's a round apartment, didn't you notice? All the rooms connect to each other and to the living room. Let's talk while I do the food thing."

Lori began doing the food thing, which meant heating up a large pot of chili on the range. Bennett opened two cans of beer and poured them into very delicate Pilsner glasses she provided.

They each took a long draught and Lori wound up with a foam mustache. He pointed at it and she laughed and blotted it away with a napkin.

She motioned Bennett out of the kitchen. "Let's sit in the living room while the chili warms up."

They did. She made small talk about the apartment and then got to the point.

"I think there's a way to go with this...this investigation."

"I'm listening."

Lori took another sip, and continued. "Okay. When did each of them have this heart attack?"

Bennett thought a moment. "While they were viewing their old films," he said.

"And what does that suggest to you?"

Bennett shrugged. "How about," he said very slowly, "they were triggered by something they saw in the films."

Lori's face lit up. "Exactly! You've thought about it, too."

"No," Bennett said, "I just thought of it now."

"Doesn't matter," Lori explained. "We're on the same wave length. The key to these deaths lies in the films they were viewing. Don't you think?"

"I don't know." Bennett stirred his beer with his right forefinger. "But it's a thought. It's an avenue to pursue."

Lori nodded, her eyes glistening. Then she suddenly jerked herself straight in her seat and said, "Oh my gosh!" She rushed out to the kitchen and rescued the chili from a fiery grave.

It tasted burnt, but it was still good.

Bennett had a second bowl, and a third glass of beer. Then he rose to go.

"When can I see you again?" Lori asked.

"Isn't it the guy who says something like that?" Bennett replied, in an old-fashioned sort of way.

"Yeah. Right. I'll call you tomorrow."

Then he thought about what she had just said. "Business." And he added, "No, you call me."

"Right," Lori smiled.

That's the way they left it. Lori closed the door behind him and hummed around the apartment. Bennett went down the elevator, got into his car, and drove home. He hoped he was not falling for that rich, proud, inaccessible broad. He hoped he was not. But he guessed he was.

Chapter 7

Everyone knew that after the death of Peter Olson, the group showing of old classic films was doomed. Even if the remaining members had wanted them to continue, the pressure from the police now investigating the matter formally, and their own concerned friends and relatives would have made it impossible.

Sylvia Carl-Stapleton had enjoyed the little get-togethers more than anyone else had. Time had not been as kind to her as it had been to Rita Reno. She had not aged gracefully. She had refused to go gently into that sweet darkness, and she was fighting and scratching old age all the way into her late sixties. She had had four expensive facelifts, and she still looked every one of her sixty-six years, possibly a few more because in her loneliness, she had turned to alcohol as a palliative, and it had ravaged her health.

Like many people who find the present unacceptable and the future without promise, Sylvia had retreated into the past, the past of her youth, the past of her glamour, and her artistic and romantic triumphs. She wore young women's clothes, and affected youthful hairstyles and makeup. Her face and figure no longer complimented them, but she clung to the illusion of youth and because she had adequate financial reserves, she was able to buy some luxuries older women could not afford. These were luxuries in the form of young lovers, mostly aspiring actors, happy to barter a few months of their youth and vigor for a roof over their heads and the opportunity to meet the power elite of the film industry through this faded queen of the cinema.

Sylvia considered it more than a fair exchange. She had lived all her life in the world of illusion, and she was comfortable with the illusion that her young prot g s stayed with her because she represented fame and glamour, not because she paid their rent and bought them suitable clothes in which to attend auditions she personally arranged. They drove her cars, ate her food, and serviced her body and her insatiable ego, and quid pro that gave her no pangs of conscience.

The former occupant of the Blue Room, the spacious bedroom just off Sylvia's master bedroom, was Frank Toynbee. He now carried the Hollywood-sounding name Sylvia had bestowed on him, Masterson Tower. Sylvia renamed all her young hopefuls. She might not have done Toynbee a massive favor with that special service, but Bernie

Friedman, Cassius Trevisnki and Herman Patterdunk, his predecessors were understandably grateful.

None had gone on to any great success. But each one of them had obtained some measure of employment as a direct result of Sylvia's influence. So Tower-formerly-Toynbee accepted the older woman's guidance and grateful for it. He became Masterson Tower and in just three months in Sylvia's gracious old residence off Sunset in the Hollywood Hills, he had acquired a small but desirable part in a major movie and two modest roles in ongoing TV series.

Such arrangements were not unique in the film industry. Sylvia herself had obtained her first important film roles through the intercession of producers and directors who had been invited to savor her physical attractions in exchange for some professional advantage. The film industry abounds with willing mentors when the quid pro is sufficiently tempting.

There was much of the mentor in Sylvia. From time to time, she taught a class in Film Arts at UCLA. She waived her modest fee, and was popular with students, all-aspiring young actors and actresses. It was from these teaching assignments that she was able to obtain an endless supply of young men. There was always some good-looking young fellow with wavy hair and wide shoulders smart enough to know it helps to know someone who can open a door. Sylvia knew many someones who could open many doors. When she encountered a particularly interesting student, she would invite him over to her home to view one of her pictures.

With Masterson Tower away on location for the last three weeks and scheduled to spend a fourth week in the Arizona desert, the old house seemed terribly empty. And so

Sylvia had invited young Rodney Camper to her home to view *How Red the Rain*, the 1937 classic shot entirely on location in Kenya.

Camper looked upon the invitation as a rare opportunity but soon after he arrived, he began reading the real-life scenario accurately. Sylvia had given her butler-handyman Rolf, the night off, and the day maid, Vivian, was putting the finishing touches to a mound of tiny sandwiches, and preparing to go home. Camper was a handsome young man with a modest I.Q., but he knew the setting for a seduction scene when he saw one. Sylvia looked radiant in a gold lame dressing gown. It was similar to the one she had worn in *Love's Fiery Desire* that had graced the front covers of so many fan magazines.

Camper was also aware of the psychological transformation of his mentor. She had gone from instructor to coquette, and even moved differently.

Camper knew what she expected of him. He had heard all the stories about this turned on old broad and he believed them. He had never slept with a woman older than twenty-five before, and he wondered what it would be like. He wasn't weighing any moral considerations, only wondering about the mechanics. He wondered if a young man with his limited experience could handle someone like Sylvia, who must have had a thousand lovers and been to bed with them a million times. What could he offer that was better, or as well, or new or different? Feelings of inadequacy began seizing him as he watched her cross the room, carrying a tray with a bottle of vintage French wine and two extremely tall, thin glasses.

He had smelled her perfume even before he caught sight

of her. Why did older women wear such heavy perfume? Was it because their sense of smell had diminished with the passing years? It smelled like the same perfume that he had encountered so often when he got into the elevator of his rundown apartment building in West Hollywood. The scent always lingered through two or three elevator door openings and closings.

Sylvia offered her best seductive smile to young Camper, and he returned it. This would not be one of his favorite roles, but he would play it to the hilt. He had told his macho father that he would make it as an actor, and make it he would. If warming this old lady's bed was to be part of the dues paying, so be it.

Sylvia poured two tall drinks, almost brimful, and held her glass out for Camper for a toast while the projectionist reeled up the feature-length attraction.

"To...your career. May it be long, brilliant, and bring you all the happiness." Sylvia would like to have said, "Bring *us* all the happiness," but she had made that mistake before.

Camper smiled and nodded. He felt awkward in this woman's presence. He wanted desperately to please her, and he was afraid he would say or do the wrong thing and spoil everything.

If he could have read Sylvia's mind, it would have put his own mind to rest. She was anticipating another great erotic adventure with this latest prot g , and she had selected him carefully. He was an excellent specimen, nearly six feet tall, a finely chiseled head and thick, curly hair, broad shoulders, and even white teeth. How long would this one last before he went on to other things, other women?

No matter, he would last long enough and there would be another one to replace him, when the time came.

Tonight, that time was far off. Sylvia sat down beside Camper, sat close, and her perfume engulfed him. She showed him how to lock arms in a toast. He was awkward, but willing to learn. He would be the same when it came to sex. She would teach him much this evening.

Sylvia was famous for her skills as a hostess. Her parties were legendary. Her trysts were equally well planned and executed. Her living room looked like a movie set, deep, real leather couches and fluffy pillows placed at strategic intervals. A bearskin rug, long out of fashion in this ecologically aware era, spread across the parquet floor polished to a slickness that made less than careful walking a hazard. Sylvia long ago had opted for low lighting. It softened the lines in her face, a trick she remembered learning on a Michael Curtiz set.

These rituals had become routine, but never boring, for Sylvia. She had choreographed dozens of them. First the wine, rather rare and always French, and then some carefully selected background music set the mood. After some small talk, she would walk over and push a button triggering a mechanism that automatically lowered a motion picture screen stored in a slot in the ceiling of the living room. Then she would dim the lights even further and take her place on the couch beside her guest. She would always be careful to sit down too close to him and then pretend, coquettishly, that she had not realized what she had done. But she would not move away and they would sit there, hips and thighs touching, so close it would be only natural for him, natural and more comfortable, to place his arm either on the back of the couch or around her.

Reading all the signs correctly, Camper placed his arm around Sylvia's shoulders and then let it slip down to encircle her waist. She rewarded his action with an impish little smile as she snuggled up to him. As the opening credits rolled by, Sylvia would launch into the same kind of explanatory speech she had used so many times at UCLA film classes, explaining who was who, placing each person in his professional perspective. How scenes were shot, which were reshot several times, what special locations were used, or lighting problems were encountered--the stuff that comprises important trivia for film buffs and aspiring young actors.

Tonight, they were watching what most people acknowledged being her very best film, *How Red the Rain*, and the opening scene was gripping. It featured a beautiful, bosomy and startlingly young Sylvia Carl-Stapleton, running down a muddy country road through a blinding rain. Behind her was her lover's car smashed against a tree, and he was lying unconscious, permanently injured in the mishap. Camper had never seen the film before. Immediately caught up in the action, he was astonished to see how beautiful this woman had been in her heyday. Sylvia could sense his appreciation, and it gave her a warm glow. This would be another night to remember.

Sergeant Mark Bennett, too, would remember this night. He was painfully downing a cup of station-house coffee, black, bitter and uncomfortably hot, when the word came over his service phone: Paramedic van answering a call to the Carl-Stapleton home. Possible heart attack.

Bennett took off on a dead run for the police garage. Twenty-two minutes later, he was watching the paramedics rolling Carl-Stapleton out on a gurney and placing her carefully in the back of their van and moving off to the nearest hospital.

A much shaken Rodney Camper walked with Bennett to the living room. Bennett indicated that Camper should sit down but he was too nervous for that. He pointed at the screen and shook his head, still unable to believe what he had just experienced.

"She was fine, just fine. I just turned to her to say something about the scene we were watching and I suddenly realized, Jesus, something's wrong," he said, his eyes cast downward in grief. "I said something, I don't even know what now, and she didn't answer. I thought she was putting me on, you know, and she didn't answer and I gave her a playful punch on the arm, like, and, you know, she still didn't answer."

Bennett patted the young man's shoulder to comfort him.

"The paramedic said catatonic."

"Yeah," Camper said. "What is that?"

Bennett paused before answering. "I'm not sure. We'll find out. But now we've got to find out what put her in that state."

"It wasn't anything I did, I swear to God," Camper pleaded.

Bennett attempted to calm the young actor down. "No one is accusing you of anything, simply tell me what happened, what you said or she said or what either of you saw or heard. What?"

Camper grabbed the top of his head as if to prevent it

from flying off. And then he nervously paced. "I'm telling you it wasn't anything I said or did! I wasn't doing anything. Not anything."

"Cool it," Bennett ordered. "She must have received an awful fright. Something put her in that state and we have to find out what. I'm guessing it was something she saw in the film."

Camper looked at Bennett as if he was crazy.

"How could that be?"

"I don't know," Bennett said, attempting to explain his theory. "But if you two were alone and no one else came in the room and nothing was happening except you were watching the film, it was something she saw in the film."

That suddenly began to make sense to the young actor. He walked quickly over the couch and sat down. And, he remembered something.

"Yeah, yeah. I remember," he began to recall. "I had my arm around her. And I thought I felt her sort of, well, like stiffen sudden-like."

"And what did she say?"

Camper shook his head, much of what he remembered not making any sense.

"That's just it. Nothing. She did not say anything. Just sort of stiffened. And then I looked at her and she was staring at the screen. Like, I mean, really staring. Not just looking. And she never stopped staring."

"At what?" Bennett continued. "What couldn't she stop staring at?"

Camper nervously explained. "I'd never seen the film before until tonight. But I noticed a character on the screen, I think it was a man, and that had this unusual glow around him. It seemed like Sylvia's eyes were mesmerized in his direction, though I can't be certain. And to be honest, I'm not sure what I saw. It all happened so fast."

"What else?"

"She just kept staring, and she didn't speak again. That's the way she was when the paramedics came."

"Catatonic?" Bennett asked.

"Jesus, I guess so," Camper replied.

Bennett nodded in a way that it was clear what Camper was telling made sense to him even though it did not make much sense to the young actor.

"Okay, now understand no one suspects you of anything. No crime has occurred here. A lady has suddenly become sick. Stricken. You just happened to be here when it took place. But you'll have to come to the station with me and make out a report. All right?"

Camper did not really think he had much choice and he was not about to argue with this police officer. In his excitement, he had forgotten he had several joints in his coat pocket but he was remembering them now. And he wondered if going to the station meant they would search him. The thought drained the color from his face and if he was not nervous during Bennett's examination he was now.

"Could we do it tomorrow?" Camper begged.

Bennett seemed surprised. "Why?"

Camper held his stomach to fake an illness. "I feel kind of sick, after all this, you know?"

Bennett had seen plenty of witnesses turn cold, and he was not about to buy this young actor's performance.

"I think you can hold up. You got something else on your mind?"

Camper dropped the facade, and tried honesty instead. "Okay, I got some joints in my pocket. Jesus, there it is."

Camper reached in his pocket and Bennett caught his hand before he could extricate the marijuana.

"Kid, I didn't see anything in your pocket and I don't give a shit what's there or what isn't there. Okay?"

Camper breathed a huge sigh of relief.

"You mean it?"

"I mean it."

Camper brightened and the color returned to his face, and his stomach suddenly felt much better. "Thanks, thanks a lot, if you know what I mean."

Bennett merely smiled. "I know what you mean. Let's go."

Pete Bellingham, a uniformed patrolman, was standing outside as they emerged from the house. Bennett told him to pick up the movie projector and the film and bring them to his car. Bellingham was glad to oblige. Placing them in the back seat, Bennett thanked the officer and drove off.

***

Lori Matrix was watching Charley Burnside, the veteran film editor, cutting thirty-one minutes out of a film that had been in theatrical release and was not part of a package bought for television viewing.

Film editing fascinated her, and Burnside was the senior editor at the station, an old pro who liked the young anchorwoman. He looked in her eyes when he talked to her. And he never made any sexual references. He was one of the few men at the studio in whose presence she felt she could relax.

"Calling what we do film editing," Charley was saying, "is like calling a woodpecker a wood carver."

Lori laughed at the comparison. "Come on, Charley, you used to cut features before you started cutting up news features."

"A thousand years ago," Charley joked. "I've been on pension from the studios for almost three years now."

"I didn't know they retired film editors when they got to be forty," Lori cracked.

Charley accepted the compliment gladly, even though he looked all seventy-one years of his age.

"Thanks. You may be the only person in the world who knows I lie about my age, always making myself twenty-five years older than I really am."

Charley continued to work as he and Lori talked. He had just finished editing some scenes from the first reel of the movie and was about to reel up the second reel. The editing room, no bigger than a cracker box, was overflowing with film reels and old movie posters, some from Hollywood's golden age, which adorned the walls. Charley was a wealth of knowledge, and Lori frequently tapped his brain to learn as much as she could about the business.

"So what's the secret to taking thirty-one minutes out of a film that ran 120 minutes in its original form?" she asked.

"Easy," Charley explained. "Be ruthless. I eliminate all unnecessary exposition--explanation of what's going, what happened, or what's going to happen. Then, I get rid of any subplots we don't really need."

"Like what?"

"Like it's a 'Marcus Welby' episode, okay? The main story is about this girl who gets what appears to be a fatal disease but her records get mixed up with somebody elses and she'll be all right in the end. But one subplot has a seventy-two-year-old circus acrobat dying of terminal acne and another has the Mafia trying to corner the market in bedpans."

"I think I saw that flick," Lori murmured.

"Right...Okay, I cut the old broad and the Mafia hoodlums and stick with the general story."

"And if that isn't enough?"

"I take the last sentence off each speech that has more than one sentence in it."

"Swell," Lori said offhandedly. "So if the girl says, 'John, I want you to marry me. I'm pregnant,' you take out 'I'm pregnant.'"

"Sure."

Lori could not believe what she was hearing. "You're kidding."

"Yes, I'm kidding," Charley laughed. "But, I really do shorten speeches. I'm brutal. I have to be. You'd be surprised how often you can do that without harming the story one bit. And another thing, I sometimes get rid of people I don't like. Just last night, I was able to cut every scene of a desert picture in which Victor Mature plays an Arabian prince. I figure I ought to get a public service award for that!"

The editing room phone rang while Lori was still laughing.

"For you, Lori."

Charley sat very still in front of his maze of editing

equipment while Lori talked.

"Yes. Yes. You bet, I'd really like to. Thanks. I will. Right away."

Lori handed the phone back to Charley and he replaced it on the wall hook next to him.

"Don't tell me," Charley offered. "It was from a man. A man you like."

Lori blushed in a way that Charley could say he was right. "You sly dog," she said. "Right on both counts."

Lori rose from her chair and hurriedly moved toward the door. But first, she planted a surprise kiss on Charley's cheek.

"Catch you later, Charley." And she fast walked out the door.

Still feeling her kiss on his cheek, Charley called after her as she started down the hall.

"Tell him to treat you right or I'll do to him what I did to Victor Mature!"

Chapter 8

Before she left the newsroom, Lori knew what Bennett wanted to talk to her about. The Los Angeles News Bureau wire had bulletined the following story:

Sylvia Carl-Stapelton, star of nearly one hundred feature films of the thirties and forties, collapsed in her Brentwood home tonight and was rushed to Brentwood Community Hospital where she's described in good condition, a staff physician said. Carl-Stapleton was suffering from exhaustion and would probably remain hospitalized for several days. The veteran actress was the recipient of two Academy Awards and was a part-time lecturer on film at UCLA. Carl-Stappetton has no living relatives.

Lori noted that the name appeared three times, spelled differently each time. Par for the course, she thought. She could hear her newspaperman father's cynical laugh now.

One thing Lori did not learn from the story was that Sylvia was catatonic. She learned that from Bennett who called and asked her to join him in a booth at Mama Simone's on Argyle Street in Hollywood.

Lori had hooked a ride to the cocktail lounge from Porcupine Harris. The Porsche was back in the garage for repairs.

Porcupine was the least skilled cameraman at the station, but the best equipped. He acquired the nickname because he had so many antennas on his station wagon. Porcupine could receive police and fire and ambulance calls. He had a radiotelephone and special communications for aircraft and ship to shore contacts, as well as a CB radio, a siren and a loudspeaker. Porcupine could talk to anyone in the world without leaving his car. The trouble was that when he reached someone he rarely had anything to say. Unfortunately, Porcupine had an I.Q. that matched his hat size.

Lori thanked Porcupine for the lift and hurried inside. Bennett was talking to Mama Simone as she came in. Mama was a handsome black man about sixty years old. He had taken early retirement from his postal inspector's job and bought this place. Harry Dawson liked the name of the place so kept it. The last Mama Simone was Gertrude Steinbecker, so why should Harry Dawson feel embarrassed?

90

Bennett introduced Lori and ordered two scotch and sodas. Then he got down to business.

"Yeah, catatonic. No telling when I can talk to her and let me tell you something, I'm ready to try anything. That's four in a row, all just about the same way. Three heart attacks and now this, about as close as you can come to a fatal heart attack and live."

Lori took a sip of her drink and thought about what Bennett had said. She was thinking the same way. Actually, she always had. These incidents connected, somehow.

"Look, we're agreed that it's not coincidence, that something very strange has happenedis happening. Okay. And we're agreed it's directly connected with these films, these specific films that have special significance for each of the people involved."

Lori cradled her drink and carefully paused to think out her thoughts. She continued.

"Whatever happens, happens when they're looking at them. But when A is looking at A's film, only A is affected, not B or C or D. Right? So why don't we take each of the films that's been involved in each of the incidents and examine them as carefully as can be done?"

Bennett sat quietly for a moment and absorbed Lori's idea of how to proceed. On the surface, it seemed crazy to think that anything could possibly be contained in the films that had resulted in three identical deaths and a fourth, near fatal incident. But what other options did he have?

"Okay," he said. "But we ought to have some kind of experts on hand for that, shouldn't we?

"Maybe. Maybe." Lori stopped to reflect for a moment and came up with a logical candidate. "Good God, I'm in the film business. I know a man who knows more about film than anyone in the world does. His name is Charley Burnside and he works for us, but he used to be with Paramount and Columbia and MGM and God only knows who else."

Bennett reached for his drink, and then paused before answering.

"Will he help out? I mean, is a fee involved or something like that?"

Lori shook her head. "He's a friend. I'll buy him dinner."

Bennett corrected her. "You mean *we'll* buy him dinner."

Lori smiled. "Okay, well buy him dinner. When can you set it up?"

Bennett took one last sip, and ordered a second drink. Lori waved the waiter off; she was fine. She was still nursing her first drink. The second drink arrived and Bennett reached for his wallet.

The waiter motioned for him to put it back. "This is on Mama Simone," he said.

Genuinely touched, Bennett raised his glass and said, "Tell Mama I'll return the favor someday."

The waiter turned and walked over to the next table. Bennett picked up the conversation, full steam.

"I'll try to rent one of those editing rooms on Cahuenga or Cole, you know, where all those little production companies do their editing. How about that?"

Lori had a better idea. "Hey, we lease facilities on Cole. Let me set up some viewing and editing time at our place, and we can probably freeload the time."

Bennett smirked, and then quipped, "The taxpayers of Los Angeles humbly accept this attempt to save them a buck.

Such things are so rare these days." He then raised his glass for a toast and Lori raised hers. They touched glasses and Bennett turned up the charm.

"Is it a deal?"

"It's a deal, sergeant."

Lori lost herself in Bennett's blue eyes and almost forgot why she was there. She stared curiously at the hard-boiled detective who in the beginning seemed so unapproachable. Underneath that hard shell, she was sure there was a real gentleman, the kind any woman would desire. For a brief moment, she let her emotions get the best of her. And before she could catch herself, she almost gave her feelings away.

"When are you free?"

Bennett had not detected her adoring gaze. His mind was still on the case.

"Free?" Bennett answered. "When is your editor friend free?"

"Charley works nights. I bet I can get him tomorrow morning. Does that give you enough time to round up the prints?"

Bennett saw no reason why her idea would not work. "I've got every one of them in my office. I confiscated them as possible evidence. How about we meet at this place of yours on Cole early tomorrow morning?"

"Not too early," Lori pleaded, who by now had brushed aside her feelings for Bennett. "I've got to anchor the 11 o'clock news tonight."

They settled on ten o'clock, and Lori got up and used a booth phone to call Charley. When she returned, her smile told Bennett that the answer was "yes."

Bennett wanted to celebrate. "How about another drink?"

"Not when I have to anchor."

Bennett nodded and thought how beautiful she looked tonight. Then again, she was always beautiful. What was different about that?

Lori pulled into the Fantasy Film Company editing studio's parking lot at precisely ten o'clock the next morning. She was pleased to see the old Dodge Neon was already there, and so was a late model Buick. She and Charley Burnside got out and went inside and Bennett, she discovered, had brought more than the film.

"Lori Matrix," he motioned to the man next to him. "Larry Ponds."

They shook hands. "And this is Charley Burnside, the editor."

Ponds was the projectionist who had run the films for the old actors film group and the night Carl-Stapelton went into a catatonic state. He was a beefy, red-faced man about fifty, and even though it was still mid-morning, Lori caught the faint but pungent odor of alcohol on his breath.

Bennett had met Ponds before following two of the film screenings. He found him to be completely cooperative and totally harmless, even though the man's incessant twitching bothered him. His neck always seemed to spasm uncontrollably whenever he spoke.

Cobey Swanson, the manager of the facility, introduced himself all around and he obviously was thrilled to have Lori Matrix in his little shop. Swanson was used to meeting student filmmakers, has-been actors trying to parlay a B production into a comeback, low-budget documentary makers, and producers of boring religious films. To have a major news star in his place was a signal honor, and he had sprung for two dozen doughnuts and had a huge pot of fresh coffee that was ready for pouring.

Swanson had placed a half dozen chairs in a semi-circle in front of a small screen that showed the ravages of time and even bore marks of the untimely deaths of a few flies for whom life stopped suddenly last summer.

They did not look at each film in its entirety. They watched it only up to and through the key scenes that had seemed to trigger the reactions that caused the untimely deaths of the victims and the catatonic state of Carl-Stapelton.

In between the films, as Ponds carefully took down one reel and put up the next, they discussed the films and agreed that did not detect anything unusual in any of them. Burnside's comments were all very expert and interesting, but added nothing to dispel the mystery or to shed any further light on it. The whole thing seemed to be an exercise in futility until a sudden thought struck Lori and she expressed it. It came to her after they watched the last film, *How Red the Rain*. Ponds' was in another room rewinding the film and Swanson had drifted to the next room to handle another customer.

"What if...no."

Bennett looked at her curiously. "What if what?"

"It's crazy," she said, waving her hands in the air.

"So what isn't?" Bennett retorted. "Go ahead with your thought."

"All right," she said. "What if these films, the ones that were shown to the group, had been, I don't know, altered somehow."

"Altered how, and why?"

"I don't know how or why," she continued. "But if the film is the key to the whole mystery, doesn't it make sense to suggest that the film the victims saw might be different from the film they saw before?"

Bennett considered Lori's theory but could not see how it fit.

"But it's the same film," he said.

"That's the point," Lori explained patiently. "Each one of these people has, well, had a healthy ego, right?"

Bennett nodded. And Lori continued.

"They had seen their films, what would you guess, dozens of times, a hundred times? These are their favorite moves. Each of them had their own print to show friends, and guests, and to view themselves. They knew every scene in those films by heart, had to, and yet, on one specific night, viewing the very same film they had seen God only knows how many times before, something in the film suddenly shocks them and shocks them so badly it induces a heart attack."

Suddenly, as crazy as it sounded, it made great sense to Bennett who was enthralled by her theory.

"You're right, or I think you're right. Suddenly, there's something different about a very familiar film. There has to be. There can't be any other explanation. But how different? What's different?"

Charley Burnside was fascinated, and decided to interject his thoughts on the subject.

"Could someone have gotten hold of these prints and altered them, added something? I can tell you as an editor it wouldn't be the easiest thing in the world to slip in an extra scene."

Bennett caught something in Burnside's comment that made him want to hear more.

"Mr. Burnside, could you tell by examining the film under a microscope if someone had spliced in another scene?"

Burnside laughed. "Hardly need a microscope to check that. You could easily see the splice with the naked eye. Suppose we run each film down to the point where these people reacted to a particular scene, then I'll look at it and tell you if someone tampered with the print. It's easy to do,"

Burnside took the four films and examined each one carefully. Ponds asked if his services were needed further. Bennett said no, but he might want to talk to him later.

Lori could not help but notice the T-shirt Ponds was wearing. He had obviously purchased it at a local souvenir shop. Emblazoned across the front was the hopeful message: "What I really want to do is direct."

"Hoping to make it in films someday?" Lori asked innocently, as Ponds was about to leave.

Ponds turned and smiled uneasily at her. "Why, yes." His neck spasmed as he answered and his physical contortion surprised Lori who tried hiding her emotions. By his very actions, Ponds seemed troubled, and Lori sensed it. He looked and acted like someone who found it difficult to engage in a simple conversation, and was uncomfortable around others. Lori decided not to press her luck any further, though there was something else about him that bothered her.

"Sorry. I just had to ask.

Ponds hesitated as if his mind was elsewhere. Then he blurted, "Er. Right." He laughed loudly, fluttering his eyes as he chortled, even though Lori was not trying to be funny. He mumbled something to himself as if no one else was around, shaking his head, and then quietly exited the room, heading for the nearest bar.

When Charley Burnside finished examining the films, he had bad news for them.

"I can tell you, for certain, those are the original prints. No one has added or subtracted anything from any of them. They haven't been tampered with, or altered in any way."

"You're absolutely certain of that?" Bennett asked.

Charley looked him in the eye.

"Thirty-seven years in the business."

"Right," Bennett said. "I didn't mean to offend you. I just wanted to make absolutely sure."

Charley shrugged his shoulders in an apologetic way. "That's it," he said. "Hate to shoot your theory in the head, Lori."

Lori knew Charley would tell her nothing but the truth. What would he have to hide?

"Where does that leave us?" she asked.

Bennett knew the answer to the question without blinking an eye. "Right where we started. Nowhere."

"Unless," Lori said, thinking aloud, "it's something beyond us. Way beyond us."

Both Bennett and Charley raised their eyebrows as if on cue.

Bennett said, "And what does that mean?"

"I think she means," Charley confided, "something...unworldly." He released a nervous little laugh.

Bennett was not laughing. "Ghosts? Is that what you're talking about? Because if it is, forget it."

"I know, I know," Lori explained. "It's impossible. Superstitious. Insane. Couldn't happen."

"Right," Bennett said.

"Except that if there's nothing else, why reject it?"

Bennett aimed a forefinger at her, as if ready to explain something. Then he realized he had nothing to explain.

"Look," he said as earnestly as he could, "I don't believe in ghosts or goblins or things that bump in the night. I just don't."

Lori understood but remained steadfast in her beliefs. "And I'm not going to try to convince you there are such things, because I don't think I believe in them, either. But you will admit there are things we don't understand, that man's body of knowledge isn't complete this year, this month, and this moment. There is still room for new discoveries, new ideas, even the acceptance of bizarre old ideas."

Bennett walked over to the window and looked at the parking lot, seeing nothing.

"Lady," he said slowly, "you could get me laughed off the force."

Lori moved up behind him, and her tone was almost pleading.

"I don't *know* that it's something occult. I'm only suggesting that if every other avenue seems closed, why not at least entertain the possibility that it is, no matter how ridiculous or remote if may seem. At least, then we could deal with it better."

Bennett turned around, and took her by the shoulders. He was by no means trying to romantic. He simply did it to make his point.

"What do you mean, deal with it better?

Lori explained. "I've read a lot about extrasensory perception, poltergeists, and things like that. How about Peter Hurkos, the psychic, even police departments have used him in their investigations. And he's helped them solve a few cases, maybe a lot."

Bennett let go of Lori and tried to see her side. "Look, I don't have a closed mind, I really don't. But if you're suggesting that some kind of a ghost killed three people and sent a fourth into some kind of trauma, well, it just boggles the mind. It's just too much to accept."

"Why?" Lori asked, "simply because Mark Bennett doesn't know anything about the occult? If you know everything about nuclear energy or how to package a trip to the moon, does that mean they can't exist either?"

Bennett knew he was not going to win this kind of argument, and he was not at all sure he wanted to.

"Okay, suppose I open my mind all the way, to any possibility. What do you suggest is the next step?"

Lori felt a victory flush come to her cheeks.

"There is a way to proceed, a logical way. I'll call Helen Gamble at UCLA. She's an expert on the occult, parapsychology, all that stuff. I'll call her. We'll sit down with her, and just see what she has to say. If she says bunk, it's bunk. Is that a deal?"

Bennett waited a long time before answering. Then he said, "Deal." But he felt like a fool saying it.

Chapter 9

"Mark, I've contacted Professor Gamble and she says she's interested. Okay?"

Bennett was working his way back to his chair holding the receiver up to his ear. He was still switching his mental gears when he took the call.

"Okay." And okay to call me Mark, he thought.

"Well, good," Lori continued. "She said something interesting. She said she's been fascinated by everything she's read about the case and she's very anxious to talk to you and something else..."

"Something else?"

Lori was fully expecting that kind of reaction from Bennett. In fact, she purposely set him up to add some drama to the announcement she was about to make to him.

"Yes. She wants to see each of the movies and, if possible, she would like to visit each of the homes where someone died."

Bennett thought that over for a moment.

"Mark? Are you there?"

Still silence and then. "Yeah, I was just thinking. I don't know if it's too cool an idea to go tramping into those homes so soon after the deaths. She isn't thinking of one of those s ance things, is she?"

Lori laughed. He had grown to like that laugh very much in the past few weeks.

"No, nothing like that. But she said there is this thing she calls a presence. But let her explain it to you. I don't want to botch it up."

"Okay," Bennett said, sounding resigned to the fact he had to try this idea. "Let me make a few calls and get back to you."

Martha Von Tours' sister-in-law told Bennett he would have to obtain a court order to bring over a parapsychologist and Rex Hampton's cousin from Ohio just flatly said no way.

But Peter Olson's stepbrother said sure, anything that might help. So Bennett arranged to use the Olson residence the following night. He called Lori back and told her she could bring Professor Gamble but no film crew. That was agreeable to her.

Bennett hung up and wondered if not all this was a silly mistake. True, there were no clues in this case. None at all. And he was baffled and so was everyone else who was interested in it. But the occult? Come on, he must be slipping to have agreed to go along with Lori's idea. But then, as he reflected upon it further, he probably would have responded in the affirmative if she suggested they hold a meeting in Zambia and invite a polar bear and a medicine man from Oklahoma if it helped solve the case.

Professor Gamble was not anything like Bennett had imagined her to be. She was supposed to wear horn-rimmed glasses and a plain dark mannish business suit and carry a severe looking attach case. Flat-chested, too, of course.

When Lori arrived with Gamble, Bennett wondered what idiot had cast all those black-and-white B movies in which lady professors all looked like they were supposed to look.

Professor Gamble looked like a *Playboy* centerfold--Miss February, March *and* April. Stacked. Gorgeous. Instead of the mannish business suit she was supposed to be wearing, she was filling out form fitting blue jeans and a T-shirt that read, "Your Message Here." The T-shirt carried another message all by itself and Bennett got it immediately. Helen Gamble, consciously or not, was a turn on.

Lori introduced them and Professor Gamble flashed a warm almost seductive smile.

"Hope you're not disappointed to be working with a lady professor."

Bennett smiled right back. "You know you're kidding, don't you."

Lori did not look at all that pleased to see them getting along so beautifully in the first few seconds of their meeting. Bennett hoped she was jealous, but then, why would she be?

"It's a beautiful home," Helen was saying. "And... Just a bit spooky, too. Too dark, don't you think?"

Bennett gave a hint of sarcasm. "Are you from House Beautiful or the Parapsychology Department?"

They walked into the giant living room and Helen stopped in her tracks.

"This is where it happened."

She was not asking Bennett, she was telling him, so he did not respond.

Professor Gamble closed her eyes and nodded her head, as if agreeing with herself.

"Yes. Something's here," she said, holding her palms out and feeling the air in front of her.

"What?" Bennett asked, curiously.

She opened her eyes. "I don't know. Just...something. Is the film here? Can we see it now?"

Bennett steered Lori over to the projector. Then he said, "Professor, a friend of Lori's who is a film editor has made copies of the key scenes. They're spliced together now and we'll be able to show just the pertinent scenes without having to run through all the stuff that went before. That okay?"

Gamble said it was.

Bennett walked to the sidewall and flicked the light switch. Lori turned on the projector and they found chairs.

They watched again as handsome young Rex Hampton taxied his badly damaged plane to a halt and slowly, painfully extricated himself from the seat. He had just shot down his twenty-fifth German plane, but this was his closest call of all and he was bleeding from a superficial wound in his right shoulder. A young ground mechanic had jumped upon the wing to assist him down. The mechanic tenderly guided the flying ace to the ground and there was a cutaway and close up of the face of Hampton's concerned commanding officer. Then a close up of Hampton, grinning and giving the senior officer a "thumbs up" gesture to signal that he was all right. The scene then switched to a shot of the young mechanic's face soaked in youthful hero worship, and a long shot of the runway as other survivors of Hampton's shot-up scenario came limping home.

It was at this point the screen suddenly went dark and Lori stopped the projector and Bennett moved over and turned on the lights.

"That's the scene that triggered Hampton's heart attack," he explained to Professor Gamble. She gave him a quizzical look and shrugged her shoulders. The scene told her nothing. Bennett looked at Lori and she smiled self-consciously. They were both thinking the same thing. This might well prove to be an exercise in futility.

Bennett interrupted the silence. "Okay, ready for the next one?"

Professor Gamble motioned that she was and the lights went down again and they began watching a clip from the Martha Von Tours' award-winning film, *The Girl from La Jolla*.

It was a very long clip, because Martha Von Tours had succumbed quietly, wordlessly, in her seat. No one knew, nor would they ever know, exactly at what point in the film she suffered a fatal heart attack. But Bennett was certain, from his interrogation of the other members of the group, that she was apparently very much alive until the last ten minutes of the film. Rita Reno remembered exchanging a few comments on the film with her until that fatal moment. But some time between when the last minutes began, and

The End came flashing on the screen, Martha Von Tours had died.

It was an era in which the audience demanded happy endings. This was a happy ending to end all happy endings.

That spoiled, nasty star of the musical within a musical had slipped on a cake of soap in her lover's boudoir and fractured her ankle, on the very night of the big opening, of course, and who should have to go in her place but our little Ginger. And, of course, she wowed 'em from the orchestra pit to the upper reaches of the balcony. The little girl from Kansas was a big Broadway star, overnight, and, as she took her fifth curtain call, the prince stepped onto the stage from the wings, dressed, as he always in the picture, in full formal clothes with a multi-colored cummerbund that resembled the national flag of his country. The two embraced, and the presumption that they would live happily ever after was very strong indeed.

As the clip ended Lori stopped the projector, hit the lights, and both turned to look at Professor Gamble.

She looked frustrated and upset, even angry. Before either of them could speak, she let it flow.

"Now wait a minute. Please. I don't know quite what you expect of me, some kind of magic or something, I supposed, but I can't simply look at one of these films and suddenly hand you the answer you're looking for."

Bennett and Lori looked at each other and Lori said, "I'm sorry, Helen, if we've given you that impression. I don't know what we expect from you, but we certainly didn't mean to put undue pressure on you."

Professor Gamble, immediately embarrassed by her outburst, felt the need to explain herself.

"Look, I'm sorry, too. None of us knows just what we're looking for here, or what is here if it's here. I'm supposed to be an expert on ESP, and I guess I am. And I'm even a little psychic. But nothing's happening, and I'm getting no ideas at all. It's...frustrating."

Bennett walked over and put a brotherly hand on her shoulder.

"Relax. We're just shooting an arrow in the air. If it doesn't land anywhere, so, it doesn't. There's no pressure on you. None at all."

The professor smiled again and shook her head.

"Forgive me." She was asking Bennett to forgive her, not Lori. Lori had noticed that while the professor viewed the first two film clips, she had spent almost as much time studying Mark's profile as she had the films unreeling before her. Bennett was completely unaware of her attention, but then, Lori reminded herself, Bennett was a man.

Women are the best women watchers, not men. It takes a special skill and understanding of the subject that only another woman has.

"Do you want to go on, or shall we wrap it up?" Bennett asked.

The dazzling smile again of Professor Gamble directed his way.

"Oh, please, let's go on."

Peter Olson's *The Land of the Living Un-Dead* unfolded before Professor Gamble, and she found herself caught up in the eerie pyrotechnics. Lori and Bennett again saw Dr. Morda, despondent, ready to throw himself off the cliff and his concerned young assistant trying to convince him not to take his life.

After the clip ended, Professor Gamble's eyes were still riveted to the screen.

"What a performance," she said to Bennett. Lori felt like saying, "Hey, remember me? I'm in this room, too." But she said nothing.

"The next film," Bennett explained, "is the one Sylvia Cart-Stapelton was watching with young friend when she went into some kind of comatose state from which she hasn't returned yet. Okay?"

And there was a young Sylvia Carl-Stapelton again in *How Red the Rain*. Sylvia smiling. Sylvia crying. Sylvia pleading. Sylvia running in a panic through the rain. The clip lasted nearly twelve minutes. And, finally, it ended.

Bennett turned to the professor and she moved her chair closer to his.

"This one," Bennett said, "happened under different circumstances but with almost the same result. Sylvia Carl-Stapelton was entertaining this young actor in her home. She went into this, this trauma, this catatonic state, sometime during the last third of the picture. This young man..."

Lori interjected, "Rodney Camper."

"Right, Rodney Camper didn't know anything had happened to her until the picture ended. Then he discovered her. At first, he thought she had fainted but he couldn't rouse her. So he called the paramedics. And, well, she's still hospitalized and under a physician's care and twenty-four hour nursing service."

Lori, not about to shut out, added her thoughts to the conversation. "She's obviously our very best bet to explain this if she...when she...recovers."

"Yeah," Bennett said confidently. "If she doesn't know

108

what happened to the others, she at least knows what happened to herself. Or we hope she does. Something sent her into that traumatic state, and when she recovers consciousness, she ought to remember what it was. That ought to clue us in on what triggered the others."

Professor Gamble was listening in rapt attention. Lori thought she was concentrating more on Bennett's eyes and lips than on his words.

The professor put her hands behind her head and stretched, her magnificent breasts pushing against the T-shirt that show them off so well.

"Wow. It's really been interesting. Let me do this. Let me go home and think about what we've seen and heard. Frankly, I don't know if I can help at all, but I'll try."

"Fine," Bennett said understanding." As he spoke, he could not help keep his gaze off the professor's T-shirt and what lay behind it.

Professor Gamble turned, for the first time in half an hour to Lori.

"It's been extremely interesting, and I'm so glad you asked me to come."

Lori smiled warmly. Thank God for that acting-modeling training, she thought.

Then Professor Gamble turned to Bennett, giving him that same warm, seductive smile with which she had greeted him.

"Where do you live, sergeant?"

Bennett told her. Hollywood.

"I wonder," she said, boldly, "if it would be inconvenient for you to drop me off. Then Lori wouldn't have to go out of her way and I could ask you a couple dozen questions that have popped into my head in the last few minutes."

Bennett looked at Lori. Lori was still smiling, at least on the outside. Then she broke the silence. "Of course, that sounds like a good idea."

Professor Gamble shook hands with Lori, said they would be seeing each other very soon, and she and Bennett left, with Bennett taking the film clips with him. Lori looked after them, and then began preparing the projector for removal to the studio.

Professor Helen Gamble. Strange how someone can be so wrong about people. Lori at first thought she liked her because she was a successful, independent career woman who was making it in what was still a man's world. Instead, she turned out to be a simpering, man-hungry opportunist who seemed less interested in helping to solve the mystery than in trying to seduce the handsome police sergeant.

Not that Lori cared about her and Bennett. It was none of her business. God knows she had no special interest in Mark Bennett, even though she had felt attracted to him before. He was just another man.

She just did not want Bennett's interest diverted from this case, and Professor Gamble had the face and figure to divert any man from anything.

Lori's foot hit something and she looked down. It was a small, metal wastebasket.

She pulled her foot back and kicked it fifteen feet across the room.

Then she walked to the window just in time to see the old Dodge Neon wheeze up to the crest of the next hill and disappear over it.

"Damn," she muttered. "Damn, damn, damn."

Chapter 10

Bennett was pretending to write down Smokey Downey's confession when the call came in. Smokey confessed to everything on the police blotter that caught the attention of the newspapers or the 6 P.M. news, and if you could believe him, he had a bigger homicide score than a dozen Mansons and Jack the Rippers, and had stolen everything but the Brooklyn Bridge.

In reality, Smokey was a sixty-six-year-old former mental patient who had never harmed anyone in his life and had a deep-seated need for attention. When he had the time, Bennett was one of the few police officers who would listen to him.

Bennett kept nodding as Smokey related detail after detail

of how he had knocked off that Bank of America branch on Sunset Boulevard, escaping with eleven hundred in cash. It was coincidence that Smokey's account was a faithful reproduction of the story in the *Los Angeles Times* the next morning.

"Yes?" Bennett listened intently. "Yes, yes, of course. I'll contact Miss Matrix and we'll be right over. Oh, yes. Thanks very much."

It was Brentwood Community Hospital. A Dr. Parrish. Sylvia Carl-Stapelton had regained consciousness an hour ago and had asked Parrish to contact him and Lori. She wanted to talk to them immediately. The doctor said she was weak, but she could stand a brief visit.

Bennett dialed Lori's newsroom and received the usual, irritating message before he could explain himself.

"KTRB-TV, Your Action News, will you wait please?" It was not really a question because the voice on the switchboard never waited for an answer. She just put Bennett on hold along with two dozen other callers and did mysterious things. Probably poring over old travel brochures, Bennett guessed as he tapped his fingers on the edge of his desk, irritated and impatient.

"...so I ran down the street, turned the corner, and hopped on a west bound number twenty-four bus," Smokey continued.

"What?" Bennett asked, resenting the intrusion on his thoughts.

"A bus. I got away on a bus. That's why the newspapers said no one saw a getaway car. Well, sir, then..."

"Take a hike, Smokey," Bennett said, pointing Smokey toward the door.

The old man's face suddenly clouded.

"Where will I go, Sarg? I don't know where to go."

"Go to a movie."

"I ain't got the price. I really ain't."

Still holding the receiver, Bennett reached into his trouser pocket and removed a five-dollar bill.

"Put this with the eleven hundred you got in the bank robbery and it ought to buy you a ticket to a matinee down the street."

Smokey took the money, and his face brightened.

"Jeez, you're a good guy, Sarg. Thanks, but I ain't touchin' the eleven hundred. No sir. I got it socked away in a savings and loan. It's makin' me five and a quarter percent right now."

Bennett could not resist making a sarcastic remark.

"Until you knock over the savings and loan, right? Scoot, Smokey."

Smokey shuffled out and threw Bennett a salute as he went through the door. Bennett did not see it. He was staring at the ceiling. The irritating voice came back on the telephone line.

"KTRB-TV, Your Action News, will you wait--"

"No!" Bennett screamed into the phone. "Police! We went through that already! This is police business!"

There was a slight pause.

"How can I help you, sir?"

Bennett loosened the top button of his collar. "This is Sergeant Bennett, Homicide. Tell Ms. Matrix I'm calling, will you?"

"One moment, please."

Twenty-eight more seconds of finger tapping and the

voice came back on the phone. Bennett really had hoped the voice this time would be Lori's.

"I'm sorry, Sergeant, Lori is out in the field and can't be reached. But she should be calling in an hour or so."

Bennett left a message, saying he was going over to Brentwood Community Hospital. Knowing it would be mixed in with the fifteen or twenty other phone messages and fifty or sixty letters Lori received at the office each day, Bennett did not hold out much hope that Lori would be joining him.

He was wrong. Ten minutes after he arrived at the hospital, she joined him in the downstairs coffee room where Dr. Parrish had asked him to wait while he again checked Carl-Stapelton's condition.

Little beads of perspiration were sticking to Lori's usually cool forehead and she was obviously irritated.

"Goddamned toy television station!"

"Which means what?" Bennett asked coyly.

"I don't even want to talk about it," Lori snapped.

Bennett waited a couple of beats, knowing she would talk about it.

"They send me out to hell and gone, into a lettuce field near Oxnard, and I'm supposed to cover this farm workers' demonstration. I'm standing up to my kneecaps in fresh fertilizer, looking for some sign of life and there's nobody there."

Bennett frowned. "They called it off?"

"No, goddamnit, the ninny on the desk got the right day but not the right date. It's a week from now."

"Everybody makes mistakes," Bennett said in a consoling voice.

Lori glared at him. "The only mistake here is they hired

one of our head salesman's weekend tricks. Great boobs. No brains."

"It's so hard to get good help these days," Bennett quipped, like a comedian delivering the punch line.

Lori finally broke into a small smile.

"Okay, I'm sorry. You probably just came from a knife fight with six fatalities and I'm telling you my big problems. What about Sylvia?"

Bennett started pacing in place. Looking at his watch, it seemed like he and Lori had already been at the hospital for hours.

"Conscious, apparently, and anxious to talk to us. Asked for us by name," he said. "This Dr. Parrish called me and then I called you. He's in with her now. Ought to be out any minute. Want some coffee? It's really rotten."

Now Lori was getting antsy. She began to fidget in her seat.

"What do you think she's got on her mind?"

Bennett shrugged. "I can't even imagine, can you?"

"No."

A nurse came out of Room 317 and a few moments later, Dr. Parrish emerged and headed for Bennett and Lori.

Bennett introduced Lori. Dr. Parrish beamed.

"I see your show every once in a while Miss Matrix. And I enjoy it."

Lori smiled and thanked him, anxious for him to begin talking about Sylvia.

"...But I didn't much care for that thing, that series, you did on socialized medicine. I'd like to talk to you about that sometime."

Lori nodded, impatiently. Then she said, "How is Sylvia? Is she...coherent?"

Dr. Parrish did not respond but used his head to indicate they should follow him to the room. He stopped outside and looked at his watch, just the way doctors do in soap operas.

"She's very weak. Five minutes. No more."

They agreed, and he turned on his heel and walked away. They looked at each other, wordlessly, and then Bennett followed her through the door.

At first, Sylvia looked right at them without a hint of recognition, and they both wondered if her attack had affected her memory. But then they realized it was her eyesight. She could not really see them until they had approached within a few feet or her bed. She smiled, wanly, and they both were shocked to see how her experience had seemed to deteriorate her. The frail little woman who had tried so hard to look younger than sixty-six years now looked like a tired seventy-five. It was the first time Lori and Bennett had seen her without makeup. There was not a trace of color in her gray face.

"Well, hello," she said, brightly. But the voice seemed very small in the large white room. "It's so nice seeing you two again."

Bennett and Lori told her how well she looked and she pretended to believe them. She made a small joke about how all the handsome young interns kept trying to undress her and give her unneeded examinations, and then, when they were seated close to her, she propped herself up and looked from one to the other with a penetrating gaze. She had been an actress all her life. She seemed to be enjoying what she had hoped were the dramatics of the situation...And she had already decided to make this scene, in which she was starring so completely, last as long as she possibly could.

"You are a handsome couple," she said, as she studied Bennett and Lori at close range."

The comment made both of them uncomfortable, but they smiled, looking at Sylvia and not at each other.

"You know, I fell in love with a police officer once. Not a city policeman, actually. He was a captain of the guards at MGM when I was there. He looked so tall and handsome in his dark gray uniform and every little trollop on the lot wanted to get her hands on him. But if you can have a star, why settle for a waitress!"

Lori and Bennett got to the point and had no interest in disputing Sylvia's logic. Bennett tried to hide his impatience but Lori was becoming increasingly aware of it.

"Sylvia," she said, "there was something else you wanted to tell us, wasn't there?"

By the expression on her face, it was apparent Sylvia understood the meaning of Lori's question. There was not much point in trying to delay it any longer. Timing is everything, on and off the stage. She could lose her audience if she left them dangling too long.

She nodded reassuringly to herself, and then she said, "I know what happened to me...that night. It may be what happened to everyone else. I'm almost sure of that."

Bennett, bursting with curiosity, remained silent.

"Please tell us everything you know," Lori persisted. "Everything you remember."

Sylvia put her head back on the pillow and stared straight at the ceiling. She remained so motionless for a few seconds that they wondered if something was wrong. But she was only setting them up for what was to come. When she spoke, the voice was even smaller than it was before, and they each leaned forward to make certain they would not miss a single word.

"It was the film. It happened right in the film."

Bennett and Lori looked at each other quizzically.

"Every one in the world, in the world, remembers that scene. Roger has cracked his head on the windshield and he's bleeding. He may die. I've got to help!"

There was a real panic in her voice as she relived the part in her mind. Bennett imagined that she probably psyched herself up this way when she was actually doing the original scene.

"I have to run through that blinding rain. It's just awful. But if I don't, Roger will die. And so, I pull myself out of the car and I don't know which way to turn. Far in the distance, I see a light. It's not from a car. It's from a house, a farmhouse, probably. I begin running. My tears mix with the rain. I loose a shoe. Then I kick off the other shoe, keep running, running, running. And then..."

Sylvia paused for a second, her eyes never leaving the ceiling. And then she let out a little shriek. It startled both Bennett and Lori.

She turned her head and looked at each of them, almost in a crazed look." It happened...right in the film."

Bennett leaned forward expectantly to calm her and make her slowly explain what that was.

"What happened? What?"

"He was there."

Bennett threw a quick glance at Lori, who was staring at

Sylvia's face, mesmerized by her performance. Then the words spilled from Sylvia's mouth.

"Bruce Baylor."

Bennett and Lori remained speechless for a moment before Lori broke the silence.

"Bruce Baylor?"

"Yes, Bruce Baylor," Sylvia repeated, before letting out a deep sigh.

Bennett and Lori waited a few moments, waited for her to resume speaking. But she remained silent.

Bennett began his own examination of the facts directing his question to Sylvia. "Who is Bruce Baylor?"

Another deep sigh followed, this one accompanied by a bronchial cough. And then Sylvia continued, now looking into their faces.

"He was a terrible young man. Egotistical. Arrogant. Not untypical of those kinds of people."

"What kinds of people," Bennett inquired further. He thought she meant male actors.

Sylvia turned up the corner of her mouth.

"He was a New York Jew. You know, how many of them are out here."

Lori bristled. So Sylvia was an anti-Semite. Well, what was so shocking about that? There were plenty of them around. And she would never suspect that the blue-eyed blonde young newswomen she seemed so fond of was also Jewish, also from New York.

"But Sylvia, I don't quite understand the connection," Lori interjected. "This Bruce Baylor, was it that just the sight of him again, even on film, so upset you that..."

"No, no, no," Sylvia explained patiently. "Yes, I was upset

to see him. But you don't understand. He was in the picture."

Bennett and Lori were reading each other's minds. The old lady was not making sense. She had not recovered as completely as Dr. Parrish had led them to believe.

Lori decided to pursue it anyway.

"Bruce Baylor was in the picture. And when his scene came up, just seeing him again

Sylvia glared at Lori so hard she stopped talking. What was wrong?

"Let me tell you, very, very slowly. Bruce Baylor was in the picture. He was in the picture the night we were looking at it. Rodney Camper will remember. He was in the picture."

Bennett rose, convinced the old woman was playing with something less than a full deck. Sylvia sensed his mood and motioned him to sit down and he did. She then tried again to explain.

"I'm not saying this very well. I'm sorry. Let me begin again. It was the prime scene in the picture. I had seen this picture, oh, fifty times before. But this was the first time it was different. This was the first Bruce Baylor was in it, don't you see?"

Her guests both sat back in their chairs at exactly the same time. She stared into their faces, and they both looked confused. Lori decided to speak up.

"Sylvia, you are saying...you are telling us...that the night you saw 'How Red The Rain' with Rodney Camper sitting at your side...you saw this Bruce Baylor in the picture and it was the first time he was ever in that particular picture?"

Sylvia nodded. "Yes, that is exactly what I am saying. That is exactly what I saw."

Bennett released air through his lips as if he had been holding his breath for five minutes. He leaned forward, trying to clarify what he was beginning to think were the inane ramblings of a very sick old woman.

"Ma'am, I am a cop and sometimes I have to talk like one. May I do that? May I ask you a few questions?"

Sylvia smiled weakly and agreed.

"Don't be offended but do you feel all right. I mean, do you feel that you have a complete grasp of...reality?"

Sylvia suddenly became defensive. "Yes, of course, I have."

"You are telling me, us, that you were watching this movie you've seen a hundred times before and on this one occasion, this very unique and special occasion, suddenly an actor who wasn't ever in the picture before is suddenly there, in front of your eyes. And he's someone you know very well."

"That is absolutely correct. Absolutely the way it was."

Bennett leaned back in his chair once more. The gesture seemed to say to Lori, there it is, she is nuts, I rest my case. Lori continued the examination without Bennetts help.

"Sylvia, then what you are trying to tell us, what you are telling us, is that you think you saw someone you know in that picture, is that right?"

Sylvia compressed her lips together. She was beginning to lose her own patience.

"I didn't think anything. I know what I saw. I saw Bruce Baylor in that picture. He wasn't supposed to be there, and the shock of it made me faint."

Read seizure, thought Bennett, but he remained silent convinced they were dealing with a mental case.

Lori pressed on. She felt she was on to something.

"You saw Bruce Baylor in the picture. He was never in before. He appeared in it, what, like magic?"

"No," Sylvia said, slowly and deliberately. "Like a ghost."

Lori paused, glanced sideways at Bennett, and continued.

"Is it possible that this young actor might have had just a modest role, a cameo, and you had forgotten about it until now?"

"No," insisted Sylvia, and now her irritation was turning into anger. "It was him all right, and he was never in the picture before. I told you that."

"But why?" Lori wondered. "Couldn't it be the way I suggest? We all have memory lapses. Why couldn't he have been in that picture and you forgot that he was?"

"Because," Sylvia said, and her actor's instinct told her she was to deliver the most significant line of this little scene, "he was dead when the picture was made!"

Bennett pursed his lips and studied his fingernails. Then he glanced at Lori. She no longer was trying to mask her suspicions that the old lady was over the rainbow.

"Sylvia, please be patient with me," Lori continued. "Baylor was not in the picture when it was made because he was dead, is that what you said and what you meant?"

"Yes."

"Then how do you account for him being in it forty years later? No, don't tell me. You think he was a ghost."

Sylvia corrected her. "Is...a ghost."

Lori shook her head.

"Is there any reason you can think the ghost of this young actor would somehow get into one of your pictures?"

Sylvia smiled without mirth. "Of course. He hated me.

Always did. No, not at first. At first, he wanted to use me."

Bennett thought, why you hypocritical old wreck, you should talk about using people, you with your stable full of young studs and promises of big careers in exchange for their favors.

Sylvia continued. "He visited me a few times in my dressing room. Oh, it was magnificent. They did things properly in those days, you know. We were...close. What I didn't know was what this brash young animal was only trying to get me to use my influence to get him promoted from the extra ranks into a speaking role in the picture."

Lori pursued that further.

"So, he wanted a favor from you but you turned him down. And he resented it."

Sylvia waved her hands in anger. "Of course he resented it. He was terribly ambitious. But he couldn't act his way out of a paper bag. Oh, he was a big, beautiful hunk of a man, all right. But that's enough. You have to act, too."

Lori was still trying to frame another question in her mind when Dr. Parrish burst into the door. He was angry.

"I told you two five minutes. And you've been here more than twenty. You'll have to stop now."

Bennett and Lori both rose at the same time. The facts that Sylvia had given them were the only evidence they had in connection with her incident and maybe the three other celebrity deaths. Now if they could only make some sense of it. Especially before the life of another movie legend was mysteriously taken. Perhaps with some more time, they would have been able to put the pieces of the puzzle together, so long as their patience with Sylvia was not exhausted first.

"We're sorry, doctor," Bennett apologized. "We really didn't realize how quickly time was going by."

Lori made her apologies, too, and Sylvia said nothing. Lori suspected the old lady was in something of a snit, angered because they did not buy her story, and aware that they thought she was a little less rational.

They moved toward the door and Lori turned around.

"Sylvia, thanks so much for talking to us. Can we talk again when you're feeling stronger?"

Sylvia nodded, and they walked out.

Dr. Parrish bade them a cool goodbye and returned to check on his patient.

Bennett and Lori walked in silence to the elevator. They waited about ninety seconds and finally the doors opened and then the elevator went up instead of down, and they both felt uncomfortable.

Finally, the doors opened on the first floor and Bennett said the first words.

"Lori."

He wanted her to look at him. And she did. Then he put his right forefinger to his right temple and said, "Scrambled eggs."

Lori's eyes flashed her disapproval.

"I'm not so sure."

"What? You're not so sure. You have to be kidding."

Lori kept talking as they walked out the hospital entrance.

"I knew you'd say that. Because your mind is closed. You can't possibly entertain the thought that something occult could have happened."

Bennett threw that line back in Lori's face.

"Can you?"

Lori glared at him. "If I say, yes, then I'm crazy. Is that it?"

"Damnit, I didn't say that," Bennett said, his voice rising. "Do you or don't you believe that the old lady believes what she told us up there?"

Lori paused for a second, and then took her stance. "Try this: I not only believe that she believes what she thinks happened, I also believe it did happen!"

Bennett thought he felt his jaw drop open.

"You mean, now we're investigating a ghost?"

Before he could force a laugh, she turned and looked him squarely in the eyes.

"You're goddamned right I do!"

Chapter 11

Captain Hansen was determined to divert Bennett from the investigation of the old movie stars. He did not like the idea of having to tie up one of his best detective division men on what was turning out to be a farce. Only the fact that Lori Matrix was interested in the Mickey Mouse case had kept him from pulling Bennett off it a long time ago.

Now, with Bennett himself admitting that the case had taken a bizarre and unbelievable turn, Hansen acted. He ordered the sergeant to report to Jules Bassett in Juvenile Division and given him a hand with a missing person's case. It was an unusual order, but hardly a unique one. Bennett had been "borrowed" for everything from stolen auto to bunco, and the Juvenile Division was hardly a first for him. But he did not look forward to it. Most missing persons wanted to be missing. Few ever met with foul play. And the majority were runaway girls, not infrequently reacting to acts of incest on the part of brothers, fathers, uncles and friends of the family.

To Bennett, most sixteen-year-old girls looked alike, but not this one. Not the girl in the photograph that Bassett was handing to him.

"Mary Ann Natter. Sixteen. Fourth week. The old man has clout, too. Big contributor to the mayor's last two campaigns."

Bennett studied the girl's features. Long, straight, blonde hair, huge blue eyes, and skin that looked like peaches and cream. Well, if not at sixteen, when?

"Why the big delay in reporting her?" Bennett inquired.

Bassett seemed to be losing interest already. He was shuffling through dozens of other photographs on his desk, all of them teenage girls, missing anywhere from two weeks to eighteen months.

"What? Oh, the old man knows police procedure, knew we wouldn't begin an investigation right away. Knows most kids return home after a short period of time on the street."

Bennett understood the importance of the case, but the facts were not completely clear.

"This one, Mary Ann," he said. "Has she run away before?"

"Six, seven times," Bassett explained while looking at another missing person's report that caught his eye.

"Jesus!"

Bassett winced. "I know, I know. So she'll come back on her own. But we have to react to a character like this or all the brass will be down on our ass, you know that."

Bennett looked away. Then he turned and faced Bassett and resigned himself to the fact he had no choice. "I'll look around."

Bassett sank heavily into his chair. He was a big man, and the chair lets him know it thoroughly resented his weight.

"Show a lot of places in your report. Every nook and cranny. Put down a lot of interviews. I don't give a shit whether you only talk to your bookie. Make it read well for Mr. Big Shot, her father."

Bennett nodded and carefully placed the eight-by-ten photograph below the first two pages of a clipboard he carried. Then he fired his right forefinger at Bassett and walked out.

A bail bondsman Bennett knew on sight was in the public booth phone outside headquarters and Bennett waited while he finished lying to his client. Then he took the sweaty phone and dialed Lori's office number.

As soon as the number connected, Bennett yelled, "No!" into the photo but the girl said, "Can you wait a moment, please?" anyway and he waited. After two-and-a-half minutes, he heard Lori's voice.

"It's me, Mark. Anything up?"

"Not on this end," Lori reported. "What about yourself?"

"I'm on missing person duty. A real barrel of laughs."

Lori had hoped he had called to talk to her about the celebrity murder case. She tried changing the subject to keep him interested.

"Anything interesting?"

"No."

"What's our next move? Any ideas?"

Bennett thought for a moment, although he had thought it all through hours before.

"I think we're nowhere."

There was an awkward pause, and when Lori spoke again, he thought he detected a definite chill in her voice.

"In other words, you're not even going to entertain the remote possibility that we're dealing with..." She paused. He figured she was going to say ghost, but did not want anyone to overhear it because she would feel foolish.

"...and an, uh, occult situation."

Bennett made no bones about his feelings.

"Whatever. Yeah. That's about the size of it."

There was movement on the other end of the phone. Lori was slipping into her chair. But she kept talking anyway.

"Then you're going to...drop it?"

Bennett bristled a little. He did not like the accusatory tone in her voice.

"I didn't say that. I'm puzzled. Christ, you ought to be, too. I just don't know what to do next and if you do, tell me."

Another pause on Lori's end, and then, "Could we talk at lunch?"

Bennett did not want any hard feelings, so, like a perfect gentleman, he compromised. "I'm getting a late start. I'd better work through lunch. How about dinner? Maybe, we could get the early bird special at the Smoke House. You save a buck and a quarter on the prime rib."

Lori said, "I know, I've had it on Saturdays. But you're forgetting what I do at five o'clock."

Bennett shook his head, impatient with himself. "Yeah. Right. You still working in that laundry?"

He could not see Lori's smile, the first of a very rotten day for KTRB's star anchorperson.

"Listen," she offered, "I'm off the air at six, my makeup is off at six fifteen, and I'll be off at six sixteen. Let's go to the Smoke House anyway and I'll buy."

"How about we go Dutch instead?" Bennett suggested.

"Dutch it is. Meet you at, what? Seven?"

"Seven."

As Lori hung up and looked up, she caught sight of Sally Greer, the six P.M. producer, popping her head around Lori's cubicle. Lori gestured for Sally to come in and take a seat as she hung up the phone.

Greer leaned toward Lori, and whispered, "Whatever happened to the story about those old movie stars?"

Lori picked up a pencil and started doodling on a blank sheet of paper as she answered. "It's in limbo, I guess," she said quietly. "The police officially ended their investigation."

Sally seemed unsurprised by Lori's answer. It seemed whenever there was a case that was too controversial or needed covering up the police announced they had ended their investigation.

Sally liked Lori. She had hoped the story would have paid off for the young anchorwoman who wanted so much to break a big one.

Happening to eavesdrop on the other side of Lori's cubicle, executive producer Billy Gamm walked in during their conversation, and made his feelings known to both of them. "Yeah, it was a bullshit story anyway. We're working on something better for you Lori."

Lori braced herself. She knew what Gamm's idea of a good story was. What would it be this time? A pizza bake-off? Another talking dog? Gamm's voice interrupted her thoughts.

"The boss has come up with this zinger, and I think it's going to work. Lori is going to do a 'This is the Life of' series and we'll shoot the first segment today."

Sally fidgeted in her seat casting her eyes at her notebook, already knowing how Lori would react to the news. The news was greeted warm acceptance about as warm as the hottest day in the North Pole.

"What do mean a 'This is the Life of' series?" she asked, creating deep grooves with her pencil on the paper as her anger intensified.

"You know, like, 'This is the Life of,' a, uh, nun," Gamm explained proudly.

Greer was not buying it either. "It sounds like Bingo. And Andy Gonzales does that kind of series over at Channel 7. Jeez, Andy has tamed tigers and climbed mountains and played firemen and cops and tunnel workers and ."

"But," Gamm said, significantly, "Andy doesn't look like our Lori. This could be a biggie."

Lori sighed and stopped doodling for a second. "Do I get to do these...things...in a bikini? I'm sure the boss would like that."

"Don't be like that," Gamm said earnestly. "When a general manager is nice enough to offer us his input we ought to be grateful for it. Many general managers wouldn't show that much interest in their news operations."

Lori bit her tongue, and resumed her doodling. Underneath she was feeling like kettle ready to boil at any second. All she could wonder was if they would ever assign her some major new stories to cover. Maybe in her life, she thought. Probably by the time she had lost her looks and her varicose veins were prominently showing.

"Today," Gamm continued, "Lori will be a fashion model."

Lori pushed down on her pencil so hard she broke it in half, and let her sarcasm show. "And I if can manage to get pregnant over the weekend, maybe I could be an expectant mother next week."

Thinking Lori was only being funny, Gamm laughed aloud. "Great idea. See what I mean, fun."

Lori jumped up from her desk and stormed out of her cubicle like a fast-moving tornado sucking papers off her desk in the air. Not before getting in a parting shot. "Excuse me. I have more important work to do. I have to go try on bikinis."

If Lori's cubicle only had a door, she would have slammed it.

***

Bennett was already sitting at the bar as Lori entered the Smoke House. He had been watching the door and was going to get up to meet her. But he started and then stopped when he saw how much attention Lori received. Almost immediately, two middle-aged couples waiting for a table recognized her and demanded autographs.

Lori signed the back of an electric light bill, the inside of a cigarette pack, and two matchbook covers.

Then she diplomatically picked her way through the

crowd and caught sight of Bennetts hand raised above the heads at the bar. She slipped beside him and gave him a quick smile. It looked forced. It was. She was in a depressed mood.

Bennett spoke first, and used humor as a way to break the ice. "Don't tell me, it's a crisis. Somebody stole your co-anchor's makeup kit."

"Not funny," Lori snapped sharply. She was TV news' worst critic, but always resented an outside joining her. "No, it's just that I'm so sick of covering nothing stories that go nowhere."

Bennett scratched his head and gave a confused look. He understood what Lori was saying, but all he could think about was an earlier conversation they had on the subject. Now what she was telling him was completely different.

"But didn't you tell me that's what made your station number one in the market?"

Lori gave no response. Instead, she watched the bartender set down two scotch and sodas. She stopped and looked down, and pushed the drinks back toward the bartender in a snit.

"I didn't order that."

Bennett glanced over at the bartender, flashed a five-dollar bill and then waved him off. "How could you," he told Lori, "you weren't here yet."

She smiled but only for a brief moment. "Okay, so I would have. But don't make decisions for me, okay?"

"Don't worry," Bennett said, visibly hurt. "Your women's lib credentials are intact. I won't tell your group leader."

Lori sat in silence and almost looked like she was about to cry. She sipped the scotch and tried to ignore all the pairs of eyes that were appraising her in the mirror of the bar.

Bennett, always aware of her celebrity, was happy to get a nod from the maitre d', and he touched her elbow.

"Our table's ready."

They did not get around to talking about the case until the entree arrived. Two prime ribs, his medium rare, hers rare.

"Yes, horseradish, please," Bennett said to the waiter.

Lori turned her conversation toward the case while Bennett waited.

"Mark, are we on dead center with Sylvia? Are we going nowhere?"

Bennett knew that was what was depressing Lori, and not her job. She had somehow learned to live with the inequities and frustrations of the work just as he had done with his job.

"We're at a dead end. And I've got more bad news." He stopped and took the horseradish from the waiter and spread some on his baked potato. Then he continued.

"My boss has declared the investigation over. No conclusion except the original one. The deaths were coincidence."

Lori's eyes flashed.

"You don't believe that, not now?"

Bennett felt uncomfortable. He did not want it to end, not because he had any faith in Lori's ghost theories, but because he felt the end of the investigation would be the end of his tenuous relationship with this beautiful woman who was stirring feelings in him he had not felt for a long time.

"I don't know what I believe," he said, and then paused for effect. "I'm willing to pursue it if you are, but I can't do it officially. It will have to be on my time off."

Lori's face sparkled in the glow of the amber lighting.

"Mark, I really appreciate that. I really do."

She reached out and touched his hand, then gave it a small squeeze. Suddenly, he felt like a schoolboy, and hoped it did not show.

"Yeah, well, I'd like to see it resolved one way or the other, just like you would."

For the first time, Lori noticed what a fine strong face Bennett had. Maybe it was the way the indirect lighting of the restaurant caught the shadow line in his jaw, or .

"Were you ever married?" It was a sudden thought, and she almost blurted it out, so much so that she sucked in her breath almost at the same time she said it.

Bennett frowned a little; it seemed so off the wall.

"No. A couple of near misses. How about you?"

Lori laughed. "Gosh, no. You know how career women are."

"No," Bennett said, softly. "How are they?"

Lori called a halt the flirtatious questioning, before one of them might say something she did not want to say or hear, not yet.

"What's your next move? I mean, with Sylvia."

Bennett picked up his glass of wine and pretended to study it against the candle on the table.

"We do a background check on this ghost fellow, this Bruce Baylor."

Lori brightened considerably. "Then, you are thinking that it's, well, at least possible. I mean what we talked about."

"If you mean do I believe in ghosts, no. But we'll check out her story just like any other story any person might tell us. The fact it has a supposed ghost in it shouldn't deter us."

Lori picked at her prime rib that had gotten cold during their conversation. She stabbed a juicy piece with her fork and stopped to answer.

"I'm not sure I understand all that, but I think I like it," she said before taking a bite. "You're a, well, very nice guy."

Bennett studied the shimmering blonde hair and the deep blue eyes. But he was determined to play it cool. This was not his woman and never could be.

"You're a nice guy, too," he said. "Let's chow. The food's getting cold."

Chapter 12

It was Saturday, and most of the offices in the 9000 block on Sunset Boulevard were dark. Theatrical agents occupied many of those offices, and most did not work more than five days a week. At least, not in the office. Many would still be working, but it would be on golf courses and tennis courses and in cocktail lounges where their actor and writer clients and producers played.

Spooky Calhoun always came down to the office on Saturdays. He was one of the few exceptions. His telephone did not ring very much any more. His most successful days were behind him now. He was sixty-two years old, and his best clients were under long-term contracts to Forest Lawn and Hollywood Memorial Park. In Spooky's salad days, he was the busiest and brightest young agent in Tinseltown. Hedda and Louella called him nearly every day and Winchell and Jimmy Fiddler frequently mentioned Spooky in their columns.

But Spooky had few clients these days. He was "old school," and he did not fit in with the new Hollywood crowd. He was not one of the "beautiful people." He still thought coke came in a glass and speed was something people should not do in their car. Spooky Calhoun was un-hip, square, out-of-it. He was a dinosaur in new Hollywood where overnight superstars in their mid-twenties were allowed to select their own directors and co-stars, impregnate young, would-be starlets, and still hold the love and affection of a movie audience that was no older and no wiser than they were.

Spooky did not fit into today's world very well either. He missed Bogie and Flynn and Gable and the Barrymores, and his once impressive list of credits had dwindled to four, all of them character actors, and three of them semi-retired. But he kept the office open because Spooky Calhoun did not know what else to do. He had never learned to play. If there was no work, he went through the motions. And frequently he gazed for long minutes at the photograph of his beloved Vera on the desk and wondered what happened to Tim, their oldest boy, who just up and left one day.

Spooky was thinking of Vera and Timmy when Bennett and Lori's knock jarred him back to the present.

"Come in." He got up and moved quickly around the desk to take Bennett's hand and guide Lori to one of the two leather easy chairs that faced the giant old mahogany desk.

Lori smiled warmly and Spooky suddenly thought of Madeline Carroll. He had not thought of that blonde beauty in years.

Lori got down to business right away. "Sergeant Bennett and I understand that you handled, were the agent for, Bruce Baylor."

"Yeah," Spooky said, his voice clear and sure. "I gave him his name, did you know that? He was Herschel Greenblatt or Goldblatt, or something like that. Can you imagine a name as Jewish as that on a marquee?"

Lori Matrix, blonde, blue-eyed anchor lady, could not imagine a name like that. However, Ann Fishbein could, and she hoped the blush she thought she felt had not surfaced.

Meanwhile, Bennett continued the questioning. "What we're hoping is that you've got a photo of this Baylor fellow and maybe a bio."

Spooky grinned wryly. "After all these years?"

Bennett shrugged, but Spooky was only having a little fun with him.

"Sure," he said, as he got up, "I checked it out after Miss Matrix phoned." Spooky went over to a creaky wooden filing cabinet and Lori and Bennett exchanged looks of anticipation.

Spooky carefully placed not one but three black-and-white stills in front of his visitors.

Two were close ups of the young actor's face, and the third was Baylor in some kind of period costume.

Lori and Bennett studied each photo briefly, passing them back and forth.

"Nice lookin' boy," Spooky offered. "I tried with him, really tried."

Lori did not let Spooky's comment die there. "Was it that he didn't have talent, or what?" she asked.

Spooky put his elbows on the desk and tapped the ends of his fingers together.

"I thought the kid had as much talent as anyone else, starting out. But he seemed to be, I don't know, unlucky. I'd set him up with a job here, and no deal. I'd set him up there and he'd audition, and lose it. Or he'd get into a flap with someone important, a casting director, or sometimes another actor."

Bennett started getting the picture. "Are you saying he was what, volatile? Hot-tempered?"

"Yeah, kind of. Oh, nice as pie with me. But then, I was his agent. He had to be. I don't know what was eating the kid. But something. Said his old man had been an actor himself at one time, back in the old Yiddish theatre in New York. The kid was determined to be a fine actor, like the old man. I never heard of the old man, you?"

Bennett and Lori shook their heads. Neither had heard of Bruce Baylor up until a few days ago.

"Anyway," Spooky continued, "he had a damned short career if you can even call it that. And then, one day, I get a call from his landlady and she says, 'Mr. Calhoun, the young lad killed himself. Left you this here note Well, the note doesn't say much except goodbye and thanks."

Bennett, always the cop, delved further into the actor's death. "Was there anything else in the note that might give you a clue as to his motivation? I mean, for killing himself?

Spooky pursed his lips and thought hard. "No. I remember it pretty well, too. Hell, only suicide note I ever got in my life, right? No, it just said, thanks for everything and either 'I've had it or I give up, something like that. No explanation."

Lori understood what Spooky was saying but there was still much she wanted to know. "I know all this is rather strange, asking questions like this about someone who's been dead for so many years, but we really do have a reason."

Spooky smiled at the pretty lady.

"I watch you on the news all the time. I saw the stories you did on the old ladies. It's pretty obvious your interest in the Baylor kid."

Not wasting a precious second, Bennett quickly interjected, "But what's obvious?

Spooky answered, "I know that Bruce Baylor had a hassle with some of those people. Maybe all of them. Hell, I may be fading fast but the old memory's good. God, he hated those people. Mostly because they were all rich and famous and successful, I guess, and here he was a struggling young actor and nobody gave a damn about him."

Bennett looked at Lori and thought, it is crazy but the pieces are fitting together. Lori had a similar thought.

"You two like to have lunch?" Spooky asked.

Bennett shook his head. "Thanks, but we've got several calls to make." Bennett rose and stuck out his hand.

"Mr. Calhoun, thanks very much. Appreciate it, really do."

Spooky smiled warmly. He liked these young people. They seemed far removed from most of the phonies that he came in contact with every day. He fixed an appreciative eye on Lori.

"Miss Matrix, I more than forty years in the business and I'd bet my house and lot against a doughnut that I could get you a major role in a movie within six weeks."

Lori smiled but demurred. "You're very nice. No, I'd rather be a monk. Do they have lady monks?"

Spooky laughed politely and turned to Bennett. "You I'd cast as a jewel thief. You know, a Raffles type or a Robert Wagner kind of reformed crook helping the cops."

"How about a cop?" Bennett said laughing at his own joke.

"No way," Spooky added. "You look too intelligent."

"Swell," Bennett said, and they shook hands again.

"Think about it, Miss Matrix," Spooky said, as they reached the door.

Lori gave him a small wave and a smile and then they were outside, waiting for the elevator.

Lori studied Bennett's face, trying to read what was on his mind. He seemed lost in his thoughts.

"What you do think?"

There was a long pause before Bennett answered.

"I think I've got a lot of thinking to do. About...ghosts. The occult. Whatever the hell we're calling all this. It's like, well, like everything logical and sane isn't working for us and the one thing that keeps coming back is that this is, well, weird."

Lori nodded. "Could we do this? Whether either of us or one of us or none of us believes it could be a ghost, could we just proceed, I mean, logically proceed, on the assumption that it could be?"

Bennett smiled. "Don't ever try to say that on the news! Yes, I think we can. I don't know any other way to keep

144

thinking about this thing. And, can we do something else, if you got the time?"

"Sure, what?"

"Could we go somewhere and talk about the occult? I want to know exactly what you believe about it, what you think is possible, or logical, or so. And I want you to help me figure out what it is I do and don't believe along the same lines. You know what I mean? Because I'm not sure that I do!"

Lori appeared happy that Bennett was now willing to consider other possibilities. "I think I know exactly what you mean, and you don't know how relieved I am to hear you say it."

The elevator finally arrived and the operator inside it looked as if he was built twenty years before the building.

"Down or up, folks?"

Bennett said, Down. It seemed the logical thing to say, since they were on the top floor. The elevator man seemed to approve. At ground level, he said what Bennett was afraid he would say.

"Have a nice day."

Outside, they paused for a moment of silence. Lori spoke first.

"There's a little park I saw when I was in this neighborhood last week."

Little was a good description of the park. Calling it a park was being kind. It was a patch of green sandwiched between an abandoned sandlot and three dilapidated apartment buildings, none of which faced the green. But it had one monumental asset. There was no one in it. Bennett and Lori sat on the grass, facing each other.

Bennett reached out and plucked the longest blade he could find and stuck it between his front teeth. He had not done that since he was a young boy.

Lori leaned back on her elbows and the position pushed her small but firm breasts hard against her silk blouse. The wind started to ripple through and do marvelous things to her long blonde hair and Bennett found himself wishing, again, that their relationship was more than professional.

"Let's really talk about this ghost business. I mean, without either of us shouting at each other."

Bennett pretended to be hurt. "I never shout. Not very loudly, anyway."

Lori laughed, and then said, "You know what I mean. I want to say something, okay. It goes like this. I'm not at all sure I believe in ghosts, but then, there are all kinds of things in this world I don't know a single thing about. I like to think I have an open mind. But not open at both ends."

Bennett gave the small joke a small smile.

"Okay, I like to think I have an open mind, too. I admit, for instance, to some superstitions, probably handed down to me from my folks. They were uneducated, but in their way, wise."

"Right," Lori said as though she understood. "I was taught to question everything, anything. And I don't think that's at all healthy."

Bennett nodded. "Fine. So?"

"So, I would naturally question the existence of ghosts. But...I don't think I'm certain about anything. There are many things in life that none of us can understand. Like, say, the native in the jungle who couldn't understand the internal combustion engine."

146

Bennett rolled over and lay on his stomach, bracing himself with his arms and staring into her bright blue eyes.

"But if the same native saw a combustion engine, saw it work, he would believe that it was there. He might now know what the hell it was, but he would know it was something."

"I agree," Lori said, "but I didn't make my point. Try this. Suppose you and I, right now, saw what appeared to be a ghost. Would you believe it was a ghost, if it looked like a ghost?"

Bennett frowned. "I don't suppose so. Maybe if the air suddenly got cold, like it does in the movies, and there was a faint smell of faded roses or something like that."

"You're putting me on," Lori said in disbelief.

"I suppose I am," Bennett countered. "So what makes you think there are ghosts?"

Lori searched for the right words. "I never said I thought there were. Look, I just think there is the *possibility* that there are. That's what I mean by keeping your mind open. To the *possibility* that there could be. Maybe there are not. But I believe anything is possible."

Bennett stopped and looked at his watch. He did not have anywhere to go; it was just a habit of being a cop. Then, trying to sound more reasonable than he really was, he said, "Once upon a time if you told someone one day man would travel to the moon they would have slapped you in the loony bin, right?"

"Right," Lori said. "Or that that one day man would split the atom, or develop wonder drugs, or thousands of women would experience multiple births, or, oh, I don't know, anything."

Bennett took the blade of grass from between his teeth and touched the end of Lori's nose with it. The unexpected gesture startled her. And then she smiled.

"As that girl in the commercial says, what are you doing?"

Bennett smiled warmly. "Just seeing if you're real."

Lori looked deep into his eyes. "I'm real."

They looked at each other for a long minute before Bennett looked away, uncomfortable, at making such advances.

"What's the matter?" Lori asked, surprised by the sudden switch in behavior.

Bennett did not look at her. "Nothing. Nothing at all. What were we saying?"

"I can't remember now. Tell me, do you believe in God?"

Bennett looked back at her.

"Do you?"

"Yes. But not in Christ. That is, not in Christ as the son of God. I think he was probably a very, very fine man, a brilliant inspired philosopher, but not the son of God."

Bennett responded, "That's what Jews believe, isn't it?

"Yes it is," Lori said, her eyes glowing as she spoke. "What do you believe?"

"I don't know if I believe in God," Bennett pondered. "I don't know."

"But you must know whether you do or not?"

Seeming a bit perturbed, Bennett said, "Why? Do I, does anyone, have to absolutely have to have his mind made up about everything?"

"No," Lori interjected. "But that's one thing everyone has made up his mind about almost from childhood. Either you believe, or you doubt, or you're absolutely certain there is no God. But I never met anyone who was, absolutely neutral about it."

Bennett wanted to get off the subject, but he did not want to offend Lori any further. So he let the conversation play itself out.

"Then if you absolutely, positively need a commitment from me to say I have an open mind about it, then here it is."

Bennett smirked when he made the comment. Lori studied him, half-smiling, "You're throwing my words back at me. You're laughing at me."

"No," Bennett insisted. "You can believe in ghosts because you believe in God. And God is a ghost. Or a ghostly being. Something or someone you can't see or hear or experience."

Lori shook her head in disagreement. "Too simple. Just too simple. You're implying that if I believe in God I must, somehow, be, well, susceptible to believing the supernatural and that just isn't so."

Bennett shrugged. "Okay. Instead of going around on this to no purpose, let's simply proceed on the assumption that there may or may not be something occult involved. We'll really keep our minds open, okay?"

"Okay," Lori agreed. "Now you're the detective, what do we do next?"

Bennett turned the question back on her. "What would the reporter do next to advance the story?"

"Easy," she explained. "Talk to everyone involved. The people who knew Bruce Baylor, who worked with him, who aggravated him."

"Right," Bennett said. "Exactly what the detective would do next. We both have the morning free. I'll set up, who? Charles Evans Fine. Tell him it's unofficial and that you'll be alone but not in your official capacity for the station, okay?"

"Good." Lori got up and began gently brushing tiny bits of grass from her slacks. Bennett had an overwhelming desire to help, but restrained himself. Lori reached down and picked up her purse.

"Ready to go?"

"Where?"

"Home."

"My home or your home?" Bennett asked, defensively. He made certain he was smiling in case she thought he was joking.

"How about this," Lori suggested matter-of-factly. "You go to your home, and I'll go to my home."

Bennett pointed playfully at her nose.

"Exactly what I had in mind."

They picked their way out of the park and found their cars. Bennett watched her climb behind the wheel and then leaned on the door, his head almost inside the car.

"Pick you up at ten?"

Lori smiled. "Suppose I pick you up at ten?"

Bennett straightened up and sighed.

Chapter 13

At the request of Sergeant Bennett, Charles Evans Fine agreed to hold a special meeting of the surviving members of the elite film club at his palatial beachfront home. The club had not met socially since Peter Olson's tragic death, and for good reason. Because of the strange circumstances surrounding the deaths of their three friends, everyone unanimously favored postponing any future screenings until the case was solved. As much as these gatherings meant to them, it was a risk no one was willing to take.

During the meeting, Bennett intended to update the actors about the case and to explore his latest theory-actually Lori's theory-that Bruce Baylor was somehow connected to the deaths of Rex Hampton, Martha Von Tours and Peter Olson. Bennett still was not so sure. He remained inwardly skeptical about Lori's theory.

No substantial evidence found had linked Baylor to the murders, if they could be called that. And the thought of a long deceased actor rising from the dead to commit such murderous acts seemed ludicrous to him, at best.

As silly as it sounded, however, Bennett felt compelled to follow through. The fact was three actors were dead, each under unusual circumstances. Ghost or no ghost, it was his responsibility to investigate all possible leads and bring whoever was responsible to trial. Even if that meant making a complete fool of himself in the process.

Lori phoned earlier to tell Fine that she was running late, and not to start the meeting without her. Her Porsche was acting up again. She tried peeking under the hood to determine the cause, but when it came to anything mechanical, she was all thumbs. A tow truck was on the way, she said, and she assured Fine that she would be there, one way or another.

Bennett arrived ten minutes ahead of schedule. Fine's lovely companion Barbara, who immediately wrapped her arms in his and escorted him inside, greeted him at the door.

"How nice to see you, sergeant, even under these circumstances," Dawes remarked.

"I'll take that as a compliment."

Dawes stopped and laughed, releasing Bennett from her grip. "You're too much for me, Sergeant Bennett. You always make me laugh. You sure we can't convince you to consider taking your act on the road."

"Now who's joking," Bennett retorted.

"**Touché**, Sergeant Bennett. **Touché**."

Dawes renewed her grasp of Bennett's arm and then ushered him into the living room. A rhapsody of sound emanating from one end of the room grew louder with each step. As they turned the corner, Bennett spotted Charles Evans Fine seated at the piano, playing his favorite show tune, "There's No Business Like Show Business." Fine was so engrossed in his music that he had not heard Bennett come in.

"Darling," Dawes said to Fine, tapping him on the shoulder. "Sergeant Bennett is here."

Fine turned around but seemed startled. The stunned expression on his face swiftly changed to a broad grin as soon as he realized who was there.

"Good morning, Sergeant," Fine said, exchanging handshakes. "Beautiful day, isn't it?"

"Yes it is, Mr. Fine. Another day in paradise."

"I tried phoning you a few minutes ago, exactly when I can't recall, but you had already left. I called everyone to re-confirm. We expect a full house this morning."

"Glad to hear it," Bennett said. "Has Miss Matrix arrived yet?"

"No, she called a few minutes ago. She's having car trouble and will be late."

Bennett smiled, then joked, "That's why I buy American."

Suddenly another figure appeared at the front door, and Dawes politely excused herself. Bennett peered over his shoulder to look. It was Bette Oliver. Fine was just beginning to explain that there was a slight possibility that Oliver might not be there, as her arthritis had been acting up and she was feeling rather poorly. Fine waved Bennett on, and he returned to his piano rhapsody. "Sergeant, you remember Bette Oliver?" Dawes introduced.

"Of course, I do," Bennett replied. "It's a pleasure to see you again."

"I must tell you sergeant that I am a little uneasy about this whole thing."

"What do you mean?"

"You know, that the killer, whoever is he, is still out there. I've had many sleepless nights, worried that I might be next. I'm very frightened."

Bennett took her right hand and gently patted it with his own. "There, there, Mrs. Oliver. Everything will be fine. We're working day and night on this case." He did not dare tell her that the case had been officially closed, and that he was acting on the case, unofficially.

Oliver appeared comforted by Bennett's reassurances. "Thank you, sergeant. I'm sorry that I got so carried away."

"It's quite all right, Mrs. Oliver. You have every right to be concerned."

At that moment, Bennett felt a quick tap on his right shoulder. Confused, he immediately turned to his left, then to his right. Standing behind him was Charles Evans Fine who had discontinued playing the piano to welcome another guest: Sylvia Carl-Stapelton. Her first public appearance since the hospital released her two days earlier, she looked peeked. Bennett gave Carl-Stapelton a warm embrace, and she firmly planted a moist kiss on his right cheek.

"Nice to see Miss Stapelton," Bennett remarked, indiscreetly rubbing the lipstick mark from his cheek with right thumb. "How are you feeling?"

"Fine. Fine. The doctors couldn't find a damn thing wrong with me."

"Imagine that?"

"That's what I said. Over a week in the hospital, and all they could tell me was that they think I suffered a mild stroke, but nobody could be sure."

Bennett listened attentively, and then looked down to check to his watch. It was three minutes to ten and still no sign of Lori. He did not want to start the meeting without her, especially since the ghost theory was all her idea.

Stapelton apologized for seeming so disoriented in the hospital. Well medicated during her stay, she admitted her mind was not always clear.

"That's okay, Miss Stapelton," Bennett said. "But are you sure you feel up for this today?"

"Honey, I've survived a lot worse things in my life." Showing her flirtatious side, she tightly squeezed his right arm, and then added, "Of course, I'd feel even safer with a strong man around to protect me."

Bennett half-smiled and then noticed a blurry figure out of the corner of his eye. Dawes was trying to flag him down. Her attempt to get his attention could not come at a better time. "I apologize, Miss Stapelton, but Barbara needs me. We'll have to chat later. If you'll excuse me."

Bennett strode over to the other side of the large living room. Barbara smiled broadly, as he approached.

"I'm sorry to bother you, sergeant, but you two have never met. This is Colleen Kantor."

"I'm a big fan of yours, Miss Kantor. I've seen all of your movies."

"Well, thank you, sergeant. You were always too busy at

the crime scenes for us to meet, but I know who you are."

"That's why they pay me the big bucks."

Kantor laughed genuinely at Bennett's attempt at humor. Without notice, she reached into a small change purse and calmly pulled out a cigarette. She asked Bennett if he would mind giving her a light. He kindly assisted, borrowing her gold-plated lighter, a memento given to her by a famous director for her Oscar-winning performance in the classic western, *Cimarron Trail*.

Taking a long puff, she cocked her head to the side, and then exhaled to keep the smoke from blowing directly into the sergeant's face.

"You know what they say about second-hand smoke these days," she mused. "I wouldn't want to be responsible for your death."

"Believe me, maam. My job will probably do that to me first."

Bennett seemed intrigued by Kantor. She had kept a very low profile of all the stars that belonged to the film club. She did not grant interviews. In fact, she rarely appeared in public.

"What's your interest in this club, Miss Kantor? Why do you come?"

"Mostly because these are my friends. We don't see each other that often, and this creates a purpose for us getting together."

Bennett found it funny that Kantor wanted to be so social. Her recluse ways were legendary throughout the Hollywood film community. He was about to pursue the matter further when Lori finally arrived. The tow truck driver had driven out of his way to drop her off. She was walking with a slight limp toward Bennett, carrying a broken heel in one hand and a maddening look on her face.

"Good, God, I can't believe I'm finally here," Lori said, catching her breath.

She quickly said hello to Kantor, then turned her attentions to Bennett.

"Are we ready to start?"

"Now that you're here, we are," he complained.

Lori decided not to respond. She could tell Bennett was irritated, but she was not sure the fact that she was the last to arrive was the reason why.

"I can see that you two have things to discuss. It was nice meeting you, sergeant."

"The feeling is mutual, Miss Kantor."

Kantor sauntered over and joined the rest of the members already seated in a half-circle in the middle of the living room. She found a comfortable high-back chair, and Lori decided to do the same. With Bennett in such a pithy mood, she left him alone to start the proceedings.

"Can I have everyone's attention, please?"

Bennett waited for everyone to quiet down. The constant chatter softened to a slight murmur, and then a sudden hush overcame the room.

"I want to thank all of you for coming. I think you all know why we are here today. I don't want to belabor anything, so I'll get right to the point. My continuing investigation into the deaths of your three dearest friends has led me to believe that they were not coincidental. Instead, we suspect that extraordinary circumstances may have been involved. And that these deaths were not of natural causes. I realize that for many of you this is a lot to swallow, and that is very difficult for each of you. But I've asked you to come here today for a very good reason."

Forgetting his manners, Bennett paused and motioned to Lori, seated between Charles Evans Fine and Rita Reno. She had arrived seconds before Lori and not been formally introduced.

"I almost forgot. You all know Lori Matrix. She's been working side by side with me on this case."

Lori stood up and joked, "It's about time." Her quip resulted in spontaneous laughter from everyone present, and an embarrassing look emerged on Bennett's face before he continued.

"Through our investigation, we have come to the conclusion that these deaths may be the work of someone from your past. Someone you each worked very closely with, I know this may sound a little crazy, but we believe this person plans to murder again."

A shocked murmur pierced the still air, and by the look on everyone's faces, it was as if they had seen a ghost.

"Wait a minute, sergeant," Fine interrupted. "I understand your theory, but I think it would be wise to take things a little slower with all of us. We're all still in a state of shock over these deaths. And at our advanced ages..."

"Speak for yourself, sweetheart," Reno laughed.

"Let me re-phrase that," Fine continued, "At our tender ages, we don't need to be needlessly alarmed."

Bennett appeared to get the point. "You're right. You're absolutely right, Mr. Fine. I respect what you're saying."

Scratching his head for a new approach, Bennett pondered Fine's comment for a minute before starting over. "This isn't easy for me. I am not totally convinced about this theory myself, but I have been asked to have an open mind about such things." He glanced at Lori who flashed a controlled smile.

Bette Oliver raised her hand, and Bennett acknowledged her. "What is it you want from us, sergeant?"

"Thank you for asking, Miss Oliver," Bennett replied. "Today, we want to discuss each of your relationships with Bruce Baylor because we think he may be somehow involved."

"That's preposterous," Reno moaned loudly. "How can a dead man be a killer?"

"Well, that's what we're hoping to find out."

Bennett knew he was treading on shaky ground. And that this theory of Lori's was bound to backfire on him unless he could come up with some solid evidence. Without any evidence, he didn't have a case.

"Who wants to be first?"

There was stone silence. Some folded their arms in disgust. Others looked down at their shoes hoping Bennett would not notice them. A few of them exchanged glances to see if anyone planned to speak. Finally, Charles Evans Fine, the good soul that he was, spoke. "Look, we have to give Sergeant Bennett a chance. He needs our help."

Guilt started to play on the minds of everyone present. A few of them started shifting around in their seats, as if they were contemplating what they would say. But still no one made a move.

Fine appeared disappointed but he did not let Bennett down. He shrugged helplessly and said he would go first. It reminded him of his acting school days; nobody ever wanted to be first to recite their readings in class but they were always glad when it was over.

"Where would you like me to begin, sergeant?"

"Very simply. What was your association like with Bruce Baylor?

Fine recounted how he and Baylor had met. They were filming a new feature-length melodrama on the 20th Century Fox lot. It was titled, *Heart of My Heart*. The film marked the first time Fine had worked at the studio, and, according to his memory, Baylor joined the cast at the last minute. An actor, whose name he could not remember, originally signed to play the part of John Clements, a successful businessman who lobbied with Fine for the love of the same woman. The actor became suddenly ill and had to bow out at the last minute.

"In the beginning, everything was very cordial between Bruce and me. Then, one day, that suddenly changed."

"How so?" Bennett inquired.

"It was after filming a love scene between me and my co-star Marilyn Kasman. She was the most desired woman in Hollywood. There was not a single actor who didn't want her."

"Go on."

"Well, Bruce got very upset with me afterwards. He said he didn't like how close Marilyn and I seemed together in the scene."

"And what did you tell him?"

"I told him, 'Nothing happened between us. We were just acting.'"

"And he said?"

Fine paused to reflect. "Nothing. He went into a violent

rage, and suddenly attacked me. He put his hands around my neck and started choking me."

By now, Fine appeared agitated. Remembering the incident left him all worked up. His face turned deep red and his body started to shake.

"It's okay, Mr. Fine. Take your time."

Barbara came over to calm Fine down. He then indicated that he was all right and wanted to continue.

"Then what happened?"

As Fine could best remember, the director, Abe Livingstone, pulled Baylor off him. Livingstone immediately sent Baylor home for the rest of the day, without pay. He shot around Baylor's scenes until he returned the following day. "Why the sudden outburst of rage?"

Fine looked down searching for answers. The strain of the intense questioning wearing him down, he gradually raised his head and gave his response.

"I didn't know it at the time but he was having an affair with Marilyn. Bruce had not been on the set but two days and started hitting on her. She found him totally charming, and he could be when he had to be, and, well, you know the rest."

Bennett kept digging deeper.

"What was your relationship like after the incident?"

"With Marilyn?" Fine asked, confused.

"No, Bruce Baylor."

"Sorry. Very cold. Icily cold, in fact. He never spoke another word to me, or I to him, during the rest of the filming."

"Did anything else happen that you can remember?"

Fine searched his memory and appeared more and more

fatigued by the battery of questions. It was some fifty years ago that he made that film and, having starred in nearly one hundred films, they all seemed the same after a while. Then his face lit up.

"Yes, there was."

"What was it?"

Fine paused as if to catch his breath. "Throughout the remaining days of filming, I began receiving death threats with my fan mail."

Fine gasped for air, and then continued. "No return address. No signature. I alerted studio security, and the police got involved. But nothing happened." Fine staggered as he completed his sentence. He looked deathly pale and weak, and Bennett noticed that he was having difficulty breathing.

"Mr. Fine, are you all right?"

"Fine," he said wheezing. "I'm fine."

"We could take five and resume."

Fine waved him off his passageway sounding restricted as he breathed. "Continue."

Bennett resumed. "Were these letters ever linked to Bruce Baylor?"

"Well, no." Fine suddenly stopped in mid-sentence. His breathing sounded more labored. "But they seemed suspicious at the time."

Pulling a white handkerchief from his pocket, Fine gingerly mopped his sweaty brow.

"Sorry," he gasped. "I'm feeling a little weak."

Just as he said that, Fine collapsed to the ground. He stopped breathing. He was dead.

Chapter 14

"Quick, somebody call the paramedics," Bennett ordered as the other actors hovered over Fine's lifeless form with looks of horror on their faces. "And nobody move."

"I'm already dialing," Lori shouted, as she dialed 911 on her cell phone.

Barbara, Fine's companion of many years, was kneeling at Fine's side stroking his receding gray hair with one hand and propping his frail head up on her knees with another.

Fine suddenly gasped, and started breathing again. Slowly his eyes began to open and he stared up at Barbara, whose face reflected what everyone was feeling.

"What happened?"

Barbara started to answer but before she could, Bennett interrupted. "It's okay Mr. Fine. You passed out. Lori's already called the paramedics."

"No, no," Fine protested. "I don't want..."

"Shhhh!" Barbara whispered quieting him. "Don't get yourself excited. I thought for sure I had lost you."

In minutes, paramedics arrived at the scene and from their initial examination, it looked as though Fine had suffered from a severe case of dehydration. "He's probably going to fine," the chief paramedic explained, "but I would advise admitting him into the hospital for more tests."

"No tests," said an agitated Fine who weakly sat up on the gurney. "I'm going to be just fine."

Barbara signed a release form and off the paramedics went. Before departing, they helped escort Fine into his bedroom so he could rest. Meanwhile, to help Fine recover, Barbara excused herself to get a glass and a pitcher of water to take into his room and to be with him

Back in the living room, where the other actors were still gathered, Bennett attempted to resume the investigation. This was no easy task given the grave circumstances that had occurred. Because of Fine's sudden health setback, many of the actors appeared worried that something would happen to them next, and unwilling to continue.

"Folks, everything is going to be fine with Mr. Fine," said Bennett who hated the redundancy of that phrase. "I'm sure if he was here he would want us to continue in the same spirit of cooperation that he had demonstrated to get to the bottom of what happened to your friends and fellow actors who have died."

Sounding more like a district attorney than a homicide

division sergeant does, Bennett pressed ahead. "So who's next?"

An eerie silence permeated the room. Bennett repeated the question. Again, there was no response. Finally, he stretched his right arm forward and, pointing a finger, selected someone by random.

"How about you, Miss Kantor?"

Kantor seemed surprised that Bennett would call upon her. It was evident by the pained expression on her face. Slow to respond, she inched forward in her chair, shuffled her feet and finally stood up.

"Guilty as charged, sergeant," she mused.

"So you knew Bruce Baylor?"

"I knew him. I knew him all right. Not that well, but well enough to know I'm glad he's dead."

"Why the hesitation Miss Kantor? You're among friends," Bennett explained.

"Do you mind?" With her right hand trembling, she held up a cigarette, seeking permission to light up.

"If nobody else objects." Kantor pulled out her favorite lighter and after taking that first puff, the trembling subsided. She remained standing, and proceeded to weave her tale.

"You want to know about Bruce Baylor. Well, you've come to the right person." Pausing, Kantor took a quick drag on the cigarette and continued, "Bruce Baylor and I were lovers."

Bennett's eyebrows rose with that one. "Really?"

"Yes, really."

"Why then if you were lovers are you so happy that he is dead?"

Kantor flicked an ash into an ashtray, and then dropped

a bombshell. "He shot me and left me for dead. He was only sorry that he didn't finish the job."

Bennett's eyes jerked wide and his whole body tensed. It was one of the few moments that he displayed any emotion.

"How did it happen?"

Kantor looked down at the smoldering cigarette and quickly took another puff. "Bruce was a character actor and so he worked at all the different studios. He and I worked together in a film on the Paramount Pictures lot. The title of the film or who starred in it isn't important. We became romantically involved."

Bennett folded his arms in front of his chest and motioned toward Kantor to continue.

"We were having problems working together. He flew into violent rages without the least provocation. Finally, I told the director either he fired him, or I wanted out of the movie."

"Did they fire him?"

"Yes. The very next day."

"What about your romance with him?

"That ended around the same time. I caught him in bed with another woman in his dressing room, I confronted him afterwards and he slapped me hard."

"What did you do next?"

"I tried slapping him back but he grabbed my wrist and began twisting it. I thought for sure that he had broken it because he twisted it so hard, but it turned out to be only a severe sprain. It was after that incident that I made my its him or else plea to the director."

"What happened after he was fired?"

"I had worked late one night. It was the final day of

filming and we were there until 11 o'clock at night. After we shot the final scene, I walked back to my dressing room to change and freshen up. Some other members of the cast and crew were going out to celebrate and I agreed to join them. After I slipped into some new clothes, I started walking to my car. The parking lot was not very well lit, and it was extremely dark..."

Kantor paused and suddenly lost her stoic composure. She placed her right hand over mouth and felt like she was going to cry.

Bennett moved toward her. He leaned over and touched Kantor on her right shoulder.

"It's all right, Miss Kantor. If you can't continue, I'll understand."

She politely pushed his hand aside, and then straightened up in her chair. "I'll be okay. Just give me a minute."

"Whenever you're ready."

Kantor took a few deep breaths, and started where she left off.

"As I said, it was extremely dark outside. When I got to my car, I began searching for my keys when I heard footsteps behind me. I spotted a shadowy figure and cried out, 'Who's there?' Whoever it was disappeared. I waited a few seconds before trying to get the door to my car opened. I heard a crunching sound on the pavement and turned around. It was him. And he was pointing a gun at me."

"Bruce Baylor?"

"That's correct."

"Goon."

Kantor slowly slid her hands down her pant legs to wipe the beads of sweat from them into the material. Her body felt cold and clammy, and she shuddered as spoke.

"He stared at me with those cold gray eyes and muttered something like, 'You think you've ruined me. Now see who's ruined.' And he shot me, not once but twice. First in the stomach, and then in the shoulder. I instantly fell against the car. In desperation, I reached out to try to hold myself up but my hands slipped. Blood was pouring out of me like water and I fell to the ground in a pool of blood. Finally, I passed out."

Bennett was amazed that a man with such a violent past was roaming the streets. He must have had friends in high places to explain how he continued to live a normal life when, in fact, he had inflicted so much pain on others.

"Was Bruce Baylor ever convicted of this crime?"

"No, he wasn't. There were no eyewitnesses and the revolver he used was never found."

"Sounds familiar." Bennett could not help but think of so many other criminals who got off because of that old refrain, "No substantial evidence."

"Did you ever hear from him again?"

"Not directly. But like Charles, I received death threats at the studio, too. The matter was taken seriously in the beginning, but then the letters suddenly stopped. So end of story."

At that moment, Bette Oliver got up from her chair to leave the room. Bennett called out after her.

"Going somewhere, Miss Oliver?"

Acting surprised, she said, "Well, no. I just thought I would get some fresh air."

"Is it fresh air you need, or is it that you have something you don't want to share?"

Oliver stood with a bewildered look her face. She was one foot from freedom, but she could tell her fellow actors did not appreciate her sudden exit.

Bennett motioned with his right hand.   "Come on, Miss Oliver. We're not here to convict anyone. Just learn the truth."

Against her better judgment, Oliver turned around and walked back to her seat. Something Kantor said had gotten under her skin, and Bennett sensed it.

"Miss Oliver, since we have no other volunteers, how about you?"

"Well, really sergeant. Is this is all really necessary?"

"It is if you hope to stay alive."

Oliver shifted back in her chair. She absorbed Bennett's comment and pondered what to do next. Guilt got the best of her, so she talked.

"Forgive me, sergeant. I didn't mean to be rude. This is very difficult for me."

"It's difficult for all us, Miss Oliver. What do you have to say?"

Oliver proceeded cautiously. She unleashed little bits of information at a time.

"Something Colleen just mentioned happened to me, too."

Bennett was all ears.

Oliver explained what happened as best as she could remember. She had appeared in more than two hundred supporting roles as a contract player at Warner Brothers. She recalled first meeting Bruce Baylor in the studio commissary. He was sitting alone, cradling a cup of lukewarm coffee and smoking a cigarette. By the number of crushed butts in the ashtray, she sensed that he had been sitting there a long time, and he appeared downcast.

"I was having lunch with someone else, an actress named Stella Davis. We were working together on a picture with Errol Flynn, one of those swashbuckling dramas. Anyway, just as Stella and I walked by Bruce Baylor's table, a man, whom we had never seen, approached his table. He said something to Bruce, something that set him off."

Oliver ended without adding anything further. Bennett prodded her to continue. "And then?"

"Well, he got up, pushed the table to the floor, and then grabbed the man by the collar. They exchanged words, and Bruce grew more heated by the minute. Finally, he decked the man. But he didn't stop there. He kept beating on him, and beating on him. The man's face was bloodied beyond recognition. Bruce had beaten him to a pulp. Studio security finally arrived to break things up."

Bennett, intrigued by the story, pressed for further details.

"Who was the man, and what did he say that set Bruce Baylor off in such a rage?"

Oliver thought for a moment. She seemed a bit more relieved, and continued. "His name was Mel Greenberg. I think he was Bruce Baylor's agent."

"Mel Greenberg?" Bennett said surprised. "I thought Spooky Calhoun was his agent?"

"He was. He was his first agent. Greenberg was his second or third, I think."

"So what did this Greenberg fellow do that made Bruce Baylor so upset?"

"Well, I didn't hear this first hand, naturally. I heard this through the studio gossip mill. Mel said something to the effect that he wasn't going to cover for Bruce any more."

"Cover for what?"

Oliver started feeling as if she had backed herself into a corner. She had maybe said too much. Yet part of her felt a great release by telling the truth.

"Bruce Baylor had a child out of wedlock with an actress whose name escapes me. She was a leading lady who was under contract at the studio, and the studio knew if the press had gotten word of the story, they would have had a field day. So they covered it up."

"But why the violent behavior?"

"Well, it goes much deeper than that. Mel had done many favors for Bruce over the years, the kind of things that agents did in those days. Supposedly, Bruce had quite a record--jailed for assault several times. He was knee-deep in debt. And impregnating one of the studio's most bankable actresses wasn't going to help his reputation any."

Bennett slowly rubbed the bottom of his chin and contemplated what Oliver just said. He remained quiet until a thought occurred to him.

"I understand what you're saying, Miss Oliver. All of what you have said is extremely helpful. But for someone who knew of this man only by seeing him in the commissary, you know more than you're telling us."

Oliver tightly pursed her lips, and froze in her chair. She sat motionless and tried not to notice the penetrating stares of others, waiting for her to comment. Seizing the moment, Rita Reno looked over at Oliver, then at Bennett. "Either you tell him, or I will," she said bluntly.

Oliver took a deep sigh, and fought back tears in her

eyes. She had done everything in her life to distance herself from Bruce Baylor and put him in her past. But the moment had come to release the tremendous burden she had carried all those years. Damn that Bruce Baylor. She had been silent long enough, It was time everybody knew her one secret.

"All right. It's true. I know more than I am letting on. Bruce Baylor and I were married."

All but Rita Reno seemed surprised. Lori sat gape open mouthed, and Bennett finally sat down. No one else could believe the news.

"It was one of those quickie marriages. We ran off to Mexico and got married in a small wedding chapel. Nobody ever knew. The press. Not even the studio. That first night was like heaven, but from then on it went downhill."

Bennett pounced on the opportunity to learn more. "How so?"

"Bruce and I became an item, okay?" Oliver stated, defensively. "I thought he married me for love. But he didn't. He married me for money. He got what he wanted then dumped me cold."

Bennett tried a more sensitive approach in his questioning, and gave Oliver all the time she needed.

"I know this is very difficult for you, Miss Oliver. And I'm sorry I have to ask you this. But did Bruce Baylor ever hurt you?"

Fidgeting with her fingers, she said, "More times than I can remember. He was an alcoholic, pure and simple. He liked to drink. He came home drunk so many times that I've tried blotting it from my memory. And, yes, he beat me. Terribly. I had to pass up acting jobs because even with makeup they couldn't hide the bruises."

Bennett allowed Oliver some space, before continuing. Then softly he asked, "How did things end between you?"

"Not good. Not good at all. I was the one who ended it. I pressed charges against him, and he served some time in jail. After that, I filed for divorce. He swore to me when the police came that night he would come back and kill me. I never saw him again after that, and then I heard about the suicide note and how he was presumed dead."

Bennett pushed himself up from his chair.

"Presumed dead?"

"That's what I said. They never found the body, as far as I know. The police made every attempt to locate the body. They even put out a search for his remains. But they came up empty handed."

Like a heavy burden lifted from her shoulders, Oliver cupped her face in her hands and began to sob helplessly. Rita Reno reached over to console her. Then she looked up at Bennett as if he was responsible.

"Sergeant, hasn't she been through enough already?"

Bennett nodded, and then walked over and put his arm around Oliver. He told her in a voice just slightly higher than a whisper, "You did the right thing."

Oliver looked up, tears streaming down her face. Between sobs, she thanked Bennett. "No. Thank you, sergeant, for helping me to confront my fears."

Bennett got up and found himself surrounded by the other actors, all waiting to offer words of comfort. Lori politely pushed her way to the front to catch up with Bennett who had turned and walked over to a large glass window with an unobstructed view of the ocean. The calmness of the deep blue sea soothed his troubled soul.

"Nice going, sergeant," Lori joked. "Remind me not to invite you to any bar mitzvahs."

Bennett appeared drawn and tired. His face was haggard with deep dark circles under his eyes. If there was ever a time he needed a Scotch and soda it was surely now.

Continuing to peer out at the untroubled waters, Bennett was trying to sort through all that was said. Then suddenly he mumbled something. His words became so garbled that Lori moved closer.

"What did you say?"

"Mel Greenberg," he mumbled again. "He's the one. We have to find him."

Almost in a trance-like state, Bennett turned around walked right past Lori.

"Where are you going?" she screamed, half-running and half-limping after him. "Wait for me."

Charles Evans Fine spotted Bennett and Lori leaving. He politely hollered after them. "Does this mean the meeting is over?"

Lori stopped and shrugged. "I guess so. Sorry we're in such a rush. Police business, you know."

Fine gave an understanding nod, smiled and waved goodbye. He chuckled and then turned to Barbara who wondered the reason for commotion. "Police business, you know." And they both laughed.

For Bennett, it was no laughing matter. His instincts told him he was on the right trail. And this time, he was listening to his senses.

Chapter 15

Bennett didn't waste any time in his search to find Mel Greenberg. Hopping into his trusty old Dodge Neon sedan, he and Lori sped from the scene straight to the Los Angeles County Records Office. If Mel Greenberg were alive, they would have a record of it, including a last known address. Then it would be only a matter of convincing Greenberg, if he was not six feet under, to discuss his past association with the dead young actor.

Keeping his eyes on the road in front of him, Bennett took a moment to reflect on the case, while Lori stared out the window deep in her own thoughts. If Bruce Baylor was the killer, he thought, he had a strong motive. Each actor, in one way or another, had frustrated his career. Each had become an enemy of him. Each had made an enemy of him. Rather than blame himself, he blamed others. Enough that he finally killed them.

Lori emerged from her silence. She was quiet for a reason. She was still upset over Bennett's strange behavior at the Fine residence prior to their leaving. She never felt so embarrassed in her life.

"Why such a rush?" Lori blurted. "Couldn't you have waited to at least say a proper goodbye?"

Bennett was kind of half-dazed and did not quite hear all of her remark.

"I'm sorry, what?"

"Back there," Lori repeated, sounding agitated. "The way you acted. I've never seen you get that way before."

"Oh, that. I don't know what happened. I just lost it, that's all."

Bennett looked dragged out. The long days and nights had finally caught up with him. He was operating purely on adrenaline and nothing else.

Lori quickly apologized. "I'm sorry. I didn't mean to keep hitting on you like that."

"Apology accepted," Bennett said, managing a slight grin. "Besides, I bruise easily."

Lori wanted to laugh but not even Bennett's best material could push a smile across her face. She hated how she lied to the assignment desk editor at the station. She told him that she was out on a special assignment, never mentioning that she was really attending a meeting of the old actors and still trying to help solve the tragic deaths of three Hollywood legends. She should have told the truth, but she knew the chief would be upset if he knew she was spending most of her time on the case. Like Bennett, she hoped that time was on their side before another actor was murdered.

The Los Angeles County Records Office was located in the heart of downtown Los Angeles near City Hall and across from the Municipal Court building. Housed in an old sky rise building built in the 1940s, the place was like the Pentagon, a maze of partitioned offices with one confusing hallway after another.

Bennett pulled up and parked the car, and he and Lori went inside. They went directly to the registrars desk, where they were greeted by a nerdy young man with wire-rimmed glasses, dressed in tacky looking plaid pants and an over starched white long-sleeve shirt buttoned up to the top.

"Can I help you?"

Bennett whipped out his badge, and introduced himself. "We're here on official police business. Were trying to locate a Mel Greenberg."

Keeping his head down the whole time and filling out paperwork, the registrar muttered softly, "Dead or alive?"

Bennett and Lori looked at each other, and then Lori said, "We're not sure. It could be either."

The man continued to look down and finished scribbling something. Then the nasal voice returned. "We have two categories. Dead or alive. Either your friend is dead. Or he is alive. He can't be both now, can he?"

Exhausted of most of his patience by now, Bennett, known for short fuse, reached over and grabbed the man by the collar. Peering straight into his eyes, each word emerged from his mouth like a tiny explosion. "Look, I am not in a joking mood. Do I look like I'm in a joking mood?"

Trying to breathe as Bennett tightened his grasp, the man squeaked, "It doesn't look like you are."

Bennett continued to let his frustrations out. 'You're a public servant. Do you know what that means?"

The man shook his head. 'You're here to serve the public. That's people like the little lady and me, taxpaying citizens. We pay your salary. That means you work for us. So when I ask for your help next time, what are you going to do?"

Squeamishly, the man replied, "Act like a public servant."

"That's right," Bennett said. "And what else?"

Gasping for air, the man could tell he had better give the right answer. "Be more polite?"

"Give this man a raise," Bennett said sarcastically. He then released the man from his grasp. "I like your attitude. You're going places. I can tell."

The man coughed and breathed deeply to restore the flow of oxygen. Weakly pointing toward the elevator, he said between breaths, "Try the library. Third floor. Someone can help you there."

Lori, who had remained quiet the whole time, smile sand said, "Thank you, you're so kind."

The man retook his seat, straightened out his collar and returned to his paperwork.

Bennett wanted to say something else but, on second thought, he had said enough He followed Lori to the elevator. They had other work to do.

Inside, Bennett ran his finger up the panel to the button for the third floor and pushed it. Lori kept silent. Bennett thought to himself, there is a first. He was waiting for her to scold him for acting so belligerently and roughing up the registrar. Instead of confronting the issue, he decided to play along. No use ruining his day anymore than it had already been.

The elevator door slid open, and Bennett and Lori could not believe their eyes. This was the place all right. However, it was bit more overwhelming than they thought. Walking straight ahead, they found themselves confronted by what seemed to be endless rows of tall metal shelves, so tall that the librarian required a ladder to climb to the top shelf. As it seemed to be throughout the building, the library was also in a state of disarray. There were literally hundreds of boxes of files in storage yet to be opened. To show how behind the times, they were they were just now beginning to computerize their records and had not even got past the letter "D."

Bennett stared helplessly at Lori, scratched his head and said, "Well, Stanley, this is another nice mess you've gotten me into."

Lori just shrugged. "I had no idea. I've never had to come here before."

"That makes two of us."

Not wasting a single minute, they approached the reference desk, and a librarian, who was at the top of the ladder putting away some files, called down to them, "I'll be right with you."

Bennett, as he often did when he became impatient, began tapping the fingers of his right hand on the oak veneered finished countertop. The woman, meanwhile, continued her slow descent down the ladder.

Lori thought to herself how fit that woman must be climbing up a ladder every day. She peered down to inspect her own legs; they were not as taut as they used to be. Unfortunately, with the demands of her job, she had little time for exercise. And what exercise she could fit in, she knew was not nearly enough.

"Phew. Sorry you had to wait so long," the woman librarian said, gasping for air and in worse shape than Lori thought. "What can I do for you folks today?"

Flashing a smile, Bennett talked slowly hoping this woman would not have the same difficulty understanding him as the young man had on the first floor. "I'm Sergeant Bennett, and we're in the middle of an investigation. We need to locate someone."

The woman smiled back and said, "And who might that be?"

Bennett and Lori blurted it out simultaneously. "Mel Greenberg."

"Oh. Okay. Well, here. Fill out this form. We have them all here. Alive. Deceased. Missing. If they lived in the county of Los Angeles, they're here."

Relieved, Bennett did not know what else to say except, "Well, thank you." He proceeded to slide over so the next person in line could be helped.

Lori asked the most obvious question before removing herself from line. "And how long will all of this take? You know, to look this person up?"

"Well, we're pretty backlogged here as you can see." Lori thought, no kidding. "About two hours. Maybe longer. Next."

This time, Lori lost her cool. She looked at the person

behind her and waved her to move back. "I'm not finished here, okay?"

Then, in a voice slightly above a whisper, Lori drew closer to the librarian and let her have it, expletives and all. "We don't have two fucking hours. We're in the middle of a murder investigation. Three people are now murdered. We're talking Hollywood legends, for Christ sake. And an actor, or his ghost, may be the killer. You obviously have to do better than that."

The words that spilled from Lori's mouth never ceased to amaze Bennett. She remained at best, unpredictable.

"I'm really sorry," the woman librarian said apologetically. "But "

"No, buts," Lori shouted at the top of her lungs. "You wouldn't want the mayor to know about the inefficiencies of your department, now would you?"

The woman kept staring at Lori and did not utter a word. She looked Lori up and down, keeping her eyes fixed on her the whole time. Then suddenly she became very animated.

"I'd know your face anywhere. Youre Lori Matrix, the news broadcaster?"

Surprised, Lori said, "Well, yes, I am."

Wiping her hair to one side, the librarian gushed. "My husband and I never miss your newscast. We're huge fans."

Completely embarrassed, Lori softened. "Well, thank you. How kind of you to say."

Leaning forward, the librarian pointed at Lori to come closer. Lowering her voice, she said, "I wouldn't normally do this for anyone. But I'll try to pull some strings. Just give a few minutes."

Lori pulled back from the counter and wisely said, "Well, if that's the best you can do."

Lori reached over and grabbed the form on which Bennett was still writing.

"I'm not finished," he said, trying to pull the paper back.

"Trust me."

Lori handed the form over to the librarian, and she disappeared in a swirl of dust. The person behind Lori was not happy. His looks said it all.

Meanwhile, in a huff, Bennett strutted over to her. "Do you mind telling me what the hell's going on?"

Acting innocently, Lori replied, "I'll tell you later."

As soon as Lori finished her comment, the librarian reappeared. "I have it. You can take a seat over there," she said pointing to a quiet room. "When you're finished, please return everything to me."

Before leaving, Lori peeked into the file. Her eyes gravitated to the first line. It read: Mel Greenberg. Occupation: Theatrical agent.

Lori beamed. "Thank you for time and trouble."

Bennett and Lori hurried over to the quiet room, closed the door behind them, and drew the curtains closed. Lori spread open the folder and they took equal time reviewing its contents.

Bennett pulled out a small writing pad from his shirt pocket and began copying down the information. Everything was listed, including Greenberg's last known address and phone number.

"Looks like he's in a rough part of town," Bennett noted. "I wouldn't allow my own mother to live there. That area is like Gang City."

Lori nodded, and then she noticed something Bennett had not. Stapled to the inside flap of the file was a small slip of paper. Yellowed and frayed around the edges, its texture was fine, not coarse. She nudged Bennett and showed him what she had uncovered.

Bennett arched his eyebrows with curiosity.

"What do you think it is?" Lori asked.

"There's only one way to find out." Bennett pulled out his car key and slid it under the staple, putting pressure underneath it to pop it loose. The staple stubbornly held its own against Bennett's brute strength until the laws of average worked in his favor.

"Got it!" Bennett enthused. "Now let's take a peek."

Bennett looked inside and was stunned what he discovered. "I wonder how this got inside here."

Lori's curiosity was piqued. "What? What does it say?"

"See for yourself."

Bennett handed the yellowed piece of paper over to Lori. Her lips moved but there was no sound as she read it to herself.

"Unbelievable. We can't tell anyone about this."

"You've got that right. You'd better let me hold on to this for safe keeping."

Lori pouted. "Oh, no. I'm part of this investigation, too. We'd better both hold on to this."

Bennett found room to compromise. "I have a better idea. I don't think anyone is going to miss this, do you? When I get back to the station, I'll make a copy and give you a copy to keep in a safe place. Deal?" Bennett extended his right hand holding it out firmly.

Lori contemplated Bennett's generous offer, and was

quick to accept. "Okay," she said. "Deal." At that, she put her hand out and took Bennett's and they shook on it.

Bennett smiled back at her, with a glint in his eyes. He studied her tanned complexion, blonde tresses and ocean blue eyes, and for a long moment got lost in her intoxicating beauty.

Lori brought him back to reality. "Everything all right, sergeant?"

The glazed look in Bennett's eyes cleared, and he shook himself out of his stupor. "Yes, I'm okay. Sorry, I was deep in thought."

Bennett for no other reason suddenly stared up at the clock. To his surprise, it was already after 1 o'clock. "Oops. I have to get back to the station. Captain Hansen will be on my ass if he thinks I'm still spending time on this case. Can I call you later tonight?"

Lori acted disappointed. "But what about Mel Greenberg?"

"Tomorrow. I promise. We'll visit him in the morning. In the meantime, I'll request 'round-the-clock police protection for the surviving members of the club. That is, if Captain Hansen will approve it."

Lori's face brightened a bit. "That would help me sleep better. I'm very concerned about their well-being."

"So am I. So am I."

Bennett quickly slid his wooden chair back on the polished linoleum floor and started to get up. Still slippery from the early morning waxing, the chair flipped from under him and he wound up on the floor, flat on his back. Lori could only laugh.

"What's so funny?" Bennett fumed.

Lori shook her head from side to side still laughing. "You. You call yourself a police sergeant."

"Not funny, Miss Matrix. I could have been very seriously injured."

Lori smirked. "Nothing a little tender loving touch couldn't cure."

Bennett looked embarrassed by her remark and did not say a word. He was a definitely attracted to Lori, but wanted to keep their relationship purely professional. He could not help but think that because they were from such different worlds they had little chance of ever sustaining any kind of serious relationship, and resisted the temptation to try.

Pulling himself to his feet, Bennett began brushing himself off, while Lori continued to laugh over the incident. "I think you've done enough damage here today, sergeant. Don't you think?"

Bennett forced a smile and said, "I couldn't agree more. Let's do this again tomorrow."

Bennett grabbed the file and returned it to the reference librarian. He wondered in the back of his mind what waited for him at headquarters. He did not count on it being good news. Everyday was the same: crime on every street corner. He just hoped today was a slow day. If not, he would have some explaining to do about his whereabouts for the last three hours.

Chapter 16

When Lori returned to the station, she found herself on the receiving end of a different kind of interrogation. Taking a side entrance, she made every effort to reach her office without being noticed. She was almost in the clear when Billy Gamm spotted in her in the hallway.

"There you are," he said, pointing in her direction. "Where have you been?"

Lori acted innocent. "On a story. What else?"

Gamm knew Lori was good at playing games, so he called her bluff. "And what story is that?"

Lori thought a moment. "An investigative story. I've been out doing research."

Gamm was not buying her story this time. His voice turned cynical. "Investigating ghosts perhaps?"

Lori suddenly became quiet. She thought, oh, god, he knows. Gamm stood there patiently waiting for an answer, and then he said, "Cat got your tongue?"

"No," Lori said, thinking fast. "I've tried keeping that story under wraps, you know. I'm glad you like the idea."

Now Gamm looked puzzled. "What idea?"

"The story, you know, that I'm researching about ghosts. It should be extremely controversial and it will make a great series. Good for ratings, high viewership, you know. I owe it all to you, of course."

Gamm scratched his head and asked quizzically. "Me? It was my idea?"

Lori knew that playing to Gamm's ego was her only way out. "Chief, you really surprise me. Don't be so damn modest. I admit it your idea for this story was a stroke of genius. People have a morbid curiosity about the supernatural."

Like most producers, Gamm was good at taking credit for things he never did. He did not remember assigning Lori to the story, but it was not unusual for stories to slip through the cracks. He therefore decided to give her the benefit of the doubt, and accept full credit.

"Now I remember. My mind has been on so many things lately," he said, with a forced smile about as sincere as a used car salesman's. "Thanks for reminding me. I'll put it on the schedule, and I'll begin talking to our promo department about running the series during sweeps month."

Lori smiled. "Great idea, Chief." Gamm walked away happily humming to himself, very upbeat. Lori returned to her office, completely exhausted. She just gave the best performance of her life.

Lori checked with her secretary. There was one message. It was an urgent message from Bette Oliver. She wanted to talk to Lori right away. Lori picked up the phone and immediately dialed the number. The phone rang once. Then twice. By the fourth ring, the answering machine picked up. Lori left a message, and told Oliver to call her at the station. She said she would be there for the rest of the day and for her to call her at any time.

Afterwards, Lori began to worry. What if Bette Oliver was calling because something was seriously wrong? Or maybe she had something to say, but wanted to talk about it privately, Lori knew she could not leave the newsroom. She had to begin editing copy for the six o'clock newscast. She acted impulsively and called Bennett right away.

"Mark, it's Lori. Bette Oliver called about a half-hour ago while we were out. She left an urgent message and I just tried phoning her. But there was no answer. I'm really worried."

Bennett said fortunately that Captain Hansen, called away on important business, would be gone for the next three days. He agreed to take care of it and drive over to Oliver's home to check things out.

"I don't know what I would do without you," Lori offered, sounding sentimental.

Bennett wasted no time responding. "When this is all over, you'll have to promise me one thing."

"What's that?"

"You and I are going to have a night out on the town and celebrate."

Lori smiled softly and said, "You're on."

Bennett started to hang up. But before he did, Lori asked him to promise something else. "Promise me, you'll call me with anything you know about Bette Oliver."

"I promise. You'll be the first to know beside myself."

Bennett hung up and grabbed his coat. He wrote down Bette Oliver's address on a slip of paper, and checked with the desk sergeant in homicide before leaving.

Oliver lived in a high rent district of Century City. Her home was far too large for just herself. It was one of those six-bedroom, two-story Spanish-style mansions built in the late 1940s during Hollywood's heyday. Oliver had had the home renovated over the years, adding a cozy foyer and private patio in the back. The clay tile roof was the original, as were the whitewashed beam ceilings and terra cotta tile floor. Bougainvillea bushes covered the front and were in full bloom, and a large neatly clipped lawn swept down to the street from the front entry.

When Bennett arrived, he noticed that Oliver's front door slightly cracked open. He knocked and decided not to enter unless he heard a friendly voice on the other end.

"Miss Oliver, are you there? It's Sergeant Mark Bennett, L.A.P.D."

The sound of footsteps on the Mexican pavers floor echoed and grew louder as the person approached. A voice boomed from behind the bleached wooden door. "Who is it?"

"Sergeant Mark Bennett."

The door opened, and a face popped around the corner. It was Bette Oliver.

"Won't you come in, sergeant. I had to make sure. I've left everything as I found it."

Bennett was not sure what Oliver meant, so he questioned her further. "I'm sorry, maam. What do you mean?'"

"Oh, you don't know. Well, I called Lori Matrix first and she left a message that she called you. I think someone's been inside my house."

Bennett's eyes widened. "How can you tell?"

Oliver escorted Bennett inside and pointed to some slivers of wood on the tile floor. "I don't ever remember seeing those there before."

Bennett pulled the door open and inspected it. He noticed some deep scratch marks to the right of the doorknob and a severe gouge in the door jam shaped like the tip to a crow bar.

"You didn't touch anything, did you Miss Oliver?"

"Not a thing, sergeant. Not a thing."

"Good. We'll dust this door for prints. Whoever it was, if he wasn't too clever, hopefully we'll get a match."

Oliver appeared relieved. She began to cry as the shock finally set in.

"I don't understand why anyone would want to do this," she said, wiping tears from her eyes. "This has always been such a safe neighborhood."

Bennett talked in comforting tones. "I'm sorry, Miss Oliver. But there's no safe haven these days. You'll find there's crime in every small town and big city. There's no escaping it."

Regaining her composure, Oliver asked Bennett to follow her. She led him into the study, where priceless mementos, family heirlooms and personal artifacts were scattered across the floor. It was a messy sight, a cleaning woman's worst nightmare.

"Somebody had a field day here all right," Bennett noted, quickly scanning the room. "Did you find anything missing?"

Oliver cried some more. It hurt inside to talk about it. Finally, she blurted it out. "Bruce Baylor."

The hair on Bennett's back instantly stood up. He was perhaps expecting a different response, maybe as if a prized antique had been stolen.

"What do you mean, Bruce Baylor?" he asked.

Oliver dried her face wiping tears with her hand and said, "My diary. I kept a diary the whole time that we were married."

Everything became a little clearer for Bennett. Why would anyone want that diary? What did it say? It had little value to anyone else. Unless there was some incriminating evidence inside that had someone worried about it falling into the wrong hands.

"Was anything else taken?" Bennett continued.

"No. Nothing else. That's all I found missing so far."

Bennett thought over his next move. He had discovered a mysterious slip of paper at the county records' office. Now a diary nobody knew about was suddenly missing. Perhaps the two were related, then again, maybe not.

"Miss Oliver, I only have one other question. Why didn't you call the police about this?"

Oliver paused for a long moment. "I didn't think it was anybody else's business. I don't need the publicity. It's hard enough..." Her voiced trailed off as the tears returned.

Bennett believed Oliver was being truthful and trusted

her word. "Very well. I understand. We'll keep this quiet. Don't touch anything until I can have somebody come out."

"Whatever you say, sergeant," Oliver shrugged. "You're the boss."

Bennett returned to the station and filed his report. Meanwhile, he dispatched a finger print team to Oliver's home to check for possible prints. The first person he called, of course, was Lori.

"What's up?" Lori asked. "Is she okay?"

"Fine. Fine. She'll be all right. But somebody broke into her house."

Lori reacted with a shocked sound in her voice. "Really. Was anything taken?"

"Strangely, nothing of any great value except for a diary."

Now Lori was really interested. "A diary. Her personal diary."

"Not just her personal diary. A diary about Bruce Baylor."

There was cold silence on the phone. Lori could not believe it either.

"That's unbelievable. But why would anyone want it?"

Sounding like a true detective, Bennett said, "Now why do you think?

Lori answered her own question before Bennett did. "There's something in that diary that someone doesn't want known.

"Bingo. You've just answered the $64,000 question."

"What are you going to do next?"

Bennett turned seriously. "Find that diary, what else?

Chapter 17

Sergeant Bennett left it with Lori that he would meet her at Mel Greenberg's downtown Los Angeles apartment at 11 o'clock the following morning. He agreed to set up the meeting and, if anything changed, he would let her know.

Bennett tried calling Greenberg after he concluded his conversation with Lori. He dialed Greenberg's phone number several times but each time there was no answer. He waited to call again as it drew closer to evening. Just when he almost gave up hope, a gravelly voice that spoke with a severe slur answered on the last ring with a loud television blaring in the background. Bennett momentarily pulled the receiver from his ear as he found the noise intrusive.

"Mr. Greenberg? This is Sergeant Mark Bennett, L.A.P.D. calling."

"Who's this?" the voice replied incoherently.

"Sergeant Mark Bennett, sir. L.A.P.D."

The voice was even less responsive than before. "I'm sorry I can't understand you."

"Perhaps if you turned down your television, you'll be able to hear me."

The man on the other end unwittingly threw down the receiver causing an irritating thumping sound that reverberated through the receiver. Bennett quickly pulled his ear away from the phone as the deafening sound penetrated his eardrum. Finally, the noise level in the background softened to a quiet murmur and the raspy voice returned.

"Your name again?"

Bennett deliberately wiped his brow, trying to remain patient. "Sergeant Mark Bennett, L.A.P.D."

"Oh, Sergeant Mark Bennett," the voice returned, as if he had just heard the question for the first time. "Why didn't you say so?"

Bennett bit down on his lip to restrain his smoldering temper. He quickly realized he was in for a long night. "Is this Mel Greenberg, the famous theatrical agent?"

The man took a long sip of something and groveled. "Why, yes it is? How did you know my name?"

"Mr. Greenberg, I work in the police department. We have ways of knowing these things."

"Oh."

Bennett could sense by the man's wavering voice and inability to comprehend a single thought that he had been drinking. He had seen this type of behavior a million times before, and this man had all the usual symptoms.

"Sir, I don"t mean to pry because I barely know you. But have you been drinking?"

Greenberg turned angry. "What would make you say that?"

"Never mind. Sorry I asked." Bennett decided to refrain from pursuing the matter further. That is all he needed was for this man to bring a lawsuit against him for slandering his good name.

"I'm not calling because you're in trouble," Bennett continued. "My partner and I..." Bennett abruptly stopped and re-phrased his response. Calling Lori his partner was stretching the truth a bit. "I mean, a friend and I would like to come and meet you tomorrow to talk about a former client of yours."

Greenberg seemed, at least for one brief moment, to understand. "Who's that?"

"Bruce Baylor."

Suddenly the brain cells that seemed dormant came to life in Greenberg's mind and his erratic behavior changed in an instant. "You know, I think someone's at my door. I wish I could help." He then started to hang up the phone, but Bennett called out, "Wait, Mr. Greenberg. Please don't hang up."

There was a long quiet pause. Only the sound of an unattended television set, playing in the background, pierced the stillness on the receiver. Then Greenberg's voice returned.

"Why shouldn't I?"

"Because we really need your help."

Greenberg grew silent again. He picked up a bottle and poured the liquidy substance into his glass, then took a few lengthy sips. "Bruce Baylor was scum," Greenberg said adamantly. "Why should I help you?"

Bennett tried the one tactic he knew worked best when all else failed: He bluffed. "Because I know something about you, Mr. Greenberg, which most people don't know."

Greenberg's voice became louder with curiosity. "You do, heh? And what's that?"

"Meet me tomorrow at 11 o'clock and you'll find out."

Greenberg considered his options and, for a brief moment, seemed resigned to the fact that he did not have any. "I guess if you put it that way."

"Believe me, Mr. Greenberg, you'll be doing your community a great public service."

Greenberg was not sold on doing any charity work. "Cut the community crap, sergeant." He took another sip of his drink and his mind seemed sharper for some strange reason. "You want my help? Then they'll be a price involved."

"A price?"

"Yes, a price.

Bennett quickly considered Greenberg's proposal. "How much are we talking about?"

"$1,000."

Now Bennett felt backed into a corner. He was not sure that he could obtain approval to pay an informant for a case that he was not even supposed to be investigating anymore. He had some people downtown that owed him some favors.

"I can do better than that, Mr. Greenberg."

"You can?"

"Well provide you and a lovely lady two tickets to the

Policeman's Charity Ball at the Ritz Carlton Hotel, all expenses paid. We'll even throw in a penthouse suite for the evening and a stash of your favorite beverage."

If wine, women and song did not work, Bennett thought, nothing else would.

"That's quite a tempting offer, sergeant. Throw in a limo and you have yourself a deal."

Bennett knew an old college buddy who owned a limousine service downtown. He was sure he could arrange something since his friend also owed him a favor.

"You're one tough negotiator, Mr. Greenberg. Consider it done." Greenberg whooped and hollered on the phone as if he had just won the California state lottery. "Sergeant, that's the best news I've had in years. I'll be happy to cooperate."

Bennett repeated the time and place, and then hung up. Privately, he had a hunch about Greenberg that he had not even shared with Lori. What it was, he was not saying. Not even to his mother.

***

When Bennett and Lori pulled up to Greenberg's apartment, they realized right away that they were not in the best part of town. The apartment building that Greenberg called home was located in a dilapidated, rat infested neighborhood on the east side of town. It was home to drunks, prostitutes, panhandlers and every kind of lowlife. Drive-by shootings were a nightly occurrence, and homes and buildings on every block had bullet holes or graffiti left by gang members marking their territories.

Greenberg lived alone in a one-bedroom studio apartment that had seen better days. His front door opened out to the fourth floor and was adjacent to a rickety winding staircase that creaked with every step. The staircase was ankle deep in trash and reeked with the smell of alcohol from countless drunken bums who took refuge on the steps from the night before.

"Nice place," Bennett said sarcastically. "Reminds me of a reform school I once knew."

Lori gave Bennett an angry look. "This is no time for jokes. Couldn't you be a bit more sensitive?"

Bennett quickly tried to make amends. "You're right. It reminds me of the county dump."

Lori sighed and gave up on refining Bennett's rough edges. He may have had a gentlemanly side to him. It is just that at this moment it was not showing.

Bennett and Lori lunged up the final step and came to Greenberg's apartment, Apartment 4A. Bennett did not waste a single second and knocked on the door while Lori surveyed the creaking wooden floor around her for intruding rats.

The door, still latched inside, opened, leaving only a small crack from which to peer out. A face appeared in the crack and eyed the couple standing there. The man unlatched the door and a voice and body appeared to match. "You must be Sergeant Bennett. I'm Mel Greenberg. Please come in."

The man who welcomed Bennett and Lori was nothing like the voice on the phone from the night before. He spoke easily and without a slur, he was clean- shaven and neatly dressed and his face smelled with an odorous aftershave that permeated the room. Standing just above five foot two inches, he was much smaller than Bennett imagined he would be, and physically much older. The man's hair was silver in color, his face heavily wrinkled and spotted, his eyes enveloped in thick bags of skin, and his nose was large and bulbous, reminiscent of that famous comedian, W.C. Fields. He also walked with a slight limp, favoring his right side, like someone who had recovered from a stroke.

Bennett surveyed the apartment as he entered while Lori felt her stomach churn in knots. It was evident to them both that Greenberg lived a dreary existence. The carpeting was threadbare. Wallpaper was torn and peeling. Cracks and fallen plaster were visible on the ceiling. The once lustrous shine of the painted white walls had severely yellowed. Half a dozen faded eight-by-ten glossy photographs, presumably of actors that Greenberg once represented hung crooked on the walls. And, as Bennett suspected, Greenberg was alcoholic. Dozens of empty bottles piled high in a comer near a small kitchen, with an army of ants feeding off the few sweet drops of liquor that remained.

"And who is this lovely lady?" Greenberg asked inquisitively.

Pivoting to his left, Bennett stretched out his right hand and said, "Lori Matrix of KTRB-TV. Mel Greenberg."

The pitch in Greenberg's voice rose in excitement. "The television anchorwoman?"

"That's right. I'm your gal."

"Well, I don't know what to say. It is a real honor to meet you."

Then pointing to an old sofa, he said, "Please have a seat."

Greenberg retreated to his favorite recliner while Bennett and Lori proceeded to sit down. The sofa was in no better shape than the rest of the apartment. The upholstery was completely shot and what little padding remained provided little support.

"As I mentioned on the phone, we are interested in talking to you about Bruce Baylor. We understand that you were his agent?

Greenberg's eyes narrowed with suspicion. "Why such an interest now, sergeant? Bruce Baylor is dead."

Lori interrupted before Bennett had a chance to answer, "Three actors have mysteriously died, almost a fourth. I'm sure you've read about it in the newspapers. We believe the lives of others are still in danger and that somehow Bruce Baylor is connected."

Greenberg inched forward in his chair. "Well, I don't know how that is possible. I filed the death certificate myself. Check for yourself."

Greenberg opened a thick manila folder marked with Bruce Baylor's name. He pulled from the folder a copy of Baylor's death certificate. Bennett and Lori read it with great interest. Their eyes moved across the page, and Bennett stopped his finger on one line.

"Date of death. February 12, 1949." Bennett acted surprised as he read the line aloud. "How can that be? Bruce Baylor's body was never found."

Greenberg nodded knowingly. "When the certificate was filed, the date of his suicide was considered as the date of his death."

Lori looked puzzled. "How can that be?"

"The police closed the case after a year long search. By then, creditors were coming from all directions like a pack of locusts, each demanding payment of past due bills. The only way to stave off creditors was make Bruce's death final.

So I petitioned the court and a death certificate was filed."

"What happened to Bruce Baylor's estate?" Bennett asked curiously. "There wasn't much left after everything was settled. I have his scrapbooks and a few personal mementos. Not much else."

Bennett probed further. Greenberg seemed alert, coherent, and willing to talk. He decided to take full advantage of him.

"How long were you Bruce Baylor's agent?"

"The last five years of his life."

"Did you ever have any problems?"

Greenberg was quick to respond. "More problems than I care to remember. He was a terribly disturbed young man."

"How so?" Lori asked.

"When I took over as his agent, he was down on his luck. He had a bad reputation as a womanizer and a violent temper. I convinced several producers who wouldn't work with him to give him a second chance. For a while, everything seemed to be working."

"Then what?" Bennett inquired.

"He lost all control of himself. He went into sudden violent rages and he was lucky that he didn't wind up in prison,"

Bennett eyed Greenberg questioningly. "If that's so, did Bruce Baylor ever talk to you about avenging certain actors in his past?"

Greenberg turned away from Bennett, giving the question careful thought. He looked blank for a moment, and then a thought occurred to him. "Well, if he did, he never told me. But I do know this. Whatever feelings he had towards others, he kept bottled up inside. It was impossible to reach him. To ever know his deepest thoughts."

Lori decided to pose the one question nobody had asked so far. "Do you think Bruce Baylor was capable of murder?"

Greenberg slumped in his chair. His face displayed a wide range of emotions, from puzzlement to anger, as he considered her question.

"Yes. Yes, I do. It was as if he was possessed by the devil. He became one bitter, evil man."

For a long moment, no one said a single word. Lori considered what else she wanted to ask. She did not feel right discussing the incidents that the other actors had told her and Bennett privately. She turned to Bennett and gave him a puzzled look as if to say, what next? Bennett quietly reached into his shirt pocket and pulled out a small slip of paper. He carefully unfolded it and handed it to Greenberg.

Greenberg reached over and grabbed a pair of reading glasses from the coffee table. Putting them on, he slowly reviewed the contents and his face turned ashen.

"How did you get this?"

"Call it luck, I guess. But I have a hunch I know what it means."

Greenberg put the note down and seemed less-than-friendly about it. "This is really none of your business."

Lori looked confused. "Would someone mind telling me what this all about?"

Bennett picked up the note and handed it to Lori. The same yellowed, torn slip of paper they had discovered while reviewing Mel Greenberg's file at the Los Angeles Country Records office. Lori's eyes widened. She began to see the connection.

"Your Bruce Baylor's father!"

Greenberg stood up and began to pace, breathing heavily. "Yes. Yes, I am." He then sighed. "Bruce changed his name because he didn't want to have anything to do with me."

Greenberg moved toward the window and peered out. He continued to talk but quickly became emotional. "I loved Bruce. I didn't mean to hurt him. It was all an accident,"

Tears welled up in Greenberg's eyes, and his voice choked as he tried to speak. "I was an abusive father. I had no self-control. I don't blame Bruce for hating me."

Bennett listened passively and remained seated. Suddenly, he broke his silence. "Mr. Greenberg, what you've done in the past is not relevant. I'm sure you will carry the burden of your pain to your grave. All I want is the truth."

Greenberg wiped the tears from his eyes, and walked slowly back to his worn out recliner. Once seated, he reluctantly re-opened the bulging manila folder. He pulled out the matching slip of paper that had been torn from the original, the one Bennett had found.

Bennett pieced the two together and his face became flush with satisfaction. It was the other half of an adoption record filed by Mel Greenberg and his wife Edna on August 11, 1914. The name of the child listed was Bruce Heidelman, changed to Greenberg following the adoption.

"My wife and I could never have children. So we decided to adopt. Bruce was our only child." Greenberg, filled with emotion, suddenly looked away.

Lori reached out and gently touched Greenberg on his

right knee to soften the blow. "It must have been very difficult," she offered. "I'm not married. But I can certainly feel your pain."

Greenberg appreciated Lori's tender touch. He turned as soft as the recliner in which he was seated. "You'll make a great wife for someone. Whoever marries you, he had better treat you right."

Bennett's face instantly turned red. Even though Greenberg's comment was not directed at him, luckily, nobody noticed. Although he and Lori were not an "item," part of him felt like they were. He felt a bond with her that he had never experienced before with any woman. He always knew what she was thinking before she even said it, and he sensed a definite chemistry between them. Whenever they were together, it was like magic. But the idea of making a long-term commitment totally frightened him.

Lori looked up at Bennett and he just smiled. He hid his feelings from her, and continued with the investigation.

"Mr. Greenberg. I think you've told us what we wanted to know. But I do have one more question."

Greenberg straightened up in his chair to stretch his back that had suddenly stiffened. "What is that, sergeant? I'm all ears."

"Do you know anything about a missing diary?"

"What diary?"

"Bette Oliver's diary?"

Greenberg scratched the back of his neck. "You really are some detective. What about it?"

It seems a bit farfetched, maybe. But you have a pretty large file there on your son. You wouldn't consider stealing that diary, now would you?"

Greenberg acted indifferent, "Now why would I do such a thing?"

Bennett leaned forward and looked Greenberg straight in the eyes, and uttered the first word that came to him. "Murder."

"Are you saying that you think I'm responsible for these deaths, sergeant? Are you crazy?"

Greenberg began to fume and quickly rose from his chair. Limping, he walked toward the door, pointing. "I think that will be all for today, sergeant. Uh, ma'am. I think you should both leave."

Lori tried to defend Bennett's actions. "Mr. Greenberg, please settle down, Sergeant Bennett is only doing his job. He didn't mean to offend you. Did you sergeant?"

Bennett remained silent. He knew he meant what he said and the last thing he wanted to do was apologize to save face. Lori tugged on Bennett's coat, trying to persuade him to speak. Finally he did.

"Look, Mr. Greenberg. I'm heading an investigation into the deaths of three famous actors. Now I'm sorry if I offended you, but try and put yourself in my shoes."

Greenberg remained upset and continued to show his anger. "You come into my home. I tell you everything I know, and this is how you thank me. By inferring that I am a murderer."

As Greenberg finished, a large rat scurried across the floor behind him into the kitchen, perhaps to feast on the army of ants and whatever morsels of food it could find. Lori instantly felt sick to her stomach. She hated rodents, bugs, anything that crawled.

Bennett withdrew his comment. By Greenberg's display of

anger, he sensed that he was telling the truth. "Okay, Mr. Greenberg. You're right. I had no reason to imply anything. I'm sorry."

Greenberg did not know what else to say. Bennett disarmed him of his only ammunition. Dropping his hand by his side, Greenberg stood silently in his place.

Meanwhile, Bennett pushed his hand deep in his coat pocket and emerged with two tickets in his hand. He waved them in the air.

"Mr. Greenberg, I made a deal and I want you to know I kept it. Here are your tickets to the Policeman's Charity Ball."

Greenberg waved Bennett off. "Forget it."

"No, really. They're yours. We had a deal."

Greenberg peered down at his feet and then looked up. "No. I can't accept them."

"Why?"

"Because you made me come to terms today with something I've carried inside of me for a very long time. I've never been honest with myself before until now. For years, I've always blamed others for my misfortune."

Greenberg raised his hands pointing at himself. "I'm 74 years old. I have nothing. Not even my health. I live in a dump. Some days I'm lucky to have running water. I have nobody to else to blame."

Lori sensed that Greenberg wanted to be alone. She nudged Bennett in his right side to get his attention. Bennett acted irritated at first until he understood what Lori was trying to tell him.

"No, Mr. Greenberg. Thank you," Bennett said. "You've helped us tremendously."

Greenberg stopped feeling sorry for himself and accepted Bennett's generous compliment.

"Your too kind, sergeant. I don't get many visitors."

Bennett and Lori rose from the sofa and inched their way to the front door. They said their goodbyes to Greenberg, and he appeared satisfied that he had made the right decision by talking to them.

"You're welcome here, anytime," Greenberg said, shaking their hands as they departed. He gave them each one last look before latching the door, and Bennett and Lori began the journey down the fragile stairs.

Making their descent, Lori was not sure how all the pieces fit. She was fresh out of clues, and now even she was not so sure about the ghost theory.

"Okay, Mr. Hot Shot Detective. What next?"

Bennett grinned and said, "Wouldn't you like to know."

"Come on," Lori smiled. "Be straight with me. I wouldn't expect anything less."

"I'm still not so sure that Bruce Baylor is dead."

Lori was genuinely surprised. The thought had not crossed her mind. "But there's even a death certificate."

"Yeah, but there's no body."

"Are you saying that Bruce Baylor faked his death?"

Bennett paused on the top of the step and glanced over at Lori.

"It's the only possibility we have left."

Chapter 18

If there were any information that could prove helpful in solving the murders, they would possibly be in the police files kept on Bruce Baylor's mysterious death. Bennett's first inclination was to locate those files and search for any possible clues leading to Baylor's whereabouts, that is, if he was still alive.

Files of previously closed cases were stored in a large warehouse located downtown, four blocks from police headquarters. The cavernous facility was larger than two football fields combined. Locked inside were millions of pieces of evidence, affidavits by witnesses, and photos of blood splattered bodies and police accounts of countless murders, suicides and homicides.

Bennett and Lori dropped in unannounced. They entered through a side door using Bennett's security pass. Inside, a balding, jolly rotund man dressed in uniform greeted them. He was Hal Jones, the facility's curator and security officer. Jones had served on the police force for thirty-four years and recently had transferred to the warehouse from the department.

Bennett was all too familiar with Jones, and it was not because of his police work. Jones was a frustrated comedian at heart. He loved telling jokes, and trying out new material on unsuspecting victims. Rumor had it he owned more comedy material than Milton Berle. Only it was difficult to say whose material was better.

Bennett often wished he had Jones' enthusiasm and zest for life. The man was always so damn cheerful, and Bennett often wondered, what his secret was. "Sergeant, I've got a new one for you," Jones said beaming.

Bennett handed the pen to Lori to sign in. "Okay, Hal, let's here it."

"Did you hear about the new government program to combat juvenile crime?"

Bennett and Lori looked at each other, and shrugged.

"Really," Bennett said helplessly. "What's that?

"They're calling it the war on puberty."

Bennett smiled, but Lori really laughed. "I never heard that one before. That's pretty good."

"I've got others. I write them myself."

Bennett indiscreetly pushed his left hand up against Lori's back to try to move her along. He had had heard most of Jones's jokes before, so many times, in fact, they were already past sounding old. Jones had such a backlog of material that he could tell jokes for hours. Only Lori did not know better.

"I'd love to hear another," she said unwittingly.

Hal's face brightened. "Really? Oh, you're in for a treat."

Bennett waited patiently as Jones slung another one.

"You know what a bigamist is, don't you?"

Lori indicated that she did not know the answer.

"An Italian fog."

Lori laughed so hard her side hurt. And Jones kept up the assault.

"Too bad Christopher Columbus didn't have Frank Sinatra's style. You know why?"

Lori looked at Jones with a blank look.

"Because if he had, he wouldn't have sailed to America. He would have sent for it."

Even Bennett could not resist laughing at that one. He personally could not stand Sinatra; he thought he was one of the most overrated performers of this century.

"I have to admit, Hal. That's pretty funny."

"Oh, sarg. That's just the tip of the iceberg." Before Bennett could stop him, Jones dished out one joke after another.

"You know they say my wife is a slower driver. The other day three people passed her up on the freeway. Two of them were walking...

"L.A. is different all right. Where else do unemployment offices have valet parking?

"Since I bought my electric toothbrush, I only have to see my dentist twice a year. But now I have to see an electrician once a month!"

By now, Lori was laughing to the point of exhaustion,

while Bennett was beginning to do a slow burn. Finally, he held out his right hand and said, "Enough, Hal. Enough. You're killing us down here."

"Oh, I'm sorry," Jones apologized. "I didn't mean to get so carried away."

"No problem. But if you keep it up any longer, we'll have you carried away."   Now Jones laughed. "Ooh, that's a good one, sarg. I'd better write that one down."

"Well, before you do, can you let us in."

"Sure, sarg. Sure. Whatever you say. I'll be right here. I won't go far. I'll be right on this very spot. Wild horses couldn't drag me away. So if you need me. You just call me. I'll..."

"I get the point, Hal. Can you please open the door?"

"Ooh, you're such a party pooper."

Jones unlocked the tall steel gate leading into the warehouse. Bennett hurried Lori along to elude any further bombardment of jokes.

What they discovered was anything like their previous experience at the Los Angeles County Records Office. Conveniently cataloged and cross-referenced by case number and victims name was every case dating back to 1930s easy reference. A small bank of personal computers, set up in a separate viewing area, linked to a master database that stored this information. Data was revised and updated quarterly, and the most recent revision was loaded on the server two weeks earlier.

Bennett knew little about computers. When it came to operating them, he did not know the return key from the on/off switch. He had yet to enter the high-tech age. He still preferred a pencil to computers, express mail to fax machines, and his oatmeal heated in a pan and not in a microwave. It is not that Bennett was not trainable; he loathed change-any change. He was not bound to admit to Lori that he was computer illiterate. So he tried faking his through it. He fumbled around on the keyboard, randomly punching a few keys. The screen remained blank. Nothing happened. He kept up the act until finally his patience wore thin.

"How do you operate this thing?"

Lori interceded. "What's wrong?

"For some reason, it isn't working.

"Let me try."

Lori sat down in Bennett's seat and instantly punched a key, accessing the main menu. The menu listed various options.

"How did you do that?"

"I'll have to show you some time. I teach private lessons."

Lori smiled, and Bennett smiled back at her. He wanted to flirt back but knew now was not the time.

Lori ran her finger down the list of options on the screen. Listed was very possible category. Murders. Homicides. Suicides. Accidental Deaths. Serial Killings. Without hesitating, she selected "Suicides." The computer instantly produced a second screen of options. She could choose the names of victims by decade.

Using the mouse, Lori highlighted the 1940s, and then hit return. In less than a second, an alphabetical list suicide victims from the 1940s appeared on the screen. The list was massive, and much larger than Lori thought it would be. There must have been tens of thousands of names featured, from a George W. Aaron to a Connie Zukor.

Lori turned to Bennett for approval. "Why don't we try here first?"

"You lead, and I'll follow," he grinned.

Bennett peeked over Lori's right shoulder as she continued. Using the scroll key, she began searching through the list, advancing to the letter B. She scanned through the limitless sea of names, in eager anticipation.

"Baylor. Baylor," she muttered to herself. "Where is he?"

Bennett and Lori kept their eyes peeled on the screen. Countless names continued to roll across the screen like an endless procession until finally.

"Bingo," Lori announced.

Lori aborted the scroll and stopped on the first Baylor listed. "Abigail Baylor."

"Abigail Baylor."

"Alfred Baylor."

"Alice Baylor."

Lori continued to read the names aloud, revealing dozens of Baylors all with first names beginning with the letter "A."

"Stop right there," Bennett said.

Lori lifted her finger off the scroll key and the cursor rested opposite of a Bruce Baylor. Bennett ran the tip of his finger across the screen. Listed were a case number and date, but neither matched the ones listed on the death certificate,

"Move on, that can't be him."

Lori moved slowly down the screen carefully reading each line. "There must be three dozen Bruce Baylors here. I didn't realize he had such a common name."

"Just our luck," Bennett groaned.

Meanwhile, Bennett's eyes roved back and forth across the screen and out of his peripheral vision, he spotted the date: February 12 1949.

"Hold it right there. That's got to be him."

Lori jotted down the case number. Meanwhile Bennett studied a map showing the locations of the files. The case number listed was in a section of files stored on the east end of the warehouse, almost two end zones away.

Bennett rose from his chair and pulled Lori away from the screen. "We've got what we need. Come on."

The two made their way down endless rows of files searching for the right file cabinet. Finally, they split up to make better time. It was like walking through the Library of Congress of police records. There was enough paper in the facility to start one big bonfire.

"Cases names beginning with the letter B are in this section over here," Bennett hollered.

Lori emerged from a different row and hurried to catch up with him. She reached Bennett just as he stopped in front of the cabinet marked "Ba-Bay."

"This is the one."

Bennett pulled open the file drawer and he and Lori simultaneously ran their fingers down both sides searching for the case number. Lori stumbled upon the file first.

"I found it. I found it."

"Settle down. Settle down. We don't know what we've found yet."

Lori laid the file on top of the file drawer and opened it in its place. Together, she and Bennett studied the contents. The case file listed Baylor's name, his occupation and cause of death. Glancing at each other, they read the listed cause together: "Suicide."

"This is him, all right," said Bennett.

The facility inside was dimly lit and Bennett had trouble reading part of the report. To shed more light on the subject, he held the file up toward the light. The light source barely cast enough watts to illuminate a large living room. As Bennett moved his hands upward, a small object fell from the folder and crashed to ground.

Lori spotted it and immediately bent down to pick it up. The object, whatever it was, was in a sealed envelope.

"Mark, what do you suppose this is?"

Bennett looked over his shoulder to see what Lori was holding. He stopped what he was doing and rushed over to get a better look.

"Go ahead. Open it," he said.

Lori delicately tried opening the envelope, ripping it slowly so the tear would not become too noticeable.

Frustrated in watching her, Bennett impatiently grabbed the envelope from her and brutally ripped it open. "Believe me, nobody's ever going to see this envelope again."

Bennett reached inside the tattered envelope and pulled out a small metal canister.

"What could it be?" Lori wondered.

"We'll both know in a minute."

The canister was sealed shut around the lid with packing tape. At first glance, Bennett was not sure what it was. Lori knew right away. "It's a film canister. You don't suppose?"

Bennett peeled the tape away and opened the lid. Inside was a small metal reel. He allowed Lori to have the honors. She pulled the reel from the can and began to unravel it.

Holding it up to the light, she peered through the frames.

"This is 16-millimeter film footage of something. Of what, I'm not sure."

"Well, there's one way to find out," said Bennett.

"Are you thinking, what I'm thinking?"

"Uh, huh."

Lori returned the film to the metal canister and Bennett placed it back inside the folder.

"Now if we can get past Uncle Miltie, we'll be all set."

Returning to the gated entrance, Jones stopped Bennett and Lori. He seemed delighted to have an audience again. Only this time Bennett made sure they left before the show started.

"Find what you were looking for, sarg?" Jones said happily.

Bennett rushed his way through the gate, dragging Lori behind him. "Sure, Hal. Sure. But we're in a big hurry."

"What you taking?"

"Nothing you're going to miss," Bennett said as he and Lori made their escape down a long narrow hallway.

"But sarg. You can't do that."

"Don't worry, Hal," Bennett shouted. "I'll straighten everything out later." By now, he and Lori were nearly out of eye's view.

"But sarg. You..."

"I promise to bring it back," Bennett echoed, as he and Lori disappeared into the darkness.

"You need to sign out."

Bennett and Lori hurried to the KTRB television studios to review the mysterious film footage. They knew that if anyone could help that it would be Charley Bumside, the station's senior film editor. Charley was a film historian of sorts. He could tell right down the nearest year when a film was produced, even what type of film stock was used.

Charley usually arrived at the station by mid-afternoon and worked through the evening. When Bennett and Lori dropped in to see him, he was in the middle of editing *Ben-Hur* for its traditional holiday broadcast.

"Well, look who's here," Charley said, looking up from his film monitor. "This is sure a surprise."

"Sorry, Charley. This is not a social call," Lori said seriously. "We need your help."

Lori went on to explain how she and Bennett had discovered a small reel of film in a police case file and their theory about Bruce Baylors possibly link to the deaths of the three Hollywood film legends. She said they believed the reel contained footage of Baylor, but with whom they were not sure.

"We're really pressed for time," Lori added. "We were wondering if you could screen this for us. I know this is very short notice."

Charley shook his head slowly with a hint of a smile. "I can't right now. I have to finish editing 'Ben-Hur' first. I'm in the middle of butchering...I mean, editing a big chariot scene that I don't think is too important to the story."

That was not the answer Lori expected. She tried again. Only this time she really put on the charm.

"Charley. It's really important. Please."

"Well. Okay. When you say it that way, how can I resist."

Charley unthreaded *Ben-Hur* from the film monitor. Using a grease pencil, he marked the chariot scene with an "x" to remind him where he left off. Lori handed him the mental canister and he reeled up the small metal reel and threaded the film through to the other side.

"All set."

Charley switched on the motorized viewer and the film began winding its way through. The frame counted down until a flickering image, somewhat out of focus, appeared. Charley adjusted the focus ring and to sharpen the image. The camera was panning on a group of actors lined up in front of the camera. They looked young and vibrant, in the early stages of their careers. Bennett and Lori did not recognize any of the people featured. Neither of them were serious film buffs. However, as the camera continued to pan, Charley's eyes widened. It was evident to him who they were and where the film had been shot.

"That's the 20th Century Fox back lot. I'd recognize it anywhere," Charley said excitedly. "And that gal on the far right of the screen is Rita Reno."

Bennett focused his eyes on the tiny monitor. He saw before him a sultry, bosomy brunette in her late 20s. She was a firecracker all right, and he could see why she was capable of sparking any man's fantasy in her day.

"And right over here," Charley continued, pointing with his forefinger. "That's Charles Evans Fine."

Just then, the film buckled in the machine and it snapped.

"Damnit," Charley growled. "Don't worry, I can fix the film. But it looks like old Betsy needs servicing. I'll look and see what's wrong. I should be able to fix her."

"How long will it take you to fix it?" Lori asked, checking her watch.

"It's hard to say," Charley groaned. "That all depends on what I find."

"And just when it looked like we were getting to the good part," Lori said, managing a small smile.

"I'll tell you what," Charley offered. "I don't have to have 'Ben-Hur' edited until the end of next week. I just like to stay ahead of schedule. I'll figure out what's wrong with the equipment. I have some spare parts around, so I should be able to fix it myself."

Lori leaned over and kissed Charley on the cheek. "I don't know what I do without you, Charley."

Charley blushed, while Bennett seemed envious. "Well, don't you worry, honey. Ol' Charley won't let you down."

Charley said he would call Lori as soon as he repaired the film editor and the film, and he would arrange another screening. With no other business left, Lori and Bennett went their separate ways. They agreed to call each other at the end of the way to plot their next move.

Bennett felt more certain that he was right all along. There was never any ghost. And he was sure he could prove it. Lori remained uncertain. She could sense that the evidence was stacked against her, but, until proven otherwise, she stubbornly refused to accept anything else.

Chapter 19

Thursday morning rolled around sooner than Lori ever imagined. She awakened feeling totally exhausted, devoid of any energy. The week had been like one wild roller coaster ride, full of ups-and-downs, and she found it difficult to get up.

Groggily, she pressed the snooze alarm for at least the seventh time and turned over in bed, pulling the covers up to her chin. As she lay there motionless, a bright ray of sunlight unsuspectingly penetrated the white puffy bedroom curtains, reflecting upon her tanned complexion. The harsh yellow-gold light spread over her face like a halo, and finally forced her eyes to open.

Bleary-eyed and beaten, Lori sat up and shook the sleep

from her eyes. Stretching her arms above her head, she yawned and shuffled to her feet, moving at a snail's pace to the kitchen. Immediately, she warmed up a cup of coffee in the microwave to give her the caffeine boost that her body so badly needed. Enjoying the hot brew, her energy suddenly lifted and she began to think more clearly. She remembered that she did not have to hurry. No story conference or staff meeting was scheduled. Peter Coyle was having root canal surgery, and it was doubtful he would be in.

Finishing her coffee, Lori drew a hot bath. The idea of soaking in the tub sounded very appealing. It was not often that she had time to spoil herself. Just as the water trickled out its last drop, the phone rang. Lori answered it. It was Bennett.

"I wasn't sure if I would still catch you at home. But thought I was worth a try."

"Well, this must be your lucky day. I was just preparing to jump into the tub."

Bennett resisted all temptation to make a flirtatious remark about how much he wished he could join her, even though the thought crossed his mind. And Lori did not seem to have any idea of what she had just said, or how she had said it.

"Look, I'm going to be stuck here for most of the day. They need my help on a case in the Juvenile Division. So I won't be able to see you until tonight. You know, at the AFI thing."

Still wiping the sleep from her eyes, Lori yawned. "Right. Right. The event honoring Colleen Kantor with the life achievement award."

"There's just no way I can break away today. I hope you understand."

Lori was beginning to feel chilled. She had nothing on but a silk robe that barely covered her tall naked body. And her bath water was beginning to cool. "Well, if that's the best you can do. Then fine. I'll see you later tonight."

Lori hung up and moved toward the bathtub. Slipping her robe off, she touched the water's surface with the tip of her toe to test the temperature. It was perfect. Easing her way in, she felt a tingling sensation as the warm water touched her cool creamy skin.

Becoming entirely relaxed, Lori closed her eyes and meditated. But her mind began to wander, and she could not help but think about the case. A jumble of ideas raced through her brain. Had she and Bennett overlooked something? Was there more to the deaths of the three actors than they had considered? Could it be Bruce Baylor was really alive? The thought alone sent chills up her spine. Was it possible that one of the surviving actors was involved? And if so, who? What about the mysterious film footage? Who else was in it? And the missing diary, what about that?

Lori shook her head as if to force the intruding thoughts from her mind. She opened her eyes with the sudden realization that her ghost theory was no longer relevant. The evidence just seemed to point in another direction, and, as much as she hated to admit it, her theory did not seem credible.

Taking a wet sponge, Lori squeezed the water from it on her face and moistened it. It was almost like a baptismal experience, and gave her a feeling of awakening. Just then, a sudden thought occurred to her. It was a hunch, but maybe it was the right hunch. The more she thought about it, the more excited she became.

Of course, why hadn't she thought of it before? It was so obvious she wanted to scream.

Lori immediately jumped to her feet as tiny drops of water trickled from her long slender body. Grabbing a towel, she quickly dried off and considered calling Bennett with the news, but suddenly changed her mind. This time, she was going alone. She had something to prove--to herself and Bennett. And nothing, or no one, was going to stop her.

Bennett felt guilty that he had let Lori down. He knew how important the case was to her, and he was only sorry that he assigned to another missing person's case. He felt guilt-ridden about another issue. He had some news about the case that he had not shared with her.

The previous afternoon after he left the television station he spent some time investigating the case on his own. He thoroughly reviewed Bruce Baylor's case file and did some follow up work that produced some unusual findings that he was reluctant to share with Lori until he determined if they had any relevance to the case.

It seemed strange to Bennett and he was surprised that he had not noticed it before, but Baylor's death certificate listed no known relatives. For a man who had at least one secret marriage and who knows how many others, the facts seemed disputable, especially given Baylor's wild reputation with women. Further confusing matters, Mel Greenberg's name was not even listed, which confounded Bennett since he was Baylor's adopted father. Again, why?

That was the least of what Bennett had found. He also uncovered an old newspaper clipping, dated February 19,

1950, one year after Baylor's death, announcing memorial services for the actor at Forest Lawn in Burbank. For someone whose body was allegedly unfound, why did anyone go to the trouble?

It is not like Baylor was well liked in the Hollywood community, or that he would have had a steady stream of admirers come to his gravesite.

Bennett checked with the mortuary and their records indicated that a private party, which requested anonymity, paid for the plot and gravestone. Little else was documented other than the plot location, and the fact that everything was paid for in cash. Bennett visited the grave of Bruce Baylor, and, sure enough, it was he. The headstone, for all its simplicity, listed the correct dates of birth and death.

During his visit to the cemetery, Bennett interviewed one groundskeeper who happened to be beautifying the grounds near Baylor's grave. He asked the middle-aged worker if he had ever seen any visitors at Baylor's gravesite. The man could not say for sure, but he seemed to think someone visited Baylor's grave once a month to leave a wreath of fresh cut flowers at the foot of the headstone. Aside from that, he knew nothing else.

Bennett was just as disturbed as Lori was. There were still too many missing pieces. This Baylor character had certainly covered his tracks, as had anyone else even remotely connected to him. There must have been a reason. He just hoped he could find out why--and soon.

***

Lori surprised Charley Bumside by her sudden appearance. He was just about to phone and tell her that the film editor was up and working again, and that he had successfully repaired the film.

"You must have ESP," he chuckled.

"No, Charley. Just a hunch. Can you reel up the film?"

"Your wish is my command."

Charley threaded the film through the loop, then said, "Where's your other half?"

"He's all tied up. I imagine he'll be upset at me for doing this without him. But I have to follow my journalistic instinct."

Charley laughed. "That's what got you to the top."

All set, Charley began rolling the film. The same countdown leader flashed across the tiny monitor, followed by the initial images of the group of actors that Lori and Bennett had already seen from the day before. Lori recognized Rita Reno and Charles Evans Fine in the group, and then some new faces appeared.

"Who's that, Charley?" she asked curiously.

Charley tried sharpening the focus. It turned out not to be the film, but his eyes that were worst for the wear. "Why that's Bette Oliver."

It was hard to believe someone that beautiful was the same woman, Lori thought. My god, how she had aged. The woman in the film was a statuesque blonde who looked like she could have doubled as a fashion model. Her long blonde tresses touched the tips of her shoulders, and the low-cut silk gown she was wearing clung to every inch of her shapely figure, highlighting every curve.

The camera panned to the next actor standing next to Oliver. He was a dark haired, handsome man wearing a striped suit and brimmed hat. Whoever he was, he looked uncomfortable. The man continuously fidgeted and smiled uneasily at the camera. And he was holding what appeared to be a newborn baby in one arm.

"That's Bruce Baylor," Charley remarked.

Lori did not seem surprised. She had a hunch it was him. Who else would be standing beside Bette Oliver?

"I wonder whose child that is." Lori thought aloud.

Charley had worked at the 20th Century Fox studios and remembered hearing that Baylor and Oliver had had a child out of wedlock. He was not positive, but he thought the birth of the child precipitated their secret marriage and that the studio managed to keep it from the press because in those days having a child without being married was enough to run anyone's career.

"Bette Oliver told us that Baylor had had a child out of wedlock with an unnamed actress," Lori thought aloud. "You don't remember who that was, do you Charley?"

Charley intensely watched the footage and answered without looking up. "That's her right there." He lifted his finger and pointed at the woman on the screen.

"Bette Oliver?"

"That's right," Charley confirmed. "She and Baylor had this affair going on. Everyone at the studio knew about it. She didn't plan on getting pregnant, however."

Lori was still in a state of shock. It never occurred to her that Oliver and the anonymous actress were one and the same.

"Was it a boy or a girl?"

Charley scratched his head. "I believe it was a boy."

Lori remained focused on the image of Baylor and his baby son. She wondered why Bette Oliver never admitted during the meeting that she and Baylor had had a son. What did she have to hide? Perhaps she was too embarrassed to discuss it, or found it too painful to talk about her relationship with Baylor any further. Lori found the news intriguing, nonetheless.

"What happened to him, the baby, I mean?" Lori inquired.

"I believe he died in a car accident several years later. I can't be certain, though. You hear so many rumors when you work at a studio that after a while you're not sure which is fact or fiction."

Lori's face suddenly turned grim. "Hmm. There's goes my theory," she muttered quietly to herself.

Charley did not hear Lori's off-the-cuff remark and kept running the film through the monitor. Just as the camera made its final pan on the other actors in the shot, the film's color turned spotted and began to fade, and the screen suddenly went black.

"That's it. I hope it gave you what you were looking for," Charley offered.

"Well, yes and no," Lori said. "It helped confirm one of my beliefs." Charley rewound the film, placed it in the metal canister and returned it to Lori.

She thanked her old friend and decided to wait to tell Bennett the news later that evening. She had work to do that could not wait. Billy Gamm had assigned her to a cover a celebrity fashion show in Century City. The story did not excite her half as much as what she had just uncovered.

Chapter 20

Colleen Kantor had anxiously waited for this night. The American Film Institute was honoring her with its Lifetime Achievement Award for artistic contributions to the film industry. Kantor was understandably flattered when the Board of Governors informed her that they had unanimously selected her to be this year's honoree.

The lavish, star-studded affair was to be held at the Beverly Hilton Hotel and broadcast, live, to a national television audience. More than 40 millions viewers expected to watch the event, and Hollywood's brightest and best-known stars would be attending, names and faces recognized by film audiences around the world. Kirk Douglas, who had worked with Kantor in a number of classic films and had known her the longest, agreed to present the award.

Bennett and Lori were surprised when Kantor invited them to the event. They hardly knew the aging film star, but it was her way of showing them her appreciation for their understanding and friendship throughout the tumultuous investigation.

Arriving by chauffeured limousine, Kantor looked radiant. She was resplendent in elegant lavender and gold sequined evening gown that sparkled as photographers' flashbulbs flashed in her direction. It reminded her of one of those grand Hollywood movie premieres. A long velvet red carpet leading from the curb to the entrance welcomed each new arrival, and two large klieg lights roved the skyline, in perfect synchronization, adding to the excitement of the evening.

The Grand Ballroom, in its entire splendor, was the site of the event. One by one, famous people, film executives and studio heads filed in to find their seats. By the number of early arrivals, it looked like a complete sell out.

Bennett had never been among Hollywood's elite before. He was accustomed to watching such events on his 19-inch Motorola color television, fortified by a light beer in one hand and a bowl of microwave butter popcorn in the other. Lori, on the other hand, had attended scores of social events involving the rich and famous, and knew fully well what to expect as well as how to act.

Scores of stars continue to arrive right up until minutes before the opening broadcast. Bennett wisely left the Dodge Neon at Lori's place and caravanned in style in her flaming red Porsche, which, for now, was in perfect working condition.

During the drive over, Lori felt compelled to tell Bennett. That she had viewed the mysterious film footage without him at the station, and what she had discovered. But it seemed like neither the time nor place, and she decided not to spoil the evening.

Lori was dressed appropriately for the occasion and looked liked she belonged among Hollywood's rich and powerful. She was wearing a blue sequined dress that slunk open in the back, practically down to her waist. Up against her long blonde hair and blue eyes, she was a remarkable sight. Bennett felt completely overdressed and out of his league. The last time he wore a black tuxedo was for his younger brother's wedding, and even that turned out to be an unhappy occasion when the bride-to-be left his brother stranded at the altar.

Escorting Lori inside, Bennett surveyed the ballroom and felt totally out of place. He had never seen so many famous movie stars in person before in his life. In one corner, there was Sid Caesar and Red Buttons, laughing and swapping stories about the good old days. Twelve feet in front of him was the ever-beautiful Raquel Welch, surrounded by a foursome of male film executives, no doubt mentally drooling over her boundless curves and well-endowed figure. Ageless film legend Kirk Douglas was engaged in a lively conversation with son Michael, whose career as an actor and producer had already eclipsed that of his famous father's. Then one of Hollywood's most talked about couples made their entrance, catching every second of Bennett's attention.

"My god, Catherine Zeta-Jones is more beautiful in person," Bennett whispered softly to Lori. "That Michael Douglas is one lucky guy."

Lori laughed, "Will you stop. They're real people like you and me."

Now Bennett laughed. "Yeah," he said peering at Zeta-Jones's low-cut, off-the-shoulder black evening dress that gave every man in the room an eye full. "How many real people do you know that dress like that?"

The announcer's voice boomed over the loudspeaker. "Will everyone please take your seat? Two minutes to show time."

Finding their table, Lori and Bennett joined the others already seated. None of the people seated at their table were from Hollywood's "A" list. They were mostly comprised of actors whose star had faded over the years, and were still trying to live off their past glories.

Just then, the twenty-piece orchestra, led by Oscar-winning composer John Williams, went into its opening number, and the show was officially underway. Jay Leno was the master of ceremonies and host of the event. It marked the first time Leon had hosted the event, and his opening monologue drove the audience into fits of laughter. Following Leno's monologue was an endless parade of stars, each of which paid tribute to Kantor for her work as an actress and for her great showmanship over the years.

Then the moment everyone had waited for finally arrived: A masterfully edited, five-minute film tribute chronicling Kantor's illustrious film career. The neatly produced retrospective featured some of the best moments and Academy Award-winning performances from than 100 films. Kantor, seated in the front row directly near the stage, became emotional as she watched Kirk Douglas, still showing effects of a stroke that initially left him disabled, walk on stage to make the presentation.

Every member in attendance, from the major superstars of today to the stars of old, stood on their feet and gave Kantor a well-deserved standing ovation before the presentation ever started. Pained by arthritis, she slowly moved to her feet and waved to the crowd, throwing kisses in every direction. A technical assistant hurried over with a microphone so everyone, including the live television audience, could hear Kantor's gracious comments, but the microphone failed to work as she mouthed her heartfelt remarks. Jay Leno, standing off to the side of the stage, could not resist quipping afterwards, "As many of you know, Miss Kantor got her start in silent movies."

Following a commercial break, the lights dimmed and the film tribute began. Lori started feeling nervous. Her stomach churned in anticipation, anticipation of something ugly. She looked at Bennett, but he seemed completely calm. Noticing her curious glance, he turned, "Are you all right?"

"Yeah, I'm okay. I just hope nothing goes wrong."

"Don't worry. The place is surrounded by police and unmarked cars, and security is so tight you would think the President of the United States is here."

The images flickered on the large video screen and there she was, a young Colleen Kantor in her first film and the first talking feature with co-star Al Jolson--from 1927. The audience turned awestruck as Kantor whirled through a lavish musical number with Jolson, performing several difficult moves that brought cheers from the audience. Many more film clips followed, each nostalgic and remarkable glimpses of a career filled with memorable performances that were bound to live on forever.

Just as the tribute neared its finale, an unusual occurrence took place on the screen. In a scene from *As God Is My Witness*, Kantor's fourth Academy Award-winning performance, a luminous, non-descript figure that kept coming in and out of focus appeared in the film. It was hard to tell who or what it was exactly, but it was evident to everyone watching. The filmy figure became more prominent, overtaking the frame and becoming larger than life.

As the image sharpened, his identity became clear. It was Bruce Baylor, and he was mouthing something to the camera and staring down from the screen at Kantor with the kind of menacing look that would strike fear into anyone. What Baylor was saying was inaudible, but his actions petrified everyone.

Sensing trouble, Lori stood up and screamed. "Stop the projector! Stop the projector!"

Bolting from his seat, Bennett came to a sudden halt and looked up at the projection booth. Peering up through the glass window, he spotted a shadowy figure slip out of plain view. Bennett hurried to catch the suspect as he fled from the scene, while Lori frantically made her way down to the stage. Meanwhile, the film tribute continued to play, and Baylor's image grew larger on screen terrifying the crowd.

Puzzled by the goings on, Douglas stared up at the screen. Turning toward the audience, he looked into the darkness for Kantor but could not locate her. "Turn up the lights!" he hollered deliriously. "Turn up the lights."

Not wasting any time, Douglas hurried off stage, with the help of his son Michael, to where Kantor sat.

Bennett made his way up the final step of the stairway and approached the projection room with great caution. Like walking on eggshells, he treaded softly toward the open door, his gun drawn, ready for anything.

Turning the corner, Bennett held his gun out in front of him and stormed the room. Inside, he discovered the projector running unattended, and not a single soul in sight. Without hesitation, he quickly turned off the projector, and then searched the tiny room for evidence. Bennett surveyed every nook and cranny and found nothing until suddenly a quick reflection of light caught his eye.

Moving back to the projector, Bennett traced the reflection to a single frame of 16-millimeter film with a torn sprocket on one side and jagged at the edge as if it had become jammed in the projector. Holding the frame up to the light, Bennett studied the image closely and what he stunned him: The specter of Bruce Baylor, the same image that somehow had made its way into the Colleen Kantor film tribute. Bennett slipped the evidence into his shirt pocket and returned to the frantic scene below.

When he arrived, Bennett found Douglas cradling Kantor in his arms. Lori had managed to claw her way through the large crowd and Bennett joined her when Douglas quietly bowed his head in disbelief.

"She's dead."

Douglas eyes instantly filled with tears and he began to sob helplessly. Few words seemed appropriate, and the legendary actor kept asking himself the same question. "Why? Why?"

Sons Michael and Peter, standing close by his side, pulled their grief-stricken father to his feet and escorted him from the scene.

Bennett then took charge. "Please. Everyone clear out. There's nothing more you can do."

Uniformed police stormed the ballroom and took control of the crowd. The audience, except for a few stragglers, disbursed from the scene in an orderly fashion. Minutes later, paramedics arrived to cart away Kantor's still form to the county morgue to perform an autopsy and determine the cause of death. "I thought you said security was tight," Lori said breaking her silence.

"It was. I can't imagine how this happened."

Lori felt like it was all her fault. Perhaps if she had told Bennett the truth none of this would have ever happened. Instead, a fourth victim was dead, and her conscious got the better part of her.

"Mark," she blurted out, "there's something I need to tell you. I think I know who's responsible for this and the three other murders."

Bennett looked at Lori with a quizzical look. He did not have the faintest idea what she meant. His mind was too preoccupied now.

"I'm sorry. What were you saying?"

"I said I think I know who is..."

At that very moment, Bennett's portable police radio, clipped to the inside pocket of his rented tuxedo, boomed with the loud voice of the PBX operator. It was not clear what the female operator was saying, but the ear-piercing static that accompanied the broadcast completely drowned out Lori's voice. Bennett immediately pulled the radio from his pocket and adjusted the volume, listening closely as the operator repeated the call.

"Attention all units," the nasal voice alerted. "Suspect headed westbound on Beverly Boulevard."

Bennett smiled confidently. "That's our suspect. Let's go."

Lori fell silent and did not know what else to say. Her first thought was to try again, but she realized it was no use. Bennett was in his cop mode and there was no stopping him now.

Bennett gave final orders to the unit of officers to seal off the area and disallow any unauthorized personnel from entering the facility. Then, grabbing Lori by the hand, with a determined look in his eyes, he said, "It's now or never."

Pulling Lori along, they ran as fast as their tired legs could carry them to the parking garage below. Loris mind was full of anxiety, but she did her best to cover. Bennett was feeling certain the end was now in sight.

"I hope your Porsche is up to the task," he said sprinting briskly. "We'll need to bum rubber to catch up with him, whoever he is."

"Don't worry," Lori replied, winded. "It's insured."

Chapter 21

Speeding from the scene, Bennett put Lori's Porsche to the ultimate test. Shifting into overdrive, he skillfully swerved in and out of heavy traffic to make up for lost time. His portable police radio kept him abreast of the situation during the high-speed pursuit. "Suspect in the vicinity of Gower Studios. All available units please respond."

"Gower Studios? Why would he be going there?" Bennett wondered aloud.

"Good question," Lori answered, tightly gripping her seat with both hands. "I think I know why."

Bennett swerved through the intersection, running the red light at break-neck speed. "And what's that?"

"The Gower Studios was once one of the busiest motion picture studios in Hollywood. After falling on hard times, in the last dozen years they've used it as a warehouse, primarily. Whoever it is has probably holed himself up there without anyone noticing."

Bennett grinned. "Not bad for a rookie investigator. You haven't been taking one of those correspondence courses have you?"

Lori laughed. "No." Her eyes widened and her voice turned serious. "But if you don't watch out, you're going to kill us both."

Bennett quickly put on the brakes as the traffic ahead came to a screeching halt. A railroad crossing sign sounding its bells and flashing its red lights had started to make its slow but steady descent. Bennett would have nearly smashed into the car in front of him if it had not been for Lori's alerting him to the urgency of the situation.

Impatiently idling in traffic, Bennett was not bound to stay for long.

"Let's see what this puppy's really made of."

Lori gulped at the thought of what Bennett was thinking. "No. Don't."

Swerving out of traffic, Bennett pushed the gas pedal to the floor, and the Porsche instantly responded. The turbo-charged sports car roared ahead, picking up speed with every second. The pressure of the moment intensified as the railroad crossing sign made its final descent. Lori did not think Bennett had a chance of making it through. She wanted to take control and have Bennett pull over, but it was too late. Tiny beads of perspiration formed above Bennett's brow as he made the final stretch. His hands felt clammy in anticipation as the railroad crossing sign sounded its final warning.

"Hold on to your underwear!"

Bennett downshifted and maneuvered the tiny red sports car across the tracks. He swerved and eluded each of the candy cane striped guardrails, and managed to race across to the other side unscathed and without a scratch.

Lori breathed a sigh of relief, but her emotions flashed from euphoria to anger in a single second.

"You could have gotten us killed!"

Bennett remained true to form. Despite the serious nature of the situation, he could not help grinning. "I've always tried to make a good impression on the first date."

Lori laughed uncontrollably, partly because she found the line funny and because she was just too tired to do anything else. "Well, you're not doing too well so far," she said between laughs.

With a clear road ahead, Bennett took advantage of the stalled traffic behind him and exceeded the speed limit. The monotone voice of the PBX operator rumbled again over the police radio. "Attention all units. Stakeout in progress at Gower Studios. Suspect considered dangerous. Proceed with extreme caution."

One block away from the scene, Bennett took a sudden detour to make better time. Pulling up to the studio, he and Lori arrived to a sea of black and whites with red lights flashing. A dozen squad cars surrounded the studio, and uniformed police stood armed and ready.

George DeCarlos, the unit commander, was standing with a bullhorn closely held up to his mouth. "We have you surrounded. Come out with your hands up."

DeCarlos' impassioned plea produced no response. Bennett and Lori squatted down next to the commander who gave Bennett a less-than-friendly greeting.

"It's about time you got here, Bennett. What took you so long?

"I guess you could say we were a little tied up."

Lori exchanged introductions with the commander, and DeCarlos updated them on the situation.

"The suspect is holed up in this old abandoned sound stage that's now used as a warehouse. My guess is that he's unarmed, but we are not taking any chances."

Lori suddenly excused herself, saying she would be right back. Returning to the car, she pulled a cellular phone from the glove compartment and immediately dialed the station. Billy Gamm was on the receiving end. "Billy, it's Lori. Listen, I don't have much time to talk. Get a mobile unit over to the Gower Studios right away. The place is swarming with police, and our 'ghost' is about to be apprehended. Hurry."

Clicking off the phone, Lori returned to the stakeout. Bennett was in the middle of a heated discussion with DeCarlos.

"Not on your life, Mark. I can't allow it, and I won't."

"You don't have any choice."

Rising to his feet, Bennett stormed the warehouse alone. DeCarlos held up his right hand and signaled to the other officers to hold their fire. Exasperated, he then turned to talk to Lori but found her missing. When he was not looking, she dashed through the ring of squad cars and joined Bennett.

"What are you doing?" Bennett said angrily "You shouldn't be here."

"We've been through this together. I'm not backing down now."

Bennett could tell that Lori stubbornly refused to leave. He knew he had no other choice but let her stay. "Whatever you do, stay right near me."

Heading toward the warehouse, Bennett and Lori found a steel door. The lock on the outside had been broken, obviously the work of whoever was inside.

Entering through the door, the warehouse was pitch dark inside and filled with an eerie silence. A musty smell permeated the place as if it had gone unattended and unused for who knows many years.

Bennett bravely led the way, and Lori remained close by his side. The door suddenly slammed shut behind them, and Lori trembled with fear. Certainly, with their presence now known, there was no turning back.

The warehouse was damp and cold and the walls creaked and moaned as if it was suffering from old age. Lori instantly began to shiver. The chilled night air penetrated her bones. "God, it's freezing in here."

Pulling her tenderly toward his firm chest, Bennett could feel her heart pounding uncontrollably, and the strong sensation of it made him want to pull her even closer. He sensed a strong sexual magnetism and as much as he had resisted he wondered what it would be like to hold her and love her through the night.

Overcome by the same romantic feelings, Lori he felt inclined to thank him with more than just meaningless words but a warm embrace and passionate kiss. She knew she was attracted to him, and he was to her. But all she could wonder was why now, and in an abandoned warehouse of all places. It seriously dampened the mood.

"Thanks, I feel better now," Lori said, considerably warmer than before. "What do you suppose we do next?"

Bennett stood and looked around. His eyes had adjusted to the encroaching darkness but he could not see a thing. He remembered that he had a flashlight in his coat pocket-- he always carried one for emergencies--and aimed the beam in front of him. He looked for a sign, anything, to help lead them in the right direction. Breaking her silence was a loud creaking sound that emanated from the walls. Lori was about to say something, but Bennett pressed his forefinger against his lips encouraging her to remain silent.

The creaking sound returned, louder than before, and Bennett listened closely. It was unlike the echoing sound they had heard earlier. This was different. It was like that irritating noise he used to hear when he visited his grandmother's house and somebody was up in the attic. It was the sound of footsteps.

As best as they could tell, there was only one doorway on the other side the building, but the sound emanated above. Lori pointed to the rafters. Bennett looked up and together they noticed a catwalk that technicians once used to adjust lighting and to move backdrops and scenery into place during the making of a movie. There was no direct way up. The wooden staircase was so badly rotted half of it had collapsed.

Dangling two feet in front of Bennett were two fifty-pound sandbags attached to a pulley assembly, which gave him an idea.

"Follow me."

Bennett grabbed the first sandbag with his hands, and

turned to Lori. "Here. Hold on to this and hold it tight. Whatever you do, don't let go."

"But why?"

"Trust me."

Bennett moved toward the second sandbag, and grabbed it with both hands. Using every muscle in his body, he pulled on his end. With each tug, Lori began to ascend, and soon was floating on air. She wanted to scream, but could not. She had not told something to Bennett. She was deathly afraid of heights.

Gripping the sandbag tightly, Bennett continued to pull. His bulging biceps rippled with each jerk of the rope. In minutes, Lori made it to the top, and nervously she stepped on to the sturdy steel walkway. Her stomach was churning, and all she thought about was throwing up.

Lori wanted to check on Bennett, but she just could not look down. She knew if she did, she would lose her lunch for sure.

Bennett was hoping she would offer to help, but instead he had to go it alone. Grabbing the rope to the sandbag, he steadily climbed to the top. His only concern was that the aging rope and pulleys would hold his massive frame as he made his ascension to the top.

Lori stood frozen in her tracks and was completely helpless. She tried looking down but each time she did her queasy stomach reminded her that it was not such a good idea.

Bennett continued to put one hand before the other as he made his climb. To his surprise, the rope remained firm and the pulleys held, and Lori was right where he thought he would find her, only she looked as white as a ghost did.

"What took you so long?" Lori asked impatiently. "I thought you'd never get here."

Bennett grinned. "I'm here now."

Getting a closer look, Bennett noticed how pale she looked, and that seemed to be clenching her stomach.

"Are you okay?"

Lori managed a small smile. "Yeah. It was always my life ambition to be a trapeze artist." Then she turned serious. "No, of course, not. I'm afraid of heights."

"Great," Bennett growled. "Why didn't you tell me?"

"You never gave me a chance."

Moments earlier Bennett was contemplating having a romantic night out, and now he could not believe it was the same person.

"Look. You stay here. I'll handle this by myself."

Propping herself up, Lori countered, "Oh, no you don't. I'm coming right with you."

Lori stood up and felt woozy as she tried to keep her balance. She was sure that as long as she did not look down, she would fine.

"Come on," she said. "Let's find this ghost, or whoever it is."

Chapter 22

Heading down the catwalk, moving carefully not to make a sound, Bennett and Lori listened for the harsh squeaking sound. It returned momentarily, and then suddenly stopped. It seemed to be coming from behind the east wall.

A blast of cold air seeping through the rafters whisked into Lori's face. It frightened her for a moment, and reminded her of the time she had visited one of those haunted houses as a child on Halloween. All that seemed missing was the wicked witch and smoldering cauldron, and cobwebs and black widow spiders to make the moment complete.

Bennett moved dauntlessly down the walkway and was near the end when his footing gave way. He slipped on a welded joint and plowed into a raised wooden platform that stood squarely in his path. For a moment, he sat there dazed, but otherwise was unharmed.

Suddenly, the ground beneath him began to shake and rumble. Bennett turned and looked up, and his eyes widened in disbelief. The force of his two hundred-pound body tumbling into the platform rocked loose a large steel barrel seated at the top. The barrel contained one hundred pounds of fire retardant, and was one of a half dozen steel drums kept in storage in the event of a fire. The corroded looking sphere began rolling in Bennett's direction. Lori felt a scream coming on but quickly covered her mouth to muffle it. It did not matter. Bennett made enough noise for both of them.

"Run for cover!" Bennett shouted.

Lori took off and the barrel, soon followed by four others that rolled down the rickety platform, spun uncontrollably toward them, picking up speed with every second. Lori was a full stride ahead of Bennett but he quickened his pace as the first barrel spun perilously closer to his heels. The spider-web grid work of the catwalk turned out to be no match for Lori either.

Sprinting at a fast clip, her heel suddenly snagged in the metal webbing and she fell instantly on her face.

"Mark," Lori screamed, panic-stricken. "Help me!"

With no time to waste, Bennett quickly swept Lori into his arms, eluding the runaway barrels by mere inches, and making it safely to the other side. The barrels crashed head on into a huge wall at the end of the ramp way, producing a loud explosion. A mushroom cloud of dust, splinters and plaster protruded into the air and, once the particles settled, Bennett realized it was the sign they had been looking for.

"Look!" he exclaimed.

Shaken from the experience, Lori shook her head and slowly rose to her feet. Her face was badly scratched and bruised and her body felt like had it been run over by a truck. Dusting herself off, she focused her eyes in the same direction as Bennett's and could not believe it either. The collapsed wall revealed a hidden passageway. All this time, they were heading in the wrong direction.

Bennett flicked on his flashlight and it betrayed him when the batteries suddenly went dead.

"Damnit. So much for you, Energizer bunny."

Tossing the flashlight aside, Bennett noticed a powerful beam of light emanating from a tiny crack in the paneled wall that was inside. He and Lori moved cautiously through the demolished wall, and searched for a secret opening.

"You start over there, and I'll work from here," Bennett ordered.

Pushing their hands against the dark mahogany panels, they hopelessly looked for an opening to the other side. Bennett slid his massive hands carefully over every groove and seam, while Lori pressed her smooth palms similarly across her end. Bennett had no luck.

But Lori succeeded when her right hand snagged a glitch in the wood and, to her surprise, the panel opposite of her suddenly opened,

"Good going Holmes. You've done it again," Bennett smiled.

Bennett went first and Lori followed. On the other side, they were amazed to discover a complete state-of-the-art production facility featuring high-tech editing, film matting, special effects and film duplicating equipment. It contained at least several million dollars worth of equipment, and equal to anything that many of Hollywood's top movie studios had.

"It looks like whoever our mystery person spared no expense," Lori noted. Bennett agreed. "I wish I had his bank account."

Suddenly, the room went dark, and a voice boomed over the loudspeaker.

"Welcome to the inner sanctum," the voice laughed menacingly. "Here for a private tour, are you?"

Lori was in no laughing mood. Her stomach was acting up again, and all she could think of was how glad she would be when this was over.

"Who are you? What do you want?" she pleaded.

The voice returned. "Nothing. Just for the truth to be known."

"What do you mean by the truth?" Bennett asked curiously.

The voice remained silent. Then following a long pause, it rumbled over the loudspeaker. "It's not that simple. It's more complicated than a few words could possibly describe."

"Give us a chance," Lori offered. "We want to help."

The voice sounded familiar to Lori. She was certain she had heard it before, but where? She searched her memory, while Bennett examined the room trying to trace the origin of the mystic voice.

Lori's sincere offer only elicited an irrational response. "You want the truth," the voice exploded in anger. "You could never accept the truth."

Lori was not sure what to say. She was not accustomed to dealing with psychos and sickos on her job. So Bennett spoke on their behalf. "Try us. What have you got to lose?"

A deep sigh penetrated the speaker box, and the voice returned but in a less combative tone.

"Look, these people deserve to die. It's punishment that fits the crime."

"What crime?" Bennett replied.

The voice hesitated to answer. Bennett persisted. "Why? Why do they deserve to die?"

The voice, racked with emotion, blasted its response. "Because they are murderers, each and every one of them."

"Murderers of whom?" Lori asked.

"Don't play games with me," the voice replied irritated. "You already know the answer to that question."

"Okay," Bennett interrupted. "Calm down. We're just here to talk. Nothing else."

"Talk is cheap," the voice retorted. "Bruce Baylor represents the injustice in our world where the true criminals are set free, and the innocent victims are penalized."

"How so?" Lori wondered aloud.

"You just don't get it, do you?" the voice said bitterly.

"You're right," Lori countered. "We don't."

The voice continued. "Bruce Baylor died not because of his actions, but because of the Hollywood system. He was blacklisted, ruined for life, by a bunch of ego-driven studio executives who never tried to understand him or his problems. If they had only given him the help he needed, everything would have been different. Instead, they looked at him like a bad investment and cashed him in, replacing him with some other neophyte actor with average talent and

253

average intelligence who they could mold and manipulate any way they wanted. All because of a few actors he thought were his friends."

Lori's eyes widened. That voice. It could not possibly be who she thought it was. Then she saw the connection.

"Look, whoever you are," Bennett remarked. "That's still no reason to murder anyone. It would be best if you would just show yourself and put an end to this whole unfortunate misunderstanding."

A nearly undetectable crackle of static pierced the loudspeaker, but the voice remained stone silent. Lori proved to be the icebreaker.

"Sergeant Bennett is right," Lori reasoned. "Beside, what's done is done. Give yourself up. We know who you are, and why you are doing this. Hasn't this gone on long enough?"

Bennett glanced at Lori with a puzzled look on his face. He did not know the killer's identity, and thought she was bluffing.

The voice returned, defensive as ever. "You couldn't possibly know my name."

"Think again," Lori countered. "We've met before. Oh, sure, it wasn't a long meeting, but you appeared to be a troubled man as you are now. You were the one person who had access to the films. And by the looks of your studio, you had the capability to not only create a convincing ghost but duplicate and switch the prints without anyone ever knowing it."

"That's totally preposterous," the voice growled. "Where's your proof?"

"Oh, we have the proof all right," Lori continued. She peered over at Bennett who held the evidence in his hand, the cut piece of 16-millimeter film that he had found in the projection booth at the AFI tribute. "And it's quite evident that you had plenty of motives."

"You're a stupid fool, Lori Matrix," the voice laughed insanely. "It's awfully difficult to implicate a ghost."

Lori fell silent for a moment, and Bennett shrugged his shoulders when she looked at him with consoling eyes.

"Yes. Yes, your right," Lori answered. "But it would not be difficult to bring charges of murder against you, Mr. Ponds...Mr. Larry Ponds."

The static returned over the loudspeaker, but no voice. Bennett was more puzzled than ever. He still did not see the connection.

Suddenly, the voice returned. "How can you be so sure?"

Lori explained. "Bruce Baylor couldn't possibly be the killer. It had to be someone else who knew him. Someone who was angry and frustrated, and troubled like him. Someone who wanted revenge in the worst way. Someone who could have more motive than his own son."

Now Bennett was confused. He wondered how Lori knew.

"If my name is Larry Ponds, how could I possibly be Bruce Baylor's son?" the voice asked.

"Oh, Mr. Ponds. I'm not as stupid as you claim. You changed your name, simple as that. You changed your name because your father's reputation preceded him and, you knew until you did, you would never be able to get work in his town. You knew all about your father's past, and what you didn't know you learned from your mother."

"That's not true. It's totally untrue," the voice said. "And leave my mother out of this."

There it was. The closest thing to a confession that Lori could possibly hope for. The man's voice sensed it, too, dropping the microphone with the sound reverberating throughout the studio.

Suddenly, the pounding of footsteps, turning from a fast walk into a dead run, could be heard on the opposite site of the wall. Lori and Bennett escaped through the hidden panel, and immediately caught a glimpse of a dark burly figure hurrying across the catwalk in total darkness. They quickly took chase, and the man would not stop despite their repeated pleas.

Pausing, Bennett picked up the flashlight he had abandoned and swatted it hard with his hand. The beam of light flickered to life, and he and Lori continued the chase.

"The man was near the edge of the steel walkway, and he was stepping up on top of the rail to snag the closest sandbag and make his escape below.

Catching up to him, Bennett flashed the powerful beam in the man's face, for a moment blinded by its ray. It may have seemed like Lori was bluffing, but her theory was dead on accurate. The man holding the rope was Larry Ponds, the projectionist from the Fantasy Film Company. He was the same troubled man she remembered meeting when they first examined the films, but found nothing out of the ordinary.

"Don't take another step, or I'll jump," Ponds warned, twitching uncontrollably. "I mean it."

Bennett took charge, "Look, we just want to help. Now why don't you just come down from there?"

"And for what? To rot in prison for the rest of my life?"

Lori tried a different approach. "Mr. Ponds, I'm sorry about your father. It's unfortunate what happened, but it happened a long time ago. Isn't it time to bury the past and look to the future?"

"What future might that be?" Ponds asked doubtfully, still in a spastic fit. "All I ever dreamed of was producing and directing movies, and with the name Baylor who would ever think of giving me a chance. It was the only way. To change my name. But look at me. I'm no closer today to my dream. What's the use?"

Ponds turned to jump, but Bennett called out after him. "Don't you see what you're doing? You're repeating the same mistake your father made. Sure, he needed help. That was obvious. If he had lived, maybe things would have been different. For you and everyone else."

The rail beneath Ponds feet was moist from the ocean air. Tiny beads of moisture coveted the rail like raindrops on a windshield.

Ponds wanted to give up. He wanted to be caught. He was so confused he did not know where else to turn.

"You think this is easy for me. I never got to know my father. He died when I was very young. You can't imagine what it was like. Never to have my father around or to do all the things that fathers and sons did. My mother protected me all those years. She overcompensated for his death. She knew its effect on me. Even though they divorced, she gave me everything she possibly could. A good home. Lots of friends. A solid education. But where has it taken me?"

Ponds looked down to the deep dark depths below. He contemplated whether to end it now, or continue a life of misery.

"Come on, Mr. Ponds," Bennett pleaded. "Please get down from that rail. Let us help you. I'll do everything in my power to work with the district attorney to cop you a deal."

Lori stared at Bennett and could tell he was telling the truth. His voice sounded very sincere.

"Mr. Ponds, Sergeant Bennett is right. It doesn't have to end this way. Here, let us give you a hand."

Ponds appeared ready to give up. He started to turn himself around on the rail but suddenly lost his footing. Bennett and Lori quickly ran to help, trying to grab a hold of him with outstretched arms. It was no use. They were too late. Ponds hit the pavement below with a powerful and resounding thud, and was dead instantly.

Lori turned and sobbed helplessly in Bennett's arms. She could not stand the irony of it all as Ponds motionless body laid on the slab of cement surrounded by dark pools of blood.

Bennett whispered tenderly into Lori's ear. "It's over."

Lori continued to let out her emotions. She had experienced enough death already, but why this? Why did it have to end so tragically?

The steel doorway leading into the warehouse suddenly swung open and uniformed police swarmed the facility. DeCarlos led the charge, and immediately switched on the available light source that Bennett and Lori had failed to find, casting light on Ponds still form. He displayed little sensitivity for the man or his plight; he was just another criminal who ultimately deserved what he got in the end.

"Get this scumbag out of here," DeCarlos ordered.

Catching a glimpse of Bennett and Lori, in close company of each other, DeCarlos smiled broadly. "Well. Well, look what we have up there. Two birds in love."

Lori wiped the tears from her eyes, and started to laugh. Bennett seemed unfazed and considered the source.

"You know, you could really give us a hand by getting us down from here," Bennett barked.

"It will be my pleasure," DeCarlos said, bowing like a servant. "And would you and the lovely lady like a candlelight dinner while you're waiting?"

Bennett laughed, and Lori felt instantly better. She was relieved the incident was finally over. Bennett turned toward her as the splattered remains of Ponds attracted the morbid curiosity of investigating officers.

"Tell me. How did you know?"

Lori's eyes blinked and they looked tired. "Know what?"

"That Larry Ponds was the killer."

Her energy spent, every bone in Lori's body ached. "Can I take a rain check and tell you tomorrow?"

"Sure," Bennett said concerned. "Promise?"

"Promise." Lori crossed her fingers over heart. "Scout's honor."

The mobile unit from KTRB had arrived outside, ready for Lori to beam her exclusive story to a live television audience. With Bennett's tuxedo still wrapped neatly over her shoulders, she made her way down from the catwalk assisted by a trio of officers, all of whom seemed more than willing to help. Bennett made his descent without any assistance, while Lori went before the bright lights to report the story of her life.

Chapter 23

C aptain Hansen returned a day earlier than scheduled hoping he would find a complete report from Bennett on his desk by late afternoon. He had heard from the other investigators at the scene about the unusual twist of events that had taken place during his absence, and he arranged a private meeting with Bennett to hear all the details.

Bennett strutted into the station the next morning, treated like a hero. "Nice work, sergeant," the front desk operator said. "Can I have your autograph?"

With kudos and praise heaped on him from every direction, Bennett was not used to receiving such glowing recognition.

"Hey, Mark," shouted Hugo Rodriguez, a fellow homicide detective. "Better ask for a raise, buddy. Get it while you can."

Bennett flashed a tired but appreciative smile. "Thanks for the advice."

The commotion drew the attention of Captain Hansen, who suddenly popped his head out of his office.

"Mark. Do you have a second?"

Bennett did not sense any hostility in Hansen's voice. He was like a different person, accommodating and sincere. "Well, if you have the time."

"Sure. Sure. Why would you ever think otherwise?"

Bennett just about flipped in his shoes over that comment.

"The mayor wants to see me this afternoon. So I'm going to have to move up our meeting.

"To when?"

"How about now?"

"But Captain," Bennett noted, "I haven't even finished my report."

"Look. Don't worry about it. I know you'll have it on my desk later. But I have to tell you. You amazed me. This was a brilliant piece of police work on your part. How did you do it? You know, figure it out?"

Bennett glanced at the ceiling almost as if he was searching for heavenly guidance.

"You mean, figure out who the murderer was?"

"Exactly."

Bennett inched forward in his chair and he appeared uncomfortable. He wished he could take full credit, but he knew that he owed most of that to Lori.

"Well. That's hard to say, Captain."

"Call me Hank. You can dispense with that Captain crap. You're with friends."

Bennett thought it was odd how Hansen used the word friend in the plural sense. He did not see any one else in the room.

"Well, let's see. I got my first hunch when..."

The intercom suddenly interrupted Bennett before he made a complete fool of himself.

"Captain," the voice announced on the other end, "Lori Matrix is here to see Sergeant Bennett. Should I have her wait here?"

In a rare celebratory mood, Captain Hansen brushed off the notion. "Hell, no. Send her right in."

Hansen raised his eyebrows and glanced inquisitively at Bennett. "You two seem to have gotten awful chummy."

"Cap...I mean, Hank. It's not like at all."

"Right. You don't need a scorecard to figure out who's batting and who's pitching."

Like a breath of fresh air, Lori entered the room. Hansen rose immediately from his chair to greet her.

"Miss Matrix. I will forever cherish this moment."

"Well, thank you, Captain."

"Call me Hank."

Lori looked at Bennett puzzled. She knew of Hansen's reputation, and that it was not pleasant.

"Okay...Hank."

"Please have a seat."

Hansen politely pulled a chair over next to Bennett and waited until Lori took her seat. He then returned to his desk, easing back in his high-back chair, and proceeded.

"Mark was just about to tell me how he figured out who the murderer was."

"Oh, really," Lori said giving Bennett a cold glance. "Is that so?"

Bennett spoke up in his defense. "Well, actually. I was just about to tell Captain Hansen how instrumental you were in the investigation."

Lori remained silent and Bennett fidgeted nervously in his chair. "But I think Captain Hansen would probably like to hear your version of the story first."

Hansen studied every inch of Lori's statuesque physique and had other ideas on his mind.

"Well, Mark, if you insist."

Lori recounted in exhaustive detail how she and Bennett initially thought the ghost of Bruce Baylor was responsible for murders, but that she realized that could not possibly be true one morning when she was soaking in the bathtub.

Hansen really raised his eyebrows on that one. He would have given anything to be a fly on the wall watching.

"I remembered something Charley Burnside, our station's senior film editor, had said earlier about someone altering the films. It all made sense to me. The films we examined that day were not the same prints that had been shown prior to each of the murders."

Hansen was confused. "How was that possible?"

"I remembered doing a feature story about special effects in the movies, and how images could be computer matted in scenes featuring live actors. That meant there had to be two sets of prints, one doctored that featured our mysterious ghost and one without.

"But how did you know Larry Ponds was the killer?"

264

"I wasn't completely certain, I have to admit. But Larry Ponds was the only person who had complete access to the films. I didn't have an ounce of proof. But he had enough time before and after each screening to switch films and then return the originals in place without anyone ever noticing. I don't know why I hadn't thought of it before."

Hansen pondered everything Lori had said so far. But he still had his doubts.

"But how could a lowly projectionist like Ponds have the resources to pull off such an operation?"

Lori leaned forward in her chair. "His mother. She had millions to spend, and spared no expense in getting even. She was the ideal suspect. She fronted the murders using her son, a pathetic troubled man easily manipulated. He had no life, no self-esteem, and what little self-esteem he had he got by pleasing his mother."

"That's very interesting, Miss Matrix. But what tipped you off that it was truly him?" Hansen inquired.

"Well, I have to give credit to Sergeant Bennett. He and I discovered this mysterious film reel in Bruce Baylor's file."

Bennett said nothing, but just smiled.

Lori continued. "I happened to view the film, unfortunately on a day when Sergeant Bennett was busy. It featured each of the actors from the film club from when they were much younger. Bruce Baylor was in the film, and, to my surprise, he appeared with a child wrapped in his arms. I remembered Bette Oliver said Baylor had had a child out of wedlock. What she did not admit was that the baby was hers. At first, I wasn't so sure."

"What changed your mind?" Hansen asked.

"I did some investigating of my own," Lori explained, "and

I found there was no record of a Bruce Baylor, Jr., or any child, living or dead. The studio had covered it up to protect their investment in Bette Oliver, and therefore destroyed the records. It could only mean that this boy child was still alive, and that he had changed his name."

Bennett nodded as if he had heard the story before when, in reality, he was as surprised as anyone was.

"The real giveaway," Lori added, "was that ugly nervous twitch of his."

"How so?" Hansen wondered.

"After watching the film, I remembered noticing how his father had that same nervous habit, but he had it more under control. I wondered, like father like son. And then there was that laugh. I had heard it before. I remembered where. The day Ponds introduced himself to me at the Fantasy Film Company. He laughed for no reason and his laugh was maniacal sounding. It sent chills up my spine. I thought I would never hear it again until we stumbled upon that hidden studio of his and that creepy laugh of his boomed over the loudspeaker."

"Miss Matrix, you truly astound me," Hansen said in a flattering voice. "Any chance we could get you to work at the bureau?"

"Well, no. I'm a journalist at heart. It's what I was born to do. But thanks for offering."

Hansen then turned his attention to Bennett, and flashed a serious grin. "So what's your version of the story, Mark?"

Coyly, Bennett responded, "Pretty much just what your heard, but with a few added details."

"Really," Hansen said inching back in his chair. "And what might those be?"

266

Bennett paused for a brief moment, and then told his version. "Well, it seemed obvious to me from the start that this ghost business was pure malarkey. No offense to Miss Matrix, but I just didn't see how a ghost could be responsible for three...make that four murders."

"Goon."

"The day that Bette Oliver called Miss Matrix, instead of the police, to inform her that her home had been burglarized heightened my suspicions. As it turned out, we dusted the doorway to her palatial home for fingerprints. We found none. But I noticed what seemed like an obvious faux pas. Miss Oliver claimed that someone had broken in through the front door. The evidence was there all right: A gouged door jam and splinters lying at the base of the door. But it was a sloppy job."

"How so?" Hansen asked, his curiosity piqued.

"The splinters...they were a dead giveaway. They were on the wrong side of the door. They should have been outside where the forced entry was made. Instead, they were on the inside. That tipped me off that this wasn't a burglary at all, but made to look like one. Bette Oliver then became my prime suspect."

Now Lori was surprised. She did not think Bennett had the slightest idea of who was involved in the murders. Bette Oliver? Talk about a shock.

Hansen shook his head, very impressed. "Amazing. Utterly amazing."

"Oliver was definitely involved," Bennett continued. "Her son carried out the crimes, while she concocted this whole story of a stolen diary to lead us off track. She never stopped loving Bruce Baylor, despite all the horrible things he did to her. She just couldn't let go of the past, and brainwashed her son into believing that to validate her father's career that murder was the only way."

"And Bruce Baylor?"

"He's dead, as far as we know," Bennett explained. "He was connected to the local mob and was deeply in debt with them. We believe he's in a cement coffin in the Los Angeles River, but no one knows for sure. The suicide note was his, and it was his handwriting all right. It's one of these mysteries that may never be solved."

Bennett sighed and sat in total silence. Then, suddenly, without provocation, he added, "That's everything."

"Well, you'll never have to worry about Bette Oliver," Hansen said. "She was brought in for questioning an hour ago and she confessed to everything. She's already been charged with four counts of murder and one count of attempted murder."

Lori could not help but think about what the terrible tragedy it was, that four Hollywood film legends, still with so much to offer, were taken before their time And why? Because one actor's family just could not "let go." It seemed very incomprehensible, but in a world where premeditated murders and senseless killings occurred every second of every day, it was not so unlikely at all.

"What about Colleen Kantor?" Lori wondered aloud.

"The coroner's report crossed my desk early this morning," Hansen noted. "Poor woman. Heart attack. Just like all the others."

Bennett just shook his head. Lori sighed, and the atmosphere turned suddenly cold. Death was never a happy subject.

"Hey, cheer up you two," Hansen said. "It's over. The bureau and the city of Los Angeles owe you each our debt of gratitude."

Bennett stood up from his chair and the veins in neck bulged with anger. "Gratitude, my ass. Four people are dead. It doesn't change a thing."

"Come on, Mark. You don't mean that," Hansen reasoned. "Please have a seat. I'm not finished."

"Well, I'm finished, Captain." Bennett underscored the last word for affect, and then walked out the door.

Glancing at Lori, still seated, Hansen asked, "What's gotten in to him?"

"What do you think?" Lori rushed from her seat and hurried after Bennett without even saying goodbye.

Hansen sat there dumbfounded to fathom what went wrong. Perhaps for the first time in his career, he was speechless.

Chapter 24

Bennett had planned a special, intimate evening to celebrate with Lori. He formally wanted to thank her for her help in solving the case, and he thought they both could use a quiet night out.

Dining by candlelight, with the soothing sound of the ocean breaking in the distance, Bennett could not have picked a more perfect evening. Stars twinkled majestically above, and the full moon shined brilliantly on the blackened seascape.

Lori looked strikingly beautiful in a strapless, red satin evening dress that clung to every inch of her gorgeous body. Bennett could not help notice as her alluring blonde locks swept softly in the gentle ocean breeze.

Lori returned the approving gaze. Bennett was downright handsome. He was dressed in a custom-fitted powder blue dinner jacket, a white tuxedo shirt, black tie and dark slacks that made every muscle in his body ripple.

Picking at their baked soufflés, they enjoyed the spectacular ocean view from the patio of Las Bresas, one of Malibu's most exquisite French restaurants. And, best of all, they had it all to themselves.

'You really shouldn't have?" Lori beamed. "You didn't have to go to such trouble."

"Well, I admit, it's a bit of stretch for me, but I couldn't imagine someone more deserving."

Lori flashed a warm smile, and Bennett caught the sparkle of affection of in her deep blue eyes.

"Ah. Come on. It's the least I can do."

Lori smiled again and quickly changed subject. "Well, where do you go from here?" she asked inquisitively.

"Oh, I'll probably get kicked around between the homicide and juvenile divisions. Nothing different. How about you?"

Lori stabbed at a piece of souffl with her fork. "More of the same. I would like to believe this story will be the one that will make Champ Leaf and others at the station take me seriously. But I seriously doubt it."

Bennett stared thoughtfully at her. It was not anything she said or did. He just could not take his eyes off her stunning beauty.

"I think you know this already," Bennett said. "But you were really something yesterday."

Lori looked up from her souffl . "You really think so."

"I have to agree with Captain Hansen. You were

amazing. Any chance making you my permanent partner?"

They laughed, and then Lori demurred. "Thanks, but no. But your offer is very tempting."

For no other reason, Bennett suddenly started laughing.

"What's so funny?" Lori asked, laughing along.

"Nothing. Nothing you said."

"Then what?"

"I just thought of Captain Hansen's startled look when I blew out of his office today. I thought he was going to have a coronary."

Now Lori laughed. "He looked boiled and ready to burst, that's for sure."

"Call me Hank." Bennett laughed again. "What a bunch of crock."

"Yeah, *Captain,*" Lori said, mocking Bennett's parting shot.

They laughed until their sides ached, and Lori regained her composure first. She instantly glanced at Bennett. Her eyes met his, and she flashed a brilliant smile in his direction. Suddenly, she raised her glass, filled with white Chablis, and posed a toast.

"Really. I want to do this."

Bennett seemed embarrassed, even though no one else was around. He finally gave in so he would not hurt her feelings.

"Okay, what are we toasting to?"

Lori moved her glass closer to his, and thought for a moment. "To world peace."

Bennett laughed. The line seemed strangely familiar, like something he had used before.

"No, actually," Lori offered. "I was never very good at this. My father was always the one in our family who toasted on special occasions. I'm not my father, and thank god." She giggled. "But here it goes."

Lori positioned the glass firmly in front of her. "To Sergeant Bennett, a man of unquestionable courage, unwavering dedication, indisputable valor and one of the nicest gentlemen I have ever known."

Bennett's eyes sparkled with appreciation. They clinked their tall wine glasses, and Lori was about to relinquish hers when Bennett interrupted.

"We're not finished."

"Oh."

"Now it's my turn."

Bennett gazed affectionately into Lori's blue eyes, and she returned the favor. He had romanticized about this moment for many days and nights. Clearing his throat, he held his glass out slightly touching hers. Then keeping his eyes riveted on hers, he recited the first words that came from his heart.

"To Lori Matrix, the best damn television journalist, friend and the most beautiful woman I have ever met in my entire life."

Lori glowed under the soft moonlight, and Bennett remained mesmerized by her intoxicating beauty.

"You know. It hasn't been easy for me," Bennett finally admitted.

"How so?"

"To spend every waking hour thinking of you."

There, he said it. The words that he could never manage to express, and had often paralyzed him at the thought. It was as though a strange force had overtaken him. So what if they were from different worlds. He was hopelessly in love with her and, rather than question what he was feeling, he decided to follow his heart. Earlier, Lori might have seemed surprised. But after all that they had been through together, she welcomed it without any resistance.

"I don't know what to say."

"Don't say a word." Bennett fearlessly reached across the table and tenderly took her by the hand. He just let the words flow.

"I know we have had our differences," he said passionately," but I have never been more attracted to anyone than I am to you tonight."

Lori blushed and she felt all tingly inside. Could it be true? Was little Ann Fishbein falling in love? She knew she was attracted to Bennett the moment she laid eyes on him. But even she questioned the timing.

"Are you sure about this?"

Bennett rose from his seat without uttering a word. He was never more serious.

"Dance with me."

"What?" Lori said surprised.

"Dance with me."

Lori looked over her shoulder at the empty patio. "But there's no music."

"We'll make our own."

Lori giggled like a schoolgirl as Bennett moved from his chair and escorted her to the center of the brick laden patio.

Pressing his body closer to hers, he gazed into Lori's adoring eyes. They exchanged loving glances as the ocean breeze stirred around them, and their hearts fluttered in anticipation. It was the moment they had both waited for.

Bennett leaned closer and softly whispered something in Lori's ear. She giggled again, and he laughed with her. Holding her tight, Bennett then shuffled his feet, and they danced like two love struck fools with the moon and stars bearing witness.

Surely, it was a night they would never forget.

About the Author

JEFF LENBURG is a prolific and award-winning author of more than 30 books.

His works include many acclaimed celebrity memoirs and biographies, entertainment histories, and popular references that have been nominated for several awards, including the American Library Association's (ALA) "Best Non-Fiction Award" and the Evangelical Christian Publisher Association's (ECPA) Gold Medallion Award for "Best Autobiography/Biography."

Jeff has interviewed and written about Hollywood legends and cinematic lore since he was 15. This is his first novel. He makes his home near Phoenix, Arizona, with his wife Debby.

For more information about Jeff's upcoming books and the latest news, visit www.jefflenburg.com.

Also from Moonwater Press

PEEKABOO:
The Story of Veronica Lake

One of Hollywood's sultriest sirens of the 1940s, millions of fans adored her and she was the hottest ticket around, but not for long. *Peekaboo: The Story of Veronica Lake* tells the shocking, true story of this Hollywood heartthrob and star of 27 motion pictures (best known for her screen pairings with Alan Ladd) and her disastrous life off screen--a controlling mother, four failed marriages, and downward spiral due to alcoholism and mental illness--ending up broke and destitute. Fully authorized, this powerful, revealing, thoroughly updated and expanded edition, featuring exclusive interviews with friends and family members who knew her best and more than 100 illustrations, tells why.

WALK TO FREEDOM
Kriegsgefangenen #6410: Prisoner of War

Captured Army Air Corps sergeant John L. Lenburg braved a torturous eleven months of captivity before walking to freedom. In this powerful and compelling memoir, he vividly describes the inhumane treatment, the horrific conditions of his imprisonment and the remarkable acts of courage displayed by his fellow American prisoners who endured many months of mental and physical abuse, starvation and doubts they would ever see their homeland again. Now back in print, this expanded, critically acclaimed biography, includes many rare, never-before published illustrations.

www.ingramcontent.com/pod-product-compliance
Lightning Source LLC
Chambersburg PA
CBHW030256060726
47498CB00002BA/416